"Some days I feel like I've died and gone to heaven," she said quietly

Beau softened as his eyes met hers. "This is a far cry from heaven, Maggie. The trouble with you is that you've never lived anyplace where folks liked each other, and tried to make life enjoyable."

"I just know that livin' here is like being in a dream. I thank you for bein' kind to me, and for doin' all you do." Emotion welled within her and words spurted forth. "I just feel like huggin' you," she blurted. And that was probably enough to scare him off if anything ever would, she thought.

"You can if you want to," he said, his grin wide. "I'd really like to kiss you, if you wouldn't mind."

"You want to kiss *me?*" she asked incredulously. And then she laughed aloud. "Nobody ever kissed me in my life...!"

Dear Reader,

With the passing of the true millennium, Harlequin Historicals is putting on a fresh face! We hope you enjoyed our special inside front cover art from recent months. We plan to bring this wonderful "extra" to you every month! You may also have noticed our new branding—a maroon stripe that runs along the right side of the front cover. Hopefully, this will help you find our books more easily in the crowded marketplace. And thanks to those of you who participated in our reader survey. We truly appreciate the feedback you provided, which enables us to bring you more of the stories and authors that you like!

We have four terrific books for you this month. The talented Carolyn Davidson returns with a new Western, *Maggie's Beau*, a tender tale of love between experienced rancher Beau Jackson—whom you might recognize from *The Wedding Promise*—and the young woman he finds hiding in his barn. Catherine Archer brings us her third medieval SEASONS' BRIDES story, *Summer's Bride*, an engaging romance about two willful nobles who finally succumb to a love they've long denied.

The Sea Nymph by bestselling author Ruth Langan marks the second book in the SIRENS OF THE SEA series. Here, a proper English lady, who is secretly a privateer, falls in love with a highwayman—only to learn he is really an earl *and* the richest man in Cornwall! And don't miss *Bride on the Run*, an awesome new Western by Elizabeth Lane. True to the title, a woman fleeing from crooked lawmen becomes the mail-order bride of a sexy widower with two kids.

Enjoy! And come back again next month for four more choices of the best in historical romance.

Sincerely,

Tracy Farrell
Senior Editor

Carolyn Davidson

MAGGIE'S BEAU

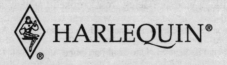

HARLEQUIN®

TORONTO • NEW YORK • LONDON
AMSTERDAM • PARIS • SYDNEY • HAMBURG
STOCKHOLM • ATHENS • TOKYO • MILAN • MADRID
PRAGUE • WARSAW • BUDAPEST • AUCKLAND

ISBN 0-373-29143-4

MAGGIE'S BEAU

Visit us at www.eHarlequin.com

Printed in U.S.A.

Please address questions and book requests to:
Harlequin Reader Service
U.S.: 3010 Walden Ave., P.O. Box 1325, Buffalo, NY 14269
Canadian: P.O. Box 609, Fort Erie, Ont. L2A 5X3

I have been blessed in many ways. I have a wonderful husband, a flock of terrific children and grandchildren, and a writing career that has fulfilled my wildest dreams. Add to that an agent who understands me and gives me absolute support, and the picture is almost complete. Except for one item.

Every published writer has an editor.
Margaret O'Neill Marbury is mine. She takes my phone calls, listens to my story ideas, encourages me on my bad days and then edits my final drafts with tender loving care. For the past seven years she and I have cooperated in a partnership that has been one of the most rewarding experiences of my life. I can only hope we survive many more such ventures as this one.

Maggie's Beau is Margaret's book, dedicated to her with all the appreciation this writer's heart can hold.

And to the man who holds my hand throughout the whole process of writing my stories, meeting my deadlines and keeping my life on an even keel, I give my thanks. I love you, Mr. Ed.

Chapter One

She was the most pathetic creature he'd ever seen. Perhaps if she were clean.... Beau Jackson shook his head. Even a bath wouldn't do much for the bitch. Even now, she was snarling and showing her teeth, in a display meant to scare him from his own barn. Sides showing clear signs of pregnancy, the dog stood spraddle-legged in the aisle and dared Beau to come one step further. He was no fool, and so instead squatted in the wide doorway and held out his hand.

"Come here, girl," he coaxed, balancing on the balls of his feet. "I'm not going to hurt you."

The dog backed up a few inches and growled again, a menacing warning. Yet her ears twitched forward, and if canine eyes could be called hopeful, Beau decided this one's could qualify. His eye caught a movement in the shadows just beyond the dog, and his brow lifted in surprise.

"Well, I'll be—looks like you got yourself a friend, honey." His words were soft, meant to pacify the bedraggled animal before him, and for a moment, she relaxed her stance, her tail moving from between her hind legs to become a flag at half-mast. Crouching beside the feed barrel, a cat shifted and lunged to its feet, wavering uncertainly for a second or two, until it caught its balance.

"I'd say you've got a problem, kitty." Beau felt his brow furrow and knew a moment of pity as he watched the gray cat move beyond the dog's shadow. Three legs held the creature erect, a scarred area, bare of hair, revealing the site of the fourth missing limb. The cat balanced on its one remaining foreleg beside the dog and watched Beau with stoic indifference.

It was a stand-off, one he could not afford to continue. The dog would either attack or back down, and it was time to give her a chance to make that decision. Beau stood slowly, one hand on the butt of his gun. "You going to let me pass, dog? Or do we have to do this the hard way?"

The dog's back ridged in protest as Beau spoke and her lips drew back over white teeth, even as a low, threatening growl announced her position.

"Damn. This isn't my first choice, pooch. But I can't let you take a chunk out of me, can I?" Beau drew his gun carefully, even as he reached for a rope that hung on the wall. If the dog lunged, he could fend it off with the heavy coil of rope, but if he couldn't manage to chase it from the barn, he'd probably have to put a bullet in its head. And that didn't sit well with him.

Not only was he opposed to putting down an animal unless there was no other choice, but it was a hell of a way to start the day. Especially since he hadn't even had his breakfast. He took one step closer, prepared for the snarl that erupted from the animal.

What he wasn't prepared for was the sight of a bare foot descending from the hayloft. It barely touched the top step of the ladder before its mate moved lower, and he was exposed to the sight of curving calves and slender feet. A drab, colorless skirt fell to cover the feminine limbs as their owner scampered to the barn floor and whirled to face him.

"Don't you shoot my dog. She's just scared you'll hurt her." The girl stepped forward, shielding the pair of animals, her narrowed eyes glittering defiance. Dark hair hung in disarray, its snarled length falling over her shoulders and partially covering her face. She snatched at the unruly mop and peered up at him.

"Who beat the tar out of you?" Beau asked, his voice quiet, even as his stomach roiled in disgust. She hadn't narrowed her eyes at him purposely. One was almost shut, its lid puffed and purpled, a bruise covering most of her cheek. Blood stained the corner of her mouth and her lips were swollen and discolored.

"None of your business." The dog moved to nudge its nose against the girl's hand and Beau watched as her fingers spread to cover the furry head. "Just let us get by and we won't bother you none." The cat stood again, and hobbled to lean against the girl's bare leg. She glanced down and reached for the wounded creature, her movement swift, her gaze returning quickly to Beau.

"I don't think I can do that, ma'am," he said quietly.

"I didn't steal nothin'," she told him sharply. "I just took a nap in your loft. We didn't touch anything."

"I wasn't worried about that." What he was concerned about was getting her and her menagerie better acquainted with the idea of eating breakfast.

She watched him warily. "If you'll move out of the way, mister, we'll be gone faster than you can blink." She took one step toward him, the dog moving to her side, the cat creeping up to wind itself around the back of the girl's neck.

"You got any belongings, miss?" Surely she hadn't arrived in his barn without some sort of baggage, aside from the creatures she protected.

Her eye twitched and she hunched her shoulders, glancing to where the ladder led to the loft. "I left my stuff up there. Forgot it."

Beau nodded. "Why don't you go up and get it, and I'll see what I can rustle up for breakfast for you and your critters."

Stock-still, she watched him, her head turning a bit as she gauged his considerable length, her gaze finally coming to rest on the gun he held. "You gonna kill my dog?"

"Not till I feed her," Beau said, sliding the pistol back into its holster.

"I don't take somethin' for nuthin'," she said firmly. "I'll earn the food."

He hesitated, but only for a moment. He'd have to let her call the shots, most likely. Otherwise, she'd be gone in a heartbeat once he turned his back. "All right, you can do that. Come on up to the house and I'll find some grub. Then you can work for a while in the garden, if you want to."

Her chin stuck out mutinously. "I'd rather clean stalls."

Beau swallowed a chuckle as she stood her ground, then shrugged. "That's up to you. I just need to have the potatoes dug and the rest of the onions pulled." At her glare, he relented. "Hey, if you'd rather clean stalls, by all means, have at it."

She turned away, reaching for one of the pitchforks on the wall and he stilled her hand with a word. "No." It was a firm command, and she was obviously used to the harsh tone he used, for she turned quickly, her expression fearful. "You can earn your food after you eat it, and after your animals get fed."

Her head nodded slowly, her hand returned to clutch at

the side of her dress and she waited. "Go ahead, mister. I'll follow you up to the house."

"Is your dog going to latch on to my leg when I turn away?" he asked, amusement coloring his words, hoping to lull her into conversation. He offered a smile and was stunned as she backed from him again.

"Maisie won't bite you if I tell her not to." She touched the dog's head and the animal sat quietly by her side. "Go ahead on. We'll follow you."

Beau turned away, walking briskly toward his house, the silence behind him tempting him to look back. She was a fey creature, without much to recommend her. Somebody had trounced her good from the looks of it. And unless he missed his guess, she'd gone hours, maybe days, without food. It was no wonder she was wary of him, with his gun slung around his waist. He'd only worn it in case he encountered the snake he'd spotted last night. Rattlers were rare around the house and barn, but he wasn't about to take any chances.

He hunched his shoulders and then stretched upward, bringing sore muscles into play. Damn, his day was shot all to hell and back and he'd hardly had time to rub the sleep from his eyes.

Maggie moved behind him, matching her steps to his, scampering as he outpaced her. Cat clung to her hair, balancing across her neck, and Maggie reached up to grasp the animal's hind legs. Beside her, Maisie moved cautiously, and as they approached the back porch of the ranch house, the dog halted and growled a warning. Maggie touched the shaggy head and looked down.

"Your dog not partial to men?" The rancher stood on the porch and turned to face her. "She can stay out here. Hell, you can all stay out here if you like. Or come on in.

It makes no matter to me." He turned from her and opened the screened door, walking into the house.

"We'll eat on the porch," Maggie said, raising her voice so as to be heard. The screened door slammed and she climbed the steps with care, her feet tender from the long hours of walking on rough ground. She should have snatched up her shoes when she'd left, but Pa had been rustling around in the next room and she'd not wanted to take a chance on being caught. She'd skinned over the windowsill and landed on the ground with a thud, then snatched up her bundle and taken off like a streak across the yard, toward the woods.

Settling against the wooden corner post, she pulled the cat from around her neck. The wound was healing well, she decided, brushing back the hair to better make out the rough stitches she'd put in place. Her mouth drew down as she recalled the horror of a steel trap and the howls of the wounded creature who'd strayed into its jaws. Pa had nailed her a good one for hiding the cat and not giving away its whereabouts, but it was worth it. Already Cat was walking pretty good. Before long, she'd be... Maggie's eyes dimmed as the creature's hopeless future loomed before her. No longer would Cat be able to hunt for food, or protect herself from predators.

"I'll take care of you. Don't you worry none," she murmured, her fingers tugging at the gray ears with tender caresses. Maisie watched from the grass below, sitting patiently, her gaze never swerving. "And you, too, Maisie." Maggie lifted her shoulders, stretching, easing the cramps from sleeping in the loft. She'd settled down near the opening, watchful of her animals, and the floor had been hard and ungiving.

In the room beyond the screened door, sounds promised the coming of a meal, or at least some sort of hastily prepared food, if she was any judge. A pan clattered, a spoon scraped, and water was pumped into a container. Who'd have ever thought a man could put together something to eat? Pa wouldn't have been caught dead dealing with the kitchen stove or making a meal for himself. But he always managed to be there when Mama dished things up.

Maggie leaned her head against the post behind her. For right now, for this moment, she was safe. If Pa was after her, she'd see him coming, for the lane was in sight. Beyond the barn, several men were heading in this direction, but they didn't seem to be on the lookout, just making their way toward a long, low building where smoke drifted from the chimney and a clanging noise seemed to be a signal of sorts. She shrank within herself, lest she be seen by the men. Three of them there were, and so far they hadn't taken any mind of her. She could hear them calling back and forth, and then they made their way through the doorway into the building next to the barn.

"If I was smart, I'd be out there eating with the hands." The big man was behind the screened door, talking to her, and here she'd been so intent on watching the yard that he'd managed to creep up on her.

"Go ahead on," she muttered, embarrassed at being caught unawares.

"I told you I'd feed you," he reminded her, and pushed the door open. "Why don't you come inside? I've put the coffee on the front of the stove and found some bread and butter and a jar of apples. There's some meat left from yesterday's dinner."

"Don't your wife cook?" Maggie asked suspiciously. "Ain't she around?"

The rancher looked at her, and shook his head. "No wife, and the cook went to be with her daughter for a couple of days. I'm making do with leftovers, but I'll probably eat with my ranch hands tonight.''

She leaned forward, peering suspiciously past him into the dim kitchen. ''You all alone in there?''

He held the door wide. ''Come take a look for yourself.''

Maggie edged closer to him, peering past his formidable bulk into the kitchen. An oblong table, covered with a checkered oilcloth centered the room, sturdy chairs positioned around it. Heat from the cookstove warmed her as she crossed the threshold, and the scent of coffee beckoned.

''You got any milk for the coffee?'' she asked, venturing to the far side of the table. A lone cup and solitary plate, with a knife and fork framing two sides, awaited her as she stood behind the chair. Her eyes widened as she beheld a pitcher filled with rich, yellow cream. ''You put the top cream in your coffee?''

He shrugged, facing her from the doorway. ''Why not? Seems like a good way to use it up.''

''My ma always had to churn it all. We drank the dregs. Never could take to the skim.'' She reached for the pitcher and then halted, aware of the grime she'd managed to gather on her skin. ''Reckon I could wash up a little first?''

''Certainly.'' He nodded toward the stove. ''There's warm water in the reservoir. I'll get it for you.''

Maggie watched as he filled a saucepan, dipping into the cavern that was attached to the side of the cookstove. He carried the pan to the sink, emptying it into a basin there, then pumped an equal amount of cool water from the well. His glance was accompanied by a small smile, and he stepped back.

''Have at it. I'll get you a towel.''

He turned to the pantry, and she moved quickly to where the luxury of warm water awaited her. A thin bar of store-bought soap lay on the wooden sinkboard and she picked it up, lifting it to her nose. The scent was clean, and she inhaled it greedily. The basin was directly beneath the pitcher pump. She moved it to one side, then pumped once, allowing the water to splash over her hands. The soap turned dark with the residue of dirt on her hands and she rubbed her fingers vigorously before she pumped again, rinsing them. No sense in letting that nice, warm water get grungy right off, she decided.

Again Maggie worked at her hands, pleased as the soap-suds dissolved her two-day collection of grime. Finally satisfied, she bent to the basin, wetting her face with both hands before she rubbed up a good amount of suds between her palms. The clean scent pleased her as she lifted her hands to her face and soaped its surface. She closed her eyes, her fingers working from forehead to chin and below, then from one ear to the other, wincing a bit as her bruises protested their cleaning. There was no help for it, she decided. The chance for real soap and warm water was an opportunity she couldn't afford to turn down. She lifted a double handful of water, splashing it against her skin, and then blew out the soap that clung to her lips.

"Here's a towel for you to use." He was beside her, and she stood erect, her heart beating furiously. His body heat touched her even as the towel was thrust into her hands. Tall and broad-shouldered, he loomed over her, and she shrank from him. Her eyes burned from soap and water combined, and she scrubbed gingerly at her face with the towel, then looked up at him, inhaling deeply for a lungful of air.

"You could scare a body to death, comin' up on them like that." Maggie's lips threatened to quiver with fright, and she would not have it. She tightened them, compressing her mouth into a thin line.

"I beg your pardon," he murmured. "I didn't mean to

frighten you." His eyes dwelt on her face, his mouth again tightening as his gaze traced her damaged skin. "I should have brought you a washcloth, too, I suppose."

What on earth was the man talking about? "Whatever for?" she asked. "I've been usin' my hands to wash with for more years than I can count."

"I always like to scrub up with…" He halted. "Never mind. Let's just get you fed and find something for your animals."

Her animals! She'd forgotten them. The towel met the sinkboard and she backed from the man, then hastened to the screened door. A sigh left her lips, an audible sound of relief. Maisie and Cat were where she'd left them, the pair of them watching and waiting patiently.

"They're fine," she announced, turning again to the table. "If you don't mind, I'll just take them out half of whatever you were gonna give me to eat."

His eyes turned dark, and he shook his head, an abrupt movement. "No. You'll eat whatever you please, and then we'll find more for the dog and cat." He motioned to the chair and she obeyed his silent command, her stomach growling as she faced the food he offered. A plate with several chunks of beef, and beside it, a Mason jar filled with cooked apples. Even as she watched, her host unwrapped a loaf of bread from a kitchen towel and placed it on a wooden board.

"You want me to slice some for you?" he asked, knife in hand.

She nodded. "That'd be welcome." The knife cut with ease through the brown crust, and white slices fell like slabs of lumber from a felled tree at the mill in town. She was pleased with the thought, and reached for a slice as he drew back. "Sure is nice and white. You musta got good flour."

"Just what my housekeeper told me to buy," he said quietly, his gaze intent on her.

She buttered the bread, using a scant portion of his supply, and heard the sound he made deep in his chest. Looking up quickly, she caught a look of anger in his eyes, a narrowed, dark glimpse into the depths of his soul. "I'm sorry if I used too much butter, mister." If he was angry about that, she could scrape it off and do without. Butter was a luxury, anyway, Ma had always said. It brought good money from the store in town. No sense wasting it on family.

He shook his head. "Use all you want. There's more where that came from." He pulled out a chair and sat across from her. He'd poured himself a cup of coffee, and she watched as he poured a generous amount of cream into it. The cream swirled and blended and he reached for a spoon, completing the process with a quick stir. Then he pushed the pitcher toward her.

"Go ahead, help yourself." His voice was gruff, even to his own ears, and Beau cleared his throat. He'd never seen such a wary creature in female form before. She was clean from the neck up and the wrists down, revealing fine skin, tanned to a golden hue. His curiosity was running rampant, becoming more aroused each moment by the creature he'd discovered. More woman than girl, now that he had a good look at her, with full breasts beneath the nondescript garment she wore. Her face held a piquant beauty, with wide-set eyes and a narrow nose. The bruising was dark around one eye, closing it to his view, but the other was dark blue, the orb circled with black. Her mouth was swollen and scraped, and she bit gingerly at the bread she held.

The thought that the brute who had damaged her flesh might have loosened teeth in the process angered Beau almost beyond his control. His hands tightened their hold on his cup, then flexing his fingers, he tightened them into fists. He'd give a bundle to lay hold of the man who had hurt her. She glanced up at him, and he caught the hint of fear she could not hide, as if she must guard against any sudden moves on his part.

Beau leaned back in his chair, then forced the corners of his mouth to curve upward. "More coffee?" he asked. "If I'd gathered the eggs this morning, I could've scrambled some for you. Never did get the knack of frying them without breaking the yolks." Nonsense talk, all of it designed to help his guest relax. Yet he saw no results.

She ate cautiously, quietly, steadily, her hand holding the fork as if it were a weapon, clutching it against her palm. Ever vigilant, she was poised on the edge of her chair, alert to his every movement. "I'd take more coffee, mister," she said after a moment, pushing her cup across the table.

She looked revived, her movements more limber, and the routine of eating had slowed. "Thanks for the food," she said, almost grudgingly, as he rose to pour steaming coffee into her cup. Her mouth pursed as she poured cream into the strong brew, and he caught a glimpse of satisfaction in her half smile. "Maybe I can milk your cow for you. To help pay for my breakfast, I mean."

Beau leaned against the kitchen cabinet, stuffing his hands into his pockets. "Why don't you stick around for a day or so, just till you get your feet under you?" Her gaze shot in his direction and she hesitated, her cup held midair.

"You need another hand around here?" She'd seen the three men near the barn, and seen a fourth ringing the bell. Surely he had help enough to run the place. And yet, hope rose within her breast. If she could hide here, just for a while. Maybe sleep in the loft and earn her grub. His lower lip protruded a bit and his eyes scanned her. She sat up straighter in the chair, then pushed away from the table and stood erect.

"I'm strong, mister. I can muck stalls and tend stock like a man."

"What's your name, miss?" he asked quietly.

She hesitated, a bit too long it seemed, for he frowned. "Don't lie to me, honey. I can spot a phony a mile away."

"I'm Maggie," she said, tilting her chin a bit, allowing him to look directly into her one good eye. "And I'm not a phony. If you don't need any more help around here, I'll earn my breakfast and be on my way."

He walked toward her and halted just beyond her reach. One hand stretched forth and she looked down at it, then back up at the somber look he wore. "My name's Beau Jackson," he offered.

The man wanted to shake her hand. Maggie shivered at the thought of giving him the chance to drag her against him. Yet, maybe that wasn't his aim. He'd had plenty of chance to haul her around if he'd been set on that course, and he'd kept his distance. Now, he held out his hand like a gentleman might, and she lifted her own to press her palm against his, allowing her fingers to curl around the wide expanse. He held her smaller hand in his, looking down for a moment. Then with a gentle movement, he squeezed, and released her from his grip.

She drew back, rubbing her palm against the side of her dress. It was warm, holding the heat from his flesh, as though the memory of his hard calluses somehow remained. "I'll go clean your barn, mister," she told him, anxious suddenly to be away from his presence. He was too big, too close for comfort.

He nodded, sliding his big hand back into his pocket. Maggie backed from him, then turned to the door. On the porch, visible through the screen, her woebegone companions sat, waiting for whatever she might offer them. Guilt struck her and she flinched. "I forgot," she said, turning quickly to face her benefactor. "You said I could feed Cat and Maisie."

"I'll get it," he told her. Beau reached for a bowl on the shelf, dumping its contents into the scrap pan in the sink. "More of the beef left over from last night," he told her. "Never seen a dog yet that didn't like stew meat." He tore up two slices of bread, adding them to the pan, then reached for a crock on top of the cookstove. What looked to be bacon grease spilled over the whole offering, and he carried it toward the door.

She opened the screen and held it wide for him to pass. He nodded his thanks. "I'll get some milk for the dog," he offered. "Looks like she'll be dropping a litter before too long."

The animals beheld the pan of food for a moment, wary of his scent, Beau supposed, then gave in to the hunger they could not hide. Ever watchful, they shared the pan, Cat finally crouching as her balance gave way.

"I thank you," Maggie said with polite formality, bowing her head. "They haven't had much to eat lately."

And neither have you. She was a prickly little thing, but her loyalty to the creatures who depended on her gave away a soft side of her nature Beau planned to exploit. He'd keep her here, for a while at least. Help her get cleaned up and find something decent for her to wear. And then, if it was the last thing he ever did, he'd find out who'd beaten the tar out of the girl.

Chapter Two

"I don't want any one of you touching that girl. And I sure don't want any of you looking her over," Beau added for good measure. "She's young and on her own, and I've told her she can stay here for a while." He paused to cross his arms across his chest as he scanned the four men before him.

Joe Armstrong, a strapping youth who lived up to his name, grinned and nodded readily. "That's all right with me. She's not much to look at, from what I saw, boss. Reckon I'll stick to Betty."

"You just better hope Betty sticks to you," Radley Bennett scoffed. "She's lookin' for a man with some money." He caught Beau's eye and sobered. "I hear you, boss. The girl looks like she's already had too much attention from someone."

"She's on the run," Beau said bluntly. "She needs a place to stay, and I don't want her feeling threatened by anyone on my ranch. She's to be left alone."

Shay agreed silently, nodding his head, dark eyes flashing, his mouth tight. Beau expected no more from the man. His face was scarred, a puckered slash marring the skin beneath his right eye, drawing his mouth up a bit when he spoke. Something he did rarely, keeping to himself, remaining silent, for the most part. But the man put in a full day's work and Beau had found no fault with him. His name was Shay, but beyond that, he was an enigma. There would be no hassle coming from Shay. Beau would bet his life on it.

He turned his gaze on Pony Taylor, short, stocky and sturdy as the Shetland horses that gave him his nickname. He'd come to Beau from a traveling circus, where he'd been a trainer of those small creatures. His talents overcame his stature, and Beau trusted him with his prized mares, knowing they were in good hands.

"I'll keep an eye out for the girl," Pony said quietly. "She'll come to no harm here."

"No one else is to know she's on the place," Beau stated, his gaze encompassing the group. "If I hear otherwise, there'll be hell to pay."

The four men nodded in unison, and Beau relaxed his stance. They were to be trusted, he was dead certain of that. He wouldn't have allowed them room in his bunkhouse if he weren't. Wearing a blue uniform for two years had taught him that the men surrounding him were his first defense. If he couldn't trust the troops he fought with, he might as well lay down his gun and call it quits. He'd chosen his ranch hands with the same thought in mind.

"She's going to clean stalls this morning," Beau stated, aware of the harsh glance shot in his direction by Pony. "Her choice," he emphasized. "I figure it'll take the best part of the morning to round up the yearlings and get them into the near pasture. Rad and Joe, you'll follow Pony's lead in sorting them out." He turned to his trainer. "You know what I'm looking for. Pick the best. I'll look over the rest for the sale."

Beau turned his gaze to Shay. "Keep an eye on things

in the barn and check that pasture gate. We can't take a chance on losing any of those yearlings.''

With nods of agreement, the men left the corral and Beau glanced over his shoulder toward the main barn. He'd be willing to bet that Maggie had been listening to his words. It had been his intent that she feel secure, and unless he missed his guess she was just beyond the double doors this very minute. He'd left her with pitchfork in hand at the far end of the line of stalls. With any luck, she'd be done with the chore in an hour or so.

It would give him time to sort out the back room, just off his kitchen, a place where she could sleep undisturbed.

She'd only caught one name—Pony. And wasn't that appropriate for a man working with horses, Maggie thought. She wondered which one of the four he was. He'd be in charge this morning. Her thoughts turned to the yearlings, those frolicking creatures who raced the wind with no thought of restraint or fear of danger. She'd come upon a herd of mares and their offspring, yearlings and weanlings alike, late the evening before, watching them as they bunched together beneath the shelter of overspreading tree limbs.

Now they were to be separated from the mares. And she wondered which of those carefree beauties Beau Jackson would keep, and which would be sold. The muscles in her arms flexed as she pitched a fork loaded with manure into the wheelbarrow. Maybe he'd let her help with the yearlings, she thought wistfully. Her mouth pulled down. Probably not. He'd think her too stupid, fit only for scut work, just like Pa had said.

She inhaled deeply. It was up to her to prove him wrong—that is, if she decided to stay on here for a few days. He'd offered her refuge, and she was mightily tempted. Too far away from the farm for Pa to find her right off the bat. And if those four ranch hands were true to their word, she'd be safe...for a while.

The wheelbarrow was heavy, and she took a fresh grip on the handles, a grunt escaping her lungs as she hefted the weight. The manure pile was fifty feet or so beyond the barn and she trudged there, her arms aching from the punches they'd received the day before yesterday. Three more trips, she figured, would do the trick, and then she'd spread fresh straw and take a gander at the rest of the barn.

The room was small, but adequate, Beau decided. The cot against the inside wall held a thin mattress, and he winced as he thought of the feather tick topping his own bed, in a room directly over this one. If she left the door open, she'd get a breeze through the kitchen. Otherwise, the air would be stifling. He eyed the outside wall. Maybe if he cut a hole, put in a window....

A shadow fell across the floor and he turned. Maggie stood in the doorway, peering past him into the storage room. A sense of relief washed through him. He'd wondered, just for a while this afternoon, if she'd cut and run. The yearlings were contained in the pasture, and their antics had kept his ranch hands hopping. One foot propped on the fence, he'd watched them sort through the herd, his mind only half aware of the melee before him. He'd walked through the barn, searched the tack room, even checked the loft, without any sign of Maggie.

A stifled sound from behind him had caused him to turn his head, looking upward at the open loft window. She'd been there, only half visible in the shadows, watching the yearlings evade the men who sorted through their numbers, following Pony's shouted instructions. One hand covered her mouth as she smothered another laugh. And he'd relaxed, chagrined at his relief.

Now, she faced him from the doorway. "Is this where you're gonna put me?" she asked bluntly.

"It's not much," he hedged, tucking his hands into his pockets. And wasn't that an understatement. "There's a cot and a table." He slid one hand from his pocket to wave at the shelves against one wall. "You can put your gear there. I'll get you a lamp."

She nodded. "I'll need one if I expect to see anything."

Almost, he caught a glimmer of humor in her eyes as he met her gaze. She stepped back and he walked past her, careful to maintain his distance. She was like a flighty young colt, all arms and legs, poised to shift and turn should he step too closely. Her forehead glistened with sweat, and she smelled of the barn, a mixture of fresh manure and animal scent. Yet, beneath that pungent aroma was a hint of woman, snagging his attention, drawing him unwillingly.

"I'll find you something else to wear. I doubt you brought much with you," Beau surmised. He allowed his eyes to measure her briefly. "You're smaller than my housekeeper, but I think something of hers might do."

"I wear pants, mostly." Her chin rose defiantly. "I've only got a dress on now, 'cause that's what I was sleepin' in when I left home."

She slept in a dress? "You always sleep in your clothes?"

"Whatever's handy," she retorted. "My pa don't hold with buyin' any more stuff than he has to." One sleeve had fallen to cover her hand and she bent her head as she rolled the cuff, hiding the ragged edge from his view.

"Then I'll ask Pony if he has anything he'd like to give you. He's not much taller than you are."

"I don't need any handouts, mister. I'm doin' fine, just like I am."

He shifted, thinking of the boiler full of water he'd put to heat on the kitchen range. "I thought you might like to have a bath and some clean clothes, what with hiding out and not..."

"I'll wash up in a bucket." Her words left no room for argument, and yet he plunged ahead, unwilling for any female to be so bereft of simple comforts.

"How about after supper? I'll fill the tub right here in your room. There's a lock on the inside of the door." He waved his hand for emphasis, pointing to where a brass hasp hung from the wooden door.

She stepped closer, peering at the shiny apparatus, then at the doorjamb, where he'd installed the rest of the lock. "You can jam a spike through there," he pointed out. "It'll hold firm." His jaw clenched at her wary look. "You'll be safe. I promise."

"You got a towel I can borrow?"

He caught a fleeting look of yearning in her eyes as she looked past him toward the range, where steam rose from the wash boiler. "Clean towels and a bar of soap." Her eyes narrowed as she shifted her gaze back to his face.

"I'll do extra, maybe clean up the garden for you, to pay my way. I swept up the barn and cleaned your tack room this afternoon." She inhaled deeply and then her shoulders rose and fell in a gesture of nonchalance. "Guess I wouldn't mind havin' a bath. You needn't bother about the clothes, though. I got a shift in my bundle. I'll wear it while I wash out my things in the bath water. You can toss them over the porch rail for me overnight, and they'll be near dry in the morning."

He'd won. And won fairly, appealing only to her need for cleanliness. Beau nodded agreeably. "I fried some ham from the smokehouse, and there's vegetables from the pantry. We'll eat in a few minutes, then I'll drag in the tub for you."

A bent spike passed from his hand to hers and she nodded, agreeing. "This'll work." Beau crossed the kitchen to the back door and Maggie watched as the galvanized tub appeared a moment later, Shay carrying one end, Beau the other.

Shay, the quiet one, withheld his glance, intent on fitting the tub through the doorway, and then with a quiet word to Beau, he left. Maggie stepped aside, allowing him room. He nodded in her direction and she watched him pass through the kitchen door to the porch. The screen slammed behind him.

"He's a strange one," she murmured, almost to herself.

"Shay won't bother you," Beau said from the doorway, where one hand leaned against the jamb. "None of my men will give you cause to complain."

She believed him, and wondered at her acceptance of his word. He'd offered her the use of his home, at least this small portion of it. Even now, water boiled on his cookstove for her benefit. Maggie snatched up a bucket by the sink and turned sharply as Beau approached, taking the handle from her fingers.

"I'll dip the water. You're too short to lift a full bucket," he told her.

She watched as he deftly tilted the pail and filled it, then carried it across the floor. Water dripped in his wake and she noticed the small, spreading pools as they turned dark against the wooden floor.

"Sophie's going to scalp me for making a mess on her floor," Beau said, returning quickly, empty pail in hand.

He filled it a second time and traced his path across the room. "I'll wipe it up when you're done."

Maggie watched him, taken by the thought of someone waiting on her in such a fashion. She'd done the toting ever since she could remember, from lugging washtubs to the yard for Ma, to carrying heavy feed sacks from the wagon to the barn. Now she stood here, perfectly healthy and able to do for herself, and a strange man was fixing her bath-water. Hot water, at that. And wasn't that a switch from scrubbing up in the creek in summer or sitting in a luke-warm second- or third-hand tub of bathwater in the cold weather.

"Maggie?" He stood before her, and she jolted, lost in the vision of lounging in a tub all for herself, without two sisters having left their scum floating atop the cooling wa-ter. "I left the soap and a couple of towels and a washrag on the table in your room. The soap is a bar I already used from, but there's plenty left. Oh," he added, his tone ca-sual, "Pony sent an old pair of pants and a shirt for you. They're on the cot."

He took a small kerosene lamp from the kitchen cabinet. "You want me to light this for you?"

It was almost too much, that a man would be so kind— and without hope of recompense. And yet, the lure he of-fered was almost beyond her ability to resist. She seized upon his final suggestion as a place to draw the line. "I can use a candle."

"There's some on the shelf," he told her, and she nod-ded. She'd seen them there earlier when she'd unloaded her meager assortment on the bottom shelf, next to her bed.

The room was small, but with the candle lit and the door closed, it felt cozy. Maggie looked around at the shadowed corners, where Beau had swept and cleaned for her benefit. The man was a strange one, taking her in the way he had, not asking questions. Her fingers slowed as she unbuttoned her dress. He smelled good, like somebody she'd seen once in town. A fellow who'd stood next to the wagon and talked to Pa, and even nodded in her direction.

Maybe it was the soap he used, she thought, reaching for the yellow bar he'd left for her. Her head bent as she sniffed at the stuff, and she grinned. That was a part of it, at least. That, and maybe his clothes, all clean and smelling of fresh air.

Her dress dropped to the floor and she slipped from her old shift, shivering as cool air touched her skin. One foot dipped in the water and she felt gooseflesh form on her arms. It was hot, probably too hot for comfort, even with the well water he'd added, but he'd left an extra pail of cold to temper it. She poured half of it into the tub, then eased herself into the water. Her eyes closed and she hunkered down, leaning forward so that her arms could be covered, her breasts enveloped with the warmth.

Bliss. Pure bliss, she decided. Bending lower, she sloshed her hair beneath the surface, then worked up a lather with the yellow soap.

Why he waited here was beyond him. She'd been behind the closed door for nearly an hour. The sun was below the horizon, his coffee was gone cold, and the lights in the bunkhouse were beckoning with the promise of a game of poker, if the muffled laughter from that direction was any indication. Yet, he waited.

The sound of metal against metal caught his attention and Beau turned his head, watching as the door creaked open. She peered around the edge, and her expression was defensive as she met his gaze.

"These clothes look close to new," she said accusingly, stepping into the kitchen.

And they'd never looked that good on Pony, he thought glumly. She'd tucked in the shirt and it clung to the curves it covered. A length of rope looped her waist, holding the loose pants in place, and she'd rolled them above her ankles.

"He told me the shirt shrank when Sophie washed it, and the pants..." Beau shrugged. He'd paid Pony two bits for the pants, but there wasn't any way Maggie could know that. She'd be volunteering to scrub the chicken coop if she thought he'd put out hard cash for her benefit.

"I'll thank him tomorrow," Maggie said quietly. "I'll hang my clothes on the porch rail myself, and then dump my bathwater." She moved past the table to the back door and he followed her progress with interest.

There was a slight hitch in her gait, as though she favored one leg, and he frowned, wondering if the clothing he'd provided covered more bruising. Her face in the lamp light gave mute evidence of painful injury, and Beau's fist clenched as he considered the beating she'd endured.

The screened door opened again and Maggie shot him a glance of inquiry. "Where'd you put the bucket? I thought it'd be on the porch."

He rose quickly, setting his coffee cup aside. "I'll empty the tub, then you can help me carry it outside."

Her mouth tightened, even as her chin tilted a bit. "I take care of myself, mister. There's no need for you to wait on me."

He hesitated, unwilling to give her cause to fear his presence. "Can we do it together?" he asked finally. "I've got a couple of pails we can fill."

Her eyes flitted over him and she nodded hesitantly. "All right. I guess so."

Beau scooped up the galvanized pail from beside the stove and entered the storeroom. A scent arose from the cooled bath water, and he inhaled it greedily. It'd been too damn long since he'd been with a female, he decided, when soap and water smelled this appealing.

He bent to his task and filled the pail, then carried it into the kitchen. "Here you go. Just dump it over the side of the porch. There's some bushes there that can use some watering."

Maggie took it from him and headed for the door, walking carefully, lest she allow the pail to slosh its contents on the floor. Beau went to the pantry door and searched for a moment before he caught sight of the second pail. Things would go quicker with the two of them at it, and he'd be better off if he stayed away from the girl. It was a sad day when a bedraggled fugitive began looking good.

In ten minutes' time the tub was sitting upside-down on the porch, and Maggie was on her hands and knees on the kitchen floor, wiping up the damp spots with a rag. She mopped at the dust of footprints with the tattered remains of a shirt Beau had provided, and, after looking around, she'd settled back on her heels.

"Guess it's as clean as it's gonna be," she said, rising to her feet.

"Thanks," Beau said from the doorway. He'd known better than to stop her from the wiping up. She'd made it clear that she wouldn't be beholden to him, and a grudging sense of respect for the girl was added to his unwilling attraction.

He cleared his throat and caught her attention. "I'm about ready to hit the sack," he said quietly, watching as her eyes widened at his words. "If you're not going out anymore tonight, I'll head on upstairs."

A flush touched her cheeks, warring with the purple blemishes below her eye. "No, I'm ready for bed."

If she'd been heading for the outhouse, he'd have

watched till she came back in, and the girl was smart enough to recognize his meaning. "If you want the outside door locked, there's a bolt you can use. That way you can leave the door of your room open for a breeze if you want to."

She shook her head. "Thanks just the same. I reckon I'll sleep better with the door shut."

Beau nodded. He'd cut a window in the outside wall tomorrow, with a shutter she could pull closed for privacy. Maybe he'd even take a trip to town and get some window glass. He turned away toward the hallway where a wide staircase swept upward. A grin curled his lip as he thought of the changes he was willing to put in place for this one small female.

"Sophie's not comin' back for a week or so."

Beau stared at Pony, his frown registering his disbelief. "Why the hell not?" he asked harshly.

"Sophie's girl took a bad turn after she birthed her baby, and Sophie sent word that she's gonna stay till the girl's back on her feet." Pony grinned, a cocky expression crossing his wizened face. "Guess your little refugee's gonna be doin' the cookin' for a while."

"She's not my little anything," Beau snapped. "She's a girl who's had a bad time, and we're giving her a bolt-hole till she decides what to do."

"She cleans up pretty good, boss," Pony said softly, his eyes sharp as they met Beau's gaze. "I watched her combin' her hair on the porch this morning." His gaze grew wistful. "Haven't seen such pretty long hair in a month of Sundays. Kinda reminded me of one of the gals who used to work on the flying trapeze. She sure was a looker."

And he'd missed that particular scene, Beau thought.

Maggie's hair had been braided and stuffed into a hat when he'd caught sight of her in the barn.

"Anybody looks better when they're cleaned up," he said harshly. "You make sure she's not pestered, understand?"

Pony nodded, wisely silent. He turned away, hot-footing it toward the barn, and Beau called after him. "Tell Maggie when she gets done with the stalls to come on up to the house. I want to talk to her."

"You didn't eat any breakfast," he said accusingly, his gaze piercing the slender female standing before him. "Looks to me like you could use some solid food in your belly." He waved at the cookstove. "I'm not much of a hand with putting together a meal, but there's biscuits made and bacon fried."

Maggie skirted him, silent as she surveyed the offerings he'd left for her. "Who made the biscuits?"

Beau bristled. "They're better than nothing. I didn't think you could afford to be fussy," he said curtly.

She picked up a biscuit and shrugged. "I'm not. I've eaten worse, that's for sure. Just wondered, that's all. My pa never lent a hand in the house. I didn't know men could do much in the way of cookin'." She bit into the flat specimen she held and hesitated, then turned to him. "Thank you kindly, mister. I don't mean to sound ungrateful."

"They're not real tender," he admitted gruffly as she made the effort to chew. "I don't know for sure how Sophie makes them. But the bacon's pretty good."

"They'll do," Maggie said, reaching for the pan he'd shoved to the back of the stove. She snatched up a strip of bacon, and Beau nodded at the table.

"I left a plate for you. And there's coffee in the pot.

From now on, you'll eat before you go out to the barn and work. Once Sophie gets back, we'll have decent meals."

Maggie took the plate to the stove, scooping the bacon from the pan, then adding another biscuit to the pile. "I can cook some," she offered. "My ma did most of it at home, but when she was laid up sometimes, I learned how to put a meal together."

Beau's ears pricked up at her words. "She's sickly?" he asked.

Maggie's gaze refused to meet his and she shook her head abruptly. "No, just once in a while, she didn't feel well."

"There's plenty of butter," he told her. "And cream ready to churn for more."

"Thank you," she said, almost formally, reaching for her knife. "I know how to do that—do the churnin'—I mean, if you want me to."

"Might be a good idea," Beau told her. "I just heard from Pony that Sophie won't be back for at least a week."

"Show me where things are and I'll get your kitchen set to rights," Maggie said, spreading butter across the surface of the biscuit in her hand. She cut him a glance and he caught a glimpse of humor there. "I'll even make the biscuits tomorrow morning, if that's all right. I can fry eggs without breaking the yolks, too."

"That'll work," Beau agreed. "Do you know how to cook a piece of beef? I'll cut off a hunk, if you know what to do with it."

Maggie shrugged her shoulders. "Just put it in a kettle with a couple of onions and some salt and pepper, I guess. If it's simmered long enough, it'll tender up pretty good."

She ate the last piece of bacon and licked her fingers. "I'll even dig your potatoes," she told him. "You'll want some in with the meat."

Beau watched in fascination as her tongue attended to a trace of bacon grease on her lips. Her fingers were slender, her hands graceful, and he was struck by the visible calluses on their palms. No woman should have to work at tasks that would leave their marks on such tender flesh.

But then, no woman should ever bear marks of cruelty such as Maggie wore. "Who hit you, Maggie?" he asked quietly.

She bent her head, as if hiding the evidence from view would daunt his curiosity. "My pa likes to use his fists sometimes," she said finally. "He says I'm sassy and don't know my place."

Beau felt his teeth clench at her words. "What did you do that made him so angry?"

She laughed, a short, bitter sound. "It didn't take much. This time was because I'd set up some pens in the woods with animals in them that I was tending, and he got mad."

"What happened to the animals?" Beau asked, even as he dreaded hearing the expected answer.

Maggie lifted her gaze to his. "He shot them. I was lucky Cat wasn't out there, or he'd have got her, too." She glanced at the stove. "I'll get myself some coffee, if you don't mind."

Beau nodded. "Go on ahead." Watching her, he felt the helpless anger build within his chest. Likely, her faint limp was evidence of her father's cruelty, he'd warrant. Maggie poured from the coffeepot and returned to the table. "Use all the cream you want," Beau told her, then watched as she poured from the pitcher.

"No one will ever hurt you here, Maggie."

She lifted defiant eyes to meet his. "I'll never let a man lay hands on me again, mister. I made up my mind when I crawled out my bedroom window that I'd got my last beating. Anyone tries to hit me ever again, and I swear I'll kill him.''

"I'll do it for you, Maggie." The words were a promise he intended to keep. Some way, somehow, he'd make certain this girl was not abused.

She drank from her cup, silent at his avowal, her eyes wary. "I'll feed my animals now, if it's just the same to you. Thought I'd give them the heel from the loaf of bread and put some bacon grease on it."

"Check with Pony. There might be some leftovers out at the bunkhouse. I think the men ate steak last night."

"You'd have done better to eat with them," she said. "I could have got along."

"I'm sure you could have," he said agreeably, "but I asked you to be my guest, and I wasn't about to leave you on your own for supper." He rose and went to the kitchen cupboard where a drawer held cutlery. A large butcher knife was there and he grasped it firmly. "I'll go on out to the barn. There's the better part of a steer hanging. I'll cut off a piece for you to cook up."

The thought of meat available and at hand was amazing to Maggie. Her mama had made do with an occasional chicken, or a rabbit when Pa was lucky with his traps. He'd swapped out butter and eggs for meat on occasion with one of the neighbors, but Maggie couldn't remember a time when meat was easy to come by. Imagine having a steer butchered and curing in the barn.

She watched as Beau left the house, then rose hastily and tended to her animals. They'd make do with bread and grease for now. She'd save scraps from the beef for later on. She cleaned the kitchen in minutes and she set off for the garden, where withered potato plants guaranteed a crop beneath the earth.

"You'd do better with a pitchfork, missy." The voice

behind her was rusty, almost harsh, and Maggie looked over her shoulder at the man who watched her. Shay held the four-tined fork in his hand, offering it to her.

She rose from the ground and stepped closer to the gate. "Thank you, sir. I thought I could just dig them out by hand, but the pitchfork will make it easier." She backed away from him and turned again to her task, aware that he watched her. The ground was soft and she lifted a mass of potatoes on the fork, then bent to shake them from the roots of the plant. Reaching into the hole she'd left, she sorted through the dirt, finding three more that had broken loose.

"You've done that before," Shay said quietly.

Maggie nodded, head bent to her task.

"You'll be safe here." Again she heard the promise of protection, and she glanced up quickly. His face was stern, the wide scar forming a forbidding barrier to an unwary glance. His eyes rested on her, and she met his gaze. No trace of male appraisal glittered there, only a calm acceptance of her presence.

"Thank you," she said formally, turning again to her chore, aware that he left as silently as he had approached. That made two men who'd promised her their protection, she thought, digging beneath another plant.

The potatoes piled up beside her as she worked, and there was a certain amount of satisfaction in the homey task. The late summer sun beat down on her head and she was grateful for the hat she'd found in the barn. In the trees surrounding the farmhouse birds sang, fluttering to the garden as she worked, pecking nearby through the overturned earth. She watched as a robin found a fat worm and leaned back, tugging it from the lump of dirt it inhabited. Her chuckle did little to daunt the red-breasted bird as he held his prize and flapped his wings, flying to the nearest tree.

The sound of her own amusement stilled her movements

and Maggie closed her eyes. She'd not found anything to smile about in longer than she wanted to consider. But this place…it put her in mind of a small piece of heaven, this sun-drenched bit of earth where she knelt. Beside her, the pile of potatoes grew ever larger as she worked, and around her a small flock of birds fluttered, reckless now in her presence. She rose, grasping the pitchfork, and they fluttered away, chirping, only to return in moments. She dug beneath a withered plant, then grasped it in one hand, shaking the harvest from its roots. There was something to be said for garden work, she decided, her movements mechanical as she moved to the next row. It gave a body time to think, made her soul feel at peace.

Sweat dripped from Maggie's eyebrow, and she rubbed her forehead with the back of one hand, looking toward the barn. Beau Jackson stood in the wide doorway, and his gaze touched hers with warmth. He nudged the brim of his hat and turned away, leading a tall mare toward the corral, but the memory of his dark eyes did not fade. He was a handsome man. Maybe if someone like him had paid her some mind she'd have taken the same route Roberta and Emily had trod, getting married and moving to town.

They'd sure grabbed at the first chance they had to clear out of the house and away from Pa's heavy hand. Ma had helped them gather their things and leave, much as she'd turned the other way when Maggie had called it quits and climbed out the bedroom window the other night.

And now Mama was left alone to bear the brunt of Pa's miserable self. Maggie bent her head, almost tempted to return, to bear some of her mother's burden. She shuddered at the very thought of going back to that hateful place. Pa would be fuming mad at having to do the field work alone as it was. She'd not give him the chance to whip her into shape again.

Never.

Chapter Three

What the food lacked in flavor it made up for in quantity, Beau decided. Pieces of beef swimming in broth with bits of potatoes made up the bulk of his meal, small pieces of carrots adding color. The onions lent seasoning, but she'd been pretty scant with salt and pepper. He shook the salt shaker over his dish with a heavy hand, aware of Maggie watching from across the table.

"Not very good, is it?" she asked quietly. "I'm not the best cook in the world."

He glanced up. "It's better than I could have done, Maggie." Another bite found its way into his mouth. "Maybe next time you just need to quit cooking it before the vegetables get…" He paused, unwilling to add to her gloom.

"Mushy," she supplied. "I probably won't be here long enough for there to be a next time, though," she said after a moment. "I don't want you to get in Dutch over me stayin' here."

"No one will know where you are, as far as I'm concerned," he told her grimly. "And if your father comes hunting you, he'll find more than his match."

She glanced up at him, and Beau caught a glimpse of beauty in the line of cheek and brow, a promise of charm in the lifting of long lashes as one eye met his gaze. Her swollen eye was still purpled, but as he watched, a tear fell from its lower lid. She blinked and her mouth trembled. "You're a nice man, Beau Jackson. I reckon you mean that."

Beau reached across the table, capturing her hand, holding it loosely within his palm. "You can stay here as long as you want to, Maggie."

She rose from the table, drawing her hand from his, and picked up her plate. "I'll wash out the wheelbarrow in the morning and load up the potatoes I dug. You got a place to store them?"

Beau nodded. "There's an old root cellar on the west side of the house. You'll want to watch for mice when you open the door. Last year we piled the potatoes against the far wall. Had pretty near enough to last past spring. They'll get soft by then and you have to cut off the sprouts, but they're fit to eat. There's a tub for carrots and a place to hang onions and such."

"There's more to dig, yet. Ma always liked to have the old plants pulled and the ground turned in the fall. I can do that tomorrow."

"Then don't plan on mucking out stalls," Beau told her firmly. "The men can tend to that. I'd rather have you at the house."

She stood at the sink, her shoulders hunched, her hands busy with the dishes. "Do you think I could help with the horses, maybe the yearlings? I've got a good touch with animals."

"We'll see," Beau said. "You might want to take a look at my milk cow in the morning. Maybe you can do something for her. She's been touchy the last couple of days at milking time."

Maggie turned to face him. "Might be she's a little milk bound. You ever use camphorated oil on her?"

Beau shook his head. "She's never had any problems before."

"You got any oil? I'll warm some up and see if it helps. You just don't want to get it in the milk. You have to wash off her bag before you commence to milkin' her."

Maybe the girl was right. It was worth a try. Beau pushed back from the table and rose. "There's a boxful of stuff in the pantry," he said. "Salves and such. Take a look. I'm pretty sure there's camphorated oil there."

Maggie wiped her hands on a towel, nodding her understanding. "I'll see what I can find. Have you milked her tonight, yet?"

"No, I'm ready to do the last of the chores now."

"Can I come with you?" she asked.

Beau nodded. "I'll wait for you."

The cow's tail twitched as Maggie sat on the milking stool. "It's only me," she murmured, her hand moving slowly over the animal's flank. She glanced up at Beau. "She got a name?"

"Not that I know of," he told her with a grin. "I just call her the cow."

"Animals do better with a name." Her hands moved together now, over the curve of the cow's belly, then to the front udder. A visible shiver passed over the creature and she shifted her near leg.

"She feels kinda hot, inflamed maybe," Maggie said quietly. "Let's try the warm oil and see if it helps by morning." One hand moved to her pocket and she withdrew a small bottle she'd warmed atop the cookstove only minutes before. She uncapped it and poured a puddle of it into her palm, then spread the pungent liquid over the bulging udder.

The cow stood still, only lowing softly as Maggie intoned words of comfort. Her voice was soft as she glanced at Beau. "You're not gonna want to use her milk tonight. I'm gonna use some of this on her teats, too."

Beau murmured agreement, crouching beside her, taking the oil from between her knees where she'd lodged it as she worked. She glanced up quickly at his touch, but he ignored her, his fingers deft as he tightened the cap and waited, silent as he listened to the soft syllables she uttered.

"I'll milk her for you," Maggie offered. "I don't think I'd ought to strip her out, though, just take milk enough to keep her comfortable."

"I'll get the pail," Beau offered, rising and moving at an easy pace. He returned in moments and put the bucket in place.

His attention was too intense, his presence too near, and Maggie shifted uncomfortably on the stool. "Haven't you got chores to do?" she asked, glancing up at him. "I can handle her just fine by myself."

He nodded and stepped back. "Leave the pail by the door when you've finished. I'll dump it."

The cow suffered Maggie's hands on her, only shifting a bit in protest. "I'm about done, cow. You'll be fine tomorrow. Just a little fever, nothing we can't take care of." The words flowed in a quiet stream, and within minutes the task was done. Putting the stool against the wall, she looked toward the back of the barn to where deep shadows held the gloom of nightfall. There was no sign of Beau.

"Must have gone out back," she murmured to herself, and then knelt down to look beneath the manger. "Come on out, Cat. I see you there." With a low chirp deep in her throat, the three-legged creature stepped cautiously past the cow and into the aisle.

"Guess I shoulda followed my own advice, Cat," Maggie murmured, bending to run her fingers through the rough fur. "Never did give you a name, did I?" She squatted next to the animal, speaking softly. "I wasn't real sure you were gonna live, you know. I didn't want to bury a critter I was attached to, and I thought if I didn't name you, it wouldn't matter so much if you died. That was pretty dumb, wasn't it?"

She stood, and the cat eyed her from her three-legged stance. "Come on, then," Maggie told her. "You can walk with me up to the house. I don't think the mister would want you inside, though."

Lifting the milk pail, she stepped to the double doors, the cat at her heels. Overhead, the stars were like silver buckshot against the sky and she tipped her head back in amazement at the sheer number of them. Perhaps she hadn't looked up lately, she decided. For more years than she could remember, she'd hung her head lest she be accused of being uppity, it seemed. But tonight she felt free, and the thrill of that discovery brought a sunburst of joy to her heart. With a light step, she set off for the house. The pail bumped against her leg, reminding her of Beau's words, and she deposited it next to the doorway, then made her way across the yard.

"She's got a good hand, don't she?" Pony stood in the shadows just inside the last stall, watching as the girl vanished in the darkness. "Do you suppose she knows what she's doin'? With the stuff she smeared on your cow, I mean?"

"We'll find out, won't we." She'd disappeared, swallowed up in the night, and then he heard the distinct sound of his screened door closing. "There's something about her

that I can't put my finger on. I saw it the other day, with
her cat and dog, and again, just now, the way she talked to
that poor crippled animal.'' He shot a glance at Pony.
''You're going to think this is far-fetched, but it's like she
understands them—and they know it.''

''Nah,'' Pony said, denying Beau's concern. ''I've seen
folks like that in the circus. Either you got it, or you don't.
Most of us don't. I kinda got the touch, with horses anyway, but there's those who have a gift.'' His voice trailed
off and he snorted. ''Now you'll think *I'm* the one goin'
out on a limb.''

The two men walked the length of the barn, a lone lantern providing light overhead. ''What you gonna do with
her, boss?'' Pony asked diffidently.

''Nothing,'' Beau answered.

''She's a pretty good-lookin' woman, ain't she?''

He shot Pony a dark look and his words were grudging.
''Yeah, I suppose so.'' Better than *pretty good,* he thought
glumly, remembering the gleam of dark hair in lantern light
as she soothed the milk cow.

''She know how to cook? I'm gettin' plumb sick of
eatin' my own fixin'.'' Pony's query held a wistful note.
''Seems like I get stuck with most of the meals. Course,
Joe don't know the first thing about food, 'cept for eatin'
it, and Radley does his share just haulin' in wood and
keepin' the ashes dumped.''

Beau noted the lack of Shay's name in Pony's litany,
then grinned as the man continued his sad tale. ''I was
thinkin' maybe she'd fill in a meal once in a while for us,
when she gets the knack real good.''

''Once she learns how to shake on a little more salt and
pepper, she won't be too bad,'' Beau told him. ''I doubt
her mother had much inspiration in the kitchen. From what

she's said, there wasn't much to be grateful for around their table.''

Pony stepped into the aisle, then bent to peer between two barrels. "I thought as much," he exclaimed softly. "I heard a noise a while ago. Looks like we got something goin' on. That mangy hound's made herself a nest."

"I saw her by the porch earlier," Beau said softly, crouching beside the other man. A soft growl issued from the darkness, and he caught a glimpse of movement in the shadows. "I wonder that Maggie didn't notice," he whispered.

"You better tell her," Pony advised. "She'll be madder'n a wet hen if you don't and she finds out." His chuckle was short. "Damned if we're not both a couple of softies, boss. Dogs been havin' litters on their own since year one. This'n will do just fine by herself."

He rose stiffly, and Beau followed suit. "You're probably right." They walked to the front of the barn, and Beau lifted the lantern from its perch. "I'll see you in the morning," he said, moving from the barn to the yard. Behind him, Pony swung the doors into place and latched them firmly.

The storeroom door was closed, and he stood indecisively, his knuckles poised to rap against the solid wood. Without warning, it swung open and Beau remained where he stood, one hand uplifted. Framed in the glow of candlelight, she resembled a nymph, her eyes startled, her body beneath the simple shift a shadowy outline. Without thinking, he clenched his hand, and she hunched her shoulders, ducking her head.

His arm dropped, the fist he'd unwittingly formed jamming against his hip. "I'm sorry. I didn't mean to startle you, Maggie."

Her chin lifted and she backed into her room, one hand

pushing against the open door, as if she would close him
out. "I was going to get a drink. I thought you were still
in the barn."

He shook his head. "Wait a minute, honey. I need to tell
you about your dog."

She froze in place. "What's wrong with Maisie?" Turning from him, she snatched at the shirt she'd placed on the
bed. "Turn away, mister. I'm gonna get dressed."

Beau obligingly turned his back on her, a grin twitching
at the corners of his mouth. If she only knew that he'd
already taken a good gander at her slender frame, outlined
by the glow of the candle behind her, she'd probably have
a fit. Not that there was a whole lot to see. She was a little
bit of a thing, built more like a child, but for the curves of
her breasts. Probably some good food on a regular basis
would fill her out nicely.

Behind him, she shoved her way past. "Where's my
dog? Is she all right?"

"Put your boots on, girl," Beau reminded her. "The
dog's all right, just holed up behind a couple of barrels. I
think she's ready to drop her litter. I thought you'd want
to know."

Her feet slid readily into the pair of boots he'd talked
Pony out of the day before, and she left the kitchen, the
spring of the screened door slamming it in place.

"Might's well join the party," Beau muttered to himself.
"There'll be no sleeping till she comes back in anyway."
Snatching the lantern from the table, he followed her out
the door, heard the murmur of voices from in front of the
barn, and then the sound of the doors opening.

"That you, Pony?" he called.

Shay appeared before him. "No, boss. I was just about
to look for the lantern. The girl says her dog's cooped up
havin' pups. Thought I'd get her some light."

"I've got this one," Beau told him.

"You want me to stick around, keep an eye on things?" Shay asked quietly.

Beau considered only a moment. "No. Go on back to the bunkhouse. I'll be here." Shay nodded and turned away. Beau watched him go. The man had either taken a shine to Maggie, or he'd appointed himself her guardian angel. And it had better be the latter.

The animals stirred, a low whinny from one of the stalls signaling a mare's unease. Beau strode the length of the aisle, and several heads turned in his direction as he passed the open stalls. Maggie crouched by the barrels, speaking softly to the creature she'd rescued.

"Want me to move those barrels?" Beau asked, hanging the lantern from a peg on the wall.

"Just the one," she responded. "It's too heavy for me to shift it alone. I already tried."

He leaned the barrel a bit and rolled it easily, giving better access to the dog's chosen spot. Maggie reached a hand toward the mongrel and Beau held his breath. It wouldn't be unheard of for a dog to bite while in the throes of labor, and the thought of Maggie's small hand left torn and bloody made him cringe inwardly. But the dog only whined, and Beau watched as a long tongue wrapped itself around slender fingers.

"I'm here, Maisie," Maggie crooned. "I'll tend to you if you need me." She settled herself cross-legged and her hands moved knowingly over the creature's swollen belly. "You got a whole mess of 'em, haven't you, girl?"

As Maggie spoke, the dog stiffened and thrust her head back, a guttural sound passing through her clenched teeth. Maggie's hands pressed and massaged, her words soft, almost indecipherable, as she comforted the straining mother-to-be. "You don't need to stay around, mister," she said after a moment, as the dog panted and closed her eyes.

"When you going to start calling me Beau?" he asked her quietly, crouching beside her.

She glanced up, and her small smile coaxed an answering grin from his mouth. "I guess now's as good a time as any," she allowed. "I'll be here a while…Beau. Why don't you go on to bed?"

"Nah, I get a kick out of watching new life come into the world," he told her. "Why don't I get us a cup of coffee, and we'll both stick around."

"Can she feed six pups? She's kinda scrawny, don't you think?" Beau leaned back in his chair, watching as Maggie stirred scrambled eggs in his large skillet. The sun was high in the sky, and they'd been in the barn until after midnight.

"She'll do fine," Maggie answered, turning to the table. "I'll feed her extra, if you don't mind. They ought to be good pups. I think the daddy's a big shepherd from the next farm to my pa's." She reached for a spoon. "You don't have a dog, do you?"

Beau shook his head. "There was one hanging around when I bought the place, but he died." He watched as scrambled eggs were turned out onto his plate. "Does Maisie belong to your pa?"

She frowned, spoon held midair. "What are you thinkin'? That I stole her?" She exhaled noisily, and stomped back to the stove. "My pa wouldn't give the time of day to an animal, let alone food to fill its belly." The skillet settled on the stove with a clatter, and Maggie went to stand before the door.

"I'm sorry," Beau said quietly. "I just need to know where the land lays, Maggie. If someone comes to my door looking for a stolen dog, I need to be sure you don't have anything to do with it.'' She was silent, and he darted a look at her.

''Maggie, come on and eat something,'' he said. ''I didn't mean to doubt your honesty, thinking you'd take a dog that wasn't yours. I had to be sure. Though to tell the truth, the poor thing doesn't look like she's worth much anyway.''

Maggie spun to face him. ''She's worth a lot to me. When I leave here, she'll be my protection.'' Her eyes glittered, and Beau motioned to the chair across the table from himself.

''Sit down. We need to talk a little bit.''

She moved across the floor and slid into the chair. ''Go ahead. Eat your eggs,'' she said. ''I'm not goin' anywhere for a while. And that's another thing I need to mention.''

Beau ate steadily, willing her to continue. She was a far cry from the female he'd coaxed into his house only three days past, and the difference was most gratifying. ''Go ahead,'' he said. ''Talk away.''

''Well, I thought I'd find enough to do for you to earn my keep till Maisie gets her pups weaned. I was worried about having to keep us safe and dry in the woods till she had them. Now, with being here and all, I thought I could work for you for the next five or six weeks.'' She broke off, her eyes seeking his, her hands clenched tightly against the tabletop.

Beau nodded, as if he considered her plan. She'd made it easy for him, given him six weeks to figure out some sort of future, and it was all he could do not to beam his approval. ''That oughta work,'' he said slowly. ''I'll need an extra hand here while a couple of my men take horses to Dodge City this month. You can...''

''You didn't answer me before.'' Her words were eager and her hands lay flat now, as she leaned forward, sitting on the edge of her chair. "Do you think I could help work with the yearlings you keep?"

"I don't want you too far from the house, Maggie. If your pa comes hunting you down, I'd just as soon he didn't see you."

She nodded, considering his words. "Maybe I could work in the corral. You know I can do barn work." Her head turned to the door as a man's voice rising in protest caught her attention from outside.

"Damn dog!"

Beau was on his feet. "I'll bet somebody set Maisie off. Probably got too close."

From the porch, Pony called his name, and Beau headed for the door. "The girl's dog won't let Joe in the barn," Pony said through the screen. "You better come on out, boss."

"I'll come," Maggie said, pushing away from the table and hurrying past Beau. She brushed against him and retreated, her glance quick. "Sorry, didn't mean to shove at you that way."

She'd flinched from him, and again Beau felt a moment's anger at the man who had instilled fear into her very being. "Run on out, Maggie," he urged her. "I can't take a chance on a dog bite. We'll have to tie her, I guess. She's not going to feel safe with those pups nursing."

Maggie ran before him, her feet flying across the packed earth. Even with the heavy boots she wore, her gait was more graceful, the limp subsiding, and Beau followed close at her heels, his eyes intent on her. She pulled up short before Joe, keeping a distance as she spoke to him.

"She won't hurt you none if I tell her who you are. Come on in with me," she urged in a rush of breath. "She needs to know you."

Joe tipped his hat back and shook his head. "I'm sorta

attached to my fingers, ma'am. I'd just as soon not have her take after me.''

Maggie looked up at Beau. ''Tell him. Tell him she'll listen to me.''

Beau nodded. ''I believe she will, Joe. Let's take a look.'' He led the way, opening the doors fully and walking toward the back of the barn, the rest trailing behind him. Maggie hurried past and spoke to the new mother in soft tones, then stood as the men approached.

''Just squat down here by me, all of you,'' she said firmly. Then, turning to the dog, she spoke the names of the men who watched, reaching with one hand to touch each of them in order, her fingers barely grazing the backs of their hands. Her other hand curled atop Maisie's head, and her monologue was continuous as she introduced each of them to the watching dog. Only as the velvet nose sniffed at the back of Joe's hand did Maisie hesitate, her low growl signifying doubt.

''I want you to be a good girl,'' she said finally, and then bent low to whisper soft phrases in the animal's ear. Maisie whined and tilted her head, then barked and stood, wagging her tail.

''I'd give a passel to know what she's sayin' to that critter,'' Pony muttered beneath his breath.

The same thought had just crossed Beau's mind, and he nodded. ''Whatever it is, I think…''

''She won't bother you none,'' Maggie said, cutting off his train of thought. ''Just leave her be, and she'll be fine.''

Joe sent her a doubtful look. ''You're sure?''

Maggie stood before the five men, dwarfed by their size. And yet, Beau thought she was, on some level, an equal. And the men seemed to consider her a bit differently than they had that first day.

''I'm more than sure. I'm dead certain,'' Maggie told

them, looking from one to another. "If you leave her a bite of your leftovers once in a while, she'll warm up. Just don't reach for her pups."

She looked across the aisle to an empty stall and her eyes lit up. "There you are, Cat. I wondered where you'd got to." From the darkened area, the lean three-legged feline hobbled toward the group, and Maggie bent to pick up her pet.

"I fed her this morning, over by the bunkhouse," Joe admitted shyly. "I figured she couldn't do much hunting on her own, what with..." He shrugged, as if unwilling to speak aloud the cat's infirmity.

"Thank you kindly." Maggie nodded at him solemnly. "I surely appreciate it."

Beau cleared his throat. "I think we've been lollygaggin' around long enough this morning. There's work to do." The men broke ranks, two of them heading for the back door and the corral, the others picking up pitchforks. "How about taking a look at the cow while we're here, Maggie?" he asked.

She was already heading in that direction and he followed. "She all right?"

Maggie squatted by the spotted Guernsey and ran her hands over the udder. She looked up at Beau and grinned. "She's not hot anymore. I wouldn't drink the milk yet, and I'd better put some more oil on her today, but she'll be fine, I think. I'll just milk her first."

He'd thought to do that chore himself, but there was no sense in arguing with success, he decided, and right now it looked like Maggie was on a roll. "I'll get the oil." He'd play nursemaid this time around, gladly, if it meant his cow was on the mend.

Supper in his kitchen was late again; the men in the bunkhouse were already doing the evening chores by the time Beau sat down at his table. The potatoes were under-done, but the steak was rare. He'd convinced Maggie to throw it in the pan and let it sear for only a minute or so before she turned it over. She'd cringed, shivering as he cut into the tenderloin, watching as the juices ran bright red on his plate.

"How can you eat that?" she asked, her nose wrinkling in disgust. "It's a wonder it's not still moving."

Beau chewed the tender morsel and swallowed. "You can fry yours to a frazzle if you like, but I want mine fit to eat."

Maggie turned back to the stove. "I want it good and dead when it goes in my stomach," she told him. The pan sizzled as she turned the piece of meat again, and finally after a few minutes, she speared it, transferring it to her plate. "That's more like it."

She helped herself to green beans, leaving Beau a second helping in the dish. "I churned butter today, and finished up with diggin' the potatoes," she said after a few minutes. "They're all in the root cellar."

"Did anyone help you?" He'd told Shay to keep an eye out for her this afternoon.

Maggie shook her head. "No. Shay offered, but I told him I could do it. He watched me from out by the barn while he was shoein' a horse." She took a bite and chewed slowly, then pushed her potatoes around on the plate. "I helped him a little bit. You don't mind, do you?"

"Not if he doesn't," Beau said. "Shay's not much for small talk. Don't have your feelings hurt if he doesn't say much."

"He didn't say anything, only nodded his head when I took hold of the mare's halter and held her steady."

"It was her first set of shoes," Beau explained. "She was probably a little spooked."

"I know. I felt like she needed someone to talk to her," Maggie explained. "So I did. But I got the potatoes done anyway."

They finished eating in silence and Beau took his plate to the sink. "I'll be out back for a while. Thanks for cooking." He left the house, noting the two men who busied themselves inside the barn. He had things to think about, he decided, veering past the bunkhouse and heading for the small peach orchard. The trees were bare of fruit and the leaves had begun to wither. It was quiet, with starlight filtering through the tree limbs overhead. Settling himself on the ground against a dark tree trunk, he bent one knee, leaning back against the rough bark. He needed to consider carefully just how deeply he was becoming involved with his little fugitive.

She was bright, but uneducated. He'd watched as she scanned through the book of recipes Sophie used on occasion. That she was unable to read the script therein was obvious. A look of utter frustration had masked her features, and he'd been appalled that anyone lacked the basic skills in this day and age. Most girls spent at least six years in schooling, sometimes more. And yet, Maggie appeared not to have been given that opportunity. He'd not wanted to embarrass her and had looked aside.

Now he considered her situation. There must be some way he could approach her, some plan he could evolve to help her. She was intelligent, despite her lack of schoolroom skills. And her innate knowledge of animals was remarkable.

Shifting against the tree, he felt a piece of tree branch beneath him and his fingers searched it out. It lay in his palm, a thickened area catching his attention, and he lifted it closer, studying the odd shape of a bole in the wood. Something about it appealed to him, and he eased his knife from his pocket as he considered the shape of his find. In the light cast from moon and stars overhead, his narrowed gaze found the suggestion of a cat within the piece of tree limb. He cut off the excess branch, then whittled at it, turning it back and forth, seeking the elusive form he'd envisioned there.

Tomorrow evening he'd sound her out, he decided. Some way, somehow, he'd ease past her distrust and persuade her to his side. She'd come a long way already, except for flinching from him twice. When he'd taken the bottle of oil from between her knees in the barn last night, she'd inhaled sharply and shivered. And again today, when she'd brushed past him, there'd been that moment of hesitation, as though she expected a blow from his hand.

His knife slipped and he sliced through the wood he held. "Damn," he muttered, the profanity not one he was given to use. His mother had frowned on cusswords, and respect for her memory kept them to a minimum in his vocabulary. This time, the single syllable was heartfelt and he repeated it.

"Damn. She thought I was going to hit her," he growled beneath his breath.

He cast aside the piece of wood he held and skimmed the ground with his left hand, seeking another scrap, but it was not to be. And then he stood, a thought piercing his mind. There were any number of likely prospects in the woodshed, just beyond the outhouse. Tomorrow he'd find one and spend some time with Maggie. He'd carve her a cat, and get her to talk to him.

Long strides carried him from the stand of peach trees toward the house. The thought of the girl there was a lure he could not resist. "I only want to help her," he whispered staunchly to himself. And his pace increased as he walked.

Perhaps she was still in the kitchen.

Chapter Four

Whittling would have to go by the wayside, Beau found upon arising the next morning. The weather looked good, a cloudless sky and hot sunshine setting his course. He'd learned early on to take advantage of fine weather and this looked to last for a couple of days.

Cutting hay was the order of the day, with the last field awaiting the mower. It was a hot, sweaty chore, one he figured to last about three days. But with five men working, the job went well, and with Maggie putting together meals of sorts, they managed to cut the field and rake it loosely, spreading it to dry by the second evening. By noon of the third day Beau looked out on the hayfield, satisfied that the sun had cooperated. With another turning by hand, the hay would be ready, once the dew burned off in the morning. They would rake it again, into rows this time, ready for the hay wagon to make its rounds.

That first evening, Beau had dragged himself atop his stallion, heading for his nearest neighbor, where he'd explained his dilemma, then begged loaves of bread from Rachel McPherson. With Sophie still not back, they were hard-pressed for fresh bread, and he was not willing to put such a demand on Maggie's talents.

Rachel had cheerfully offered to come and help her for a morning, but Beau refused, unwilling to involve his neighbor in his situation. Bad enough that he had slipped and divulged the girl's presence in his home. Swearing Rachel to secrecy, he'd headed for his place with three loaves of fresh bread and the promise of more on the morrow.

Cord McPherson had glowered from the back of his horse as Beau left, the man's possessive streak apparent. If Rachel hadn't been spoken for a few years back, Beau would have given the other rancher a run for his money. But trespassing on forbidden property was not in line with his values. Rachel was taken, and Beau was only too aware that the dark-haired beauty had eyes only for the tall rancher she'd married.

He'd carried his booty into the house and unveiled the three loaves for Maggie's inspection. She'd produced the breadboard and a knife and set to work with a will, mumbling as she cut the heel off with a vicious whack.

"There was no need to go beggin' at the neighbors. I told you I'd try my hand at baking," Maggie'd told him, slicing savagely at the loaf before her, as if his dependence on a neighbor was in some way a betrayal of her skills.

Beau winced. "Watch what you're doing, Maggie. You're making hash out of that thing."

She sniffed, stepping back to view her efforts. "I think it's too soft, that's all. Mama's bread always sliced real easy."

"Probably not so light as Rachel's," Beau surmised. "My neighbor is a good hand at baking. She'll have more for us tomorrow. You'll have to develop a lighter touch with that knife by then," he teased.

And she had, reduced to muttering about her own shortcomings as she ate with relish the bounty from Rachel McPherson's oven. Beau's only fear in the matter was that if he wasn't careful, he'd have his neighbor on his doorstep, investigating his refugee. Rachel's curiosity was potent, and he'd barely persuaded her to stay at home where she belonged. If she wasn't up to her neck with the two little ones Cord McPherson had given her, one right after the other, she'd probably have been here already.

Maggie'd done well, he decided, munching on one of the roast beef sandwiches she'd prepared for them. He sat with his back against a tree on the west side of the hayfield, where the afternoon shade was best. Sophie was due back, he figured. He'd begun looking for her the day before yesterday. He almost rued her return. Having Maggie to himself had become a habit.

Luring her closer day by day had become a challenge. And there was a certain amount of danger in that. Not that he'd been in any shape to pursue a female. Cutting hay and filling the hayloft was a job that took the starch out of a man. They cut hay at least twice a year. Sometimes if the summer was early and ran late, they managed to get in three cuttings, which provided more than enough for his own stock and some to sell off to the livery stable in town. But it was a whole lot of work crammed into three or four days, he thought glumly, and he was ripe with sweat and ready for a long soak in the galvanized tub.

Around him the scent of hay and the sounds of men's small talk lent satisfaction to his thoughts. It was his hayfield and his crew of workers, and before long Beau Jackson would be the sole name on the title to his farm. When Joe and Rad returned from Dodge City with the money from the horses he was committed to sell to the army, he'd have enough to make the final payment on his mortgage.

His gaze settled on the two men, Joe only twenty years old, Rad the elder by a decade or so. They'd proved to be worthy of his trust, and that was just about what this trip amounted to. He'd be trusting the pair of them to handle a sale he ought to have his own hand on. A faint chill of unease passed over him and he set it aside, rising to his feet, summoning the crew back to work.

"Let's see if we can get this hay in the barn by suppertime," he said. Lifting the jar of water Maggie'd provided him with to his lips, he swallowed deeply. Then watched as the four men took their places once more. The sun was hot against his back as he picked up his hay rake and lifted the first forkful of hay, tossing it easily to the waiting wagon. Around him, the men worked in harmony, Pony driving the wagon, the others pitching hay.

He bent to pick up a sheaf, testing it for dryness, satisfied that the care they'd taken in turning it to dry had given results. It wouldn't do to put green hay in the barn. Fires had been started that way, and he couldn't afford such a loss.

Maggie waited on the porch, her hands busy peeling potatoes from the bread pan she held in her lap. She was doing better these days, she decided, leaving more of the potato to be cooked, instead of tossing so much to the pigs with the parings. She quartered the specimen in her hand and tossed it into a waiting kettle of water. The sun was leaning toward the west, and the hay wagon had just made its second trip of the afternoon in and out of the barn.

She missed those minutes of laughter from the men as they transferred the hay to the loft from the big farm wagon, rued their absence as the vehicle lumbered off, back to the field. Only Pony and Rad had come back this time, the others raking and piling hay for the next load. Cat lay beside her on the porch swing and she bent her head to speak to the shy creature.

"Just you and me, Cat. Old Maisie's got herself a full-

time job with those pups, hasn't she?'' The cat looked up
from yellow eyes and a purr of content was Maggie's answer. And then the eyes narrowed and the sleek head turned
quickly to the yard, her ears pricking and twitching, one
folded, the other erect.

Even as Maggie sensed the animal's apprehension, she
heard the sound of buggy wheels against the long driveway,
and the whinny of a horse. She rose, in her haste spilling
the pan of potatoes to the porch. Then, knife in hand, she
watched as the visitors approached. A young man drove the
buggy, and at his side a middle-aged woman sat erect, holding a basket in her lap. They drew up to the porch, the
horse's nose almost within touching distance as Maggie
drew in a deep breath of relief.

And met Sophie's gaze. For it could be no one else.
Surely not the woman called Rachel McPherson, for she
was mother to two young'uns, and this woman had more
years on her than Maggie's own mother. The driver jumped
down with a nod to Maggie and scurried around the back
of the buggy, lifting his hand to assist his companion.

''You gotta be Sophie,'' Maggie said hoarsely, wishing
she'd had the presence of mind to gather the potatoes to
the pan instead of standing there like a dunderhead. For
surely that's what Pa would have called her, had he seen
her clumsiness.

''I'm Sophie all right,'' a sharp voice returned. ''And
who are you?'' Piercing eyes raked Maggie from stem to
stern, and she wished for a shroud to cover her, instead of
the pants and shirt she'd cadged from Pony. The man added
his scrutiny to that of Sophie and Maggie backed to the
door, her only thought to escape his penetrating stare.

She felt the mesh of the screen against her back and her
fingers lay flat against the wooden doorjamb. ''I'm Mag-

gie," she whispered, then cleared her throat to repeat the admission. "My name's Maggie. I've been stayin' here."

Sophie climbed the stairs, sidestepping the potatoes that blocked her path and offered the basket she carried to Maggie's care. "Take this, girl. I'll just grab a'hold of my satchel."

Turning, she took her bag from her companion and bent to plant a kiss on his cheek. "You take good care of my girl, Carmichael. You hear me?" At his abashed nod, Sophie turned back, her brow rising as she faced Maggie.

"Well, back off, girl, and I'll open the door for you to carry my baking inside. Then you better come back out here and pick up those spuds. They won't get to the kettle by themselves."

Maggie knew she was staring, sensed that her mouth was agape, and was only able to do as she was bid. By the time she'd carried the heavy basket indoors and deposited it on the table, the buggy was gone, and Sophie was trudging past her with satchel in hand, muttering words that predicted a troublesome time for Beau Jackson when he showed his face once more.

Back on the porch, Maggie gathered the potatoes and settled back on the swing, working rapidly at the peeling process, fearing her time here was soon to come to an end. She reached for last potato as the oven door clanged open in the kitchen.

"What you got in this oven, girl?" Sophie's query rang out even as Maggie heard the big roasting pan slide from place and clatter against the stovetop. The lid was lifted with a rattle and all was silent.

"Pork," Maggie said, peeling long strips of skin from the potato she held.

"Where's the onions?"

Maggie's eyes closed and she leaned her head back

against the swing. "I'll get a couple, right away," she answered, lifting the kettle from the floor and carrying it through the kitchen door.

She deposited it on the sinkboard and turned to face Sophie. "I'm not a very good cook, I'm afraid. And Beau's got me fixin' meals for all five of them, while they're bringin' in the hay."

Sophie stuck a wooden-handled fork into the pork, which Maggie noticed had browned nicely. She'd remembered the salt and pepper, and was thankful for that small favor.

"This is pret'near done, I think. Let's get the onions in right off and let them cook awhile," Sophie said. "You got some in the house?"

Maggie nodded, hurrying to the pantry. Sophie took them from her hands and whipped out a paring knife, Maggie watching in awe as the slices fell beneath the agile blade. In moments, the roaster was back in the oven and Sophie was donning a huge apron. She lifted the coffeepot from the back of the stove and gauged its weight.

"Feels like we need a fresh supply for supper. Myself, I like a cup of tea in the afternoon. You want one, Maggie?"

"Yes, oh, yes," Maggie answered, hurrying to finish the lone potato she'd abandoned minutes past. The full kettle was on the stove in moments, over the hottest area, and Maggie slapped a lid in place, then quickly lifted it to add a scant handful of salt. She'd learned that much, at least, during this long week.

Sophie arranged the flowered teapot from the kitchen buffet in the middle of the table, brought a pitcher of cream from the pantry and stuck a spoon in the sugar bowl. "Come sit down, girl. I think we need to talk," she said, choosing two cups from the half dozen that graced the top shelf of the hutch. Matching saucers held the china cups she'd admired from afar during her stay, and Maggie sat as instructed, her eyes taking in the tea party Sophie assembled with such ease.

Her mother had spoken of such a thing, recalling the years of her youth, before Edgar O'Neill stole the roses from her cheeks and the dreams from her heart. Without thinking, Maggie spoke the thoughts in her mind. "My mama told me about a tea party once."

Sophie settled herself across the table, chose a spoon from the jar and placed it on her saucer. "Did she fix tea for you?"

Maggie shook her head. "My pa said tea was foolishness." Her lips compressed as she considered her words. Sophie would think her an ungrateful daughter. "He let us drink milk, though," she said quickly.

Sophie nodded. "Where'd you come from, girl? How long you been here?"

"A week, and better," Maggie said. "Beau—I mean, Mr. Jackson said I could stay for a while." Remembering the fading bruising of her cheek and eye, Maggie looked down, and then realized her foolishness. Sophie would have long since spotted the telltale signs of a beating. And as if her thoughts had wings to the woman's mind, Maggie heard the question voiced aloud.

"Who hit you, Maggie? You got other bruises besides those I can see?" Sophie leaned across the table, pouring a stream of tea into Maggie's cup, and then her own. A spoonful of sugar was added, then a dash of cream before she offered the pitcher to Maggie. "Do you like cream?" she asked quietly.

Inviting the woman's scrutiny, Maggie lifted her head and met a kindly gaze. "I never had tea before," she admitted. "I reckon I'd like cream in it. It tastes good in coffee." Pouring a reckless amount into the delicately scented beverage seemed wasteful, but following Sophie's lead, Maggie added sugar to the brew and, choosing a spoon, stirred it with care.

Somehow there seemed to be a ritual about this occasion, and she sipped at the hot tea carefully, replacing the cup as she savored the new flavor. And then she folded her hands in her lap and prepared for what was to come. "My pa gets mean sometimes," she began.

"Your mother didn't stop him?" Sophie asked softly, even as her eyes flashed and her tone sharpened.

Maggie shook her head. "Nah. I'm the last one home and Ma knew not to put in a word or Pa would lash out at her, too. My sisters took all they could before they hightailed it last spring."

"Where'd they go?" Sophie asked, lifting her tea cup to her mouth.

"Two men from town, brothers they were, asked Emily and Roberta to marry up with them. They'd seen them on the sly, I think."

Sophie nodded. "And they were more adventuresome than you, I guess."

Maggie chanced a grin. "Yes, ma'am, they were. Pa didn't have a glimmer, till he found their empty bed one morning." Her grin became a wide smile. "He was hoppin' mad. Pret'near punched a hole in the wall, and then re-membered himself and hit me and Mama instead. Said we were to blame for not tellin' him, so he could stop them from leavin'." She recalled that day and a profound satis-faction filled her heart. "I'm glad they got away. I'm just sorry Mama took a whippin'. Laid her up for a couple of days."

Sophie stood abruptly, moving across the kitchen. Reaching the window, she turned and faced Maggie. "Land sakes, girl. You're lucky to be alive. Why did you stay so long?"

Maggie's mind filled with the image of Verna O'Neill, the woman who'd borne her. "I knew he'd take after Mama real bad once I left. But I couldn't hang on any longer, once he killed my critters."

"Your critters?"

"I had a couple of cages in the woods where I kept wild things that were hurt, and I fixed them and then let them go again. Pa found them and killed them." She shivered, recalling that day, remembering the anger that had driven her to flee. "I left that night, walked a few miles and slept in the woods. Then the second night I hid in the hayloft here in the barn, and Beau found me in the morning."

"And took you in, bless his heart," Sophie finished, nodding as if such a development was not surprising. "Does your pa know where you are?"

Maggie felt a leap of fear. "No, if he did, I'd not still be here. He'd have dragged me home already."

"Huh! I doubt Beau Jackson would allow that."

"I don't know that he could stop him, ma'am. Pa says the laws give him leave to do whatever he wants to his womenfolk. He says we're just the same as his cow and horse. We're part of his property."

"I was all set to rake you over the coals, you know." Sophie eyed Beau from her perch on the back porch. He stood on the step below, his eyes calculating her degree of aggravation. It was hard to tell. Her mouth was pursed, yet her eyes held a trace of amusement.

"Well, hello to you, too, Sophie. When'd you arrive?"

"About an hour ago," she answered. "I've been waitin' for a chance to talk to you."

"What did I do this time?" he asked after a moment,

although his better judgment had already clued him in on the problem. Maggie was nowhere to be seen, and unless he missed his guess, she was due to be the subject of this conversation. If there was to be one. From where he stood it looked like Sophie'd already met and judged the girl.

"I took one look at your guest…" Sophie began.

"She looked that way, and a hell of a lot worse, in fact, when she got here," Beau cut in. "And she's staying, Sophie. There's no argument where that's concerned."

She nodded. "By the time she told me where she got the bruises, I'd decided you were right to give her a place to stay."

"Then what's all the fuss about?" He looked past his housekeeper toward the kitchen door. "Where is she?"

"I told her to take a bath before supper, and helped her fix the tub. She didn't have any other clothes to wear, so I found her a dress of mine. She'll swim in it, but it'll do till tomorrow, and then you're goin' to town to find her something to wear from the general store. You ought to know without me telling you that it's not fitting for a young woman to be wearin' men's clothes."

Beau grinned. "You got her to agree to that?"

"Well, she didn't argue a bit about the bath part, except to worry about using up your soap, but wearin' my dress caused a bit of a problem. I cut off the bottom and made a sash for the waist. It's not fancy, but it'll do for today."

He nodded, willing to be amiable. "I need to make a trip to town, anyway, Sophie. I'll see what I can find. But I'm warning you, she'll make a fuss. She's used to wearing pants, and if she's going to be working in the barn, it's probably for the best." The thought of Maggie sashaying around the horses in a dress didn't set well with Beau. Long skirts would hamper her movements, and she'd be tripping all over herself.

"Well, we'll see," she answered. "You'd best come on in. Supper's about ready."

Beau snatched his hat off and followed Sophie inside, his gaze cutting to the storeroom door. It was closed tight and he thought of the woman inside, probably still sloshing around in the galvanized tub. She'd probably not had two baths in the same week in all of her life, up till now. And he hadn't even thought of it, hadn't even considered that she needed another change of clothing. The days of bringing in the hay had kept him going from early to late, and he'd barely kept his eyes open after supper each night. Washing up in a basin was about as good as it got when his day started at dawn and ended after dark.

"Thanks, Sophie," he murmured. He followed her to the cookstove, watching as she stirred the gravy, then lifted the lid on a kettle of succotash. The scent rose temptingly and his stomach growled accordingly. "I'm glad you're home. Maggie did her best, but we missed you."

"Don't be buttering me up, Beau Jackson. You don't look to me like you've lost any weight while I was gone." She opened the oven and slid the roasting pan out, transferring it to the stovetop. Steam rose as she lifted the cover and the scent of pork roast made his mouth water. "I'm about to make gravy," Sophie said, reaching for a platter for the meat. "Are those men ready to come in and eat?"

"They're almost done. Pony was unharnessing the team when I came up to the house. They've been spoiled the past three days, not having to do their own cooking, with Maggie fixing supper every night."

"Well, ring the bell. You got time to wash up."

Beau hung his hat by the door and stepped onto the porch, reaching for the bell rope. He tugged at it sharply and the brass bell swayed twice, the sound loud and clear. From the barn an answering call assured him it had been heard and he went back in the kitchen. The storeroom door opened, and he looked across the room to where Maggie poked her head into view. Her smile was wide as she spied him near the stove, and she stepped into the kitchen. An ill-fitting garment covered her from neck to ankles, a dress that would never be in fashion again, if Beau was any judge.

"I thought I heard you," she said quietly, glancing from Beau to Sophie, and then back. "I'm gonna empty the tub real quick, and then maybe you could help me take it outside, Beau."

He shook his head. "Leave it be till after supper and I'll dump it then. I'm going to take a bath in the kitchen later on. I've about reached my limit on scrubbing up in a pan." He rolled up his sleeves and splashed water into the sink pan.

Maggie nodded and scurried to the back door, comb in one hand. "I'll help in just a few minutes, Sophie," she said. "First I have to braid up my hair."

"You got five minutes, girl. It'll take about that long for me to make the gravy and for those men out back to hightail it up here."

Maggie hurried to the porch and bent low from the waist, allowing her long hair to cascade forward. She combed its length, working at the snarls and tugging the teeth through from her scalp to the trailing ends of her dark locks. Beau, as clean as a quick wash could make him, stood behind her, watching through the screen, his eyes drinking in the graceful lines of her arms and hands as she groomed herself. Her dress fell in voluminous folds from the strip of fabric she'd circled around her waist, and he mourned the loss of the snug-fitting trousers he'd become accustomed to seeing.

After a moment she stood erect, holding her hair in one

hand at the back of her head, then clenching the comb between her teeth, began twisting the long tresses into a braid. Her fingers worked rapidly and he watched in fascination, wondering at her ability to perform such a task. Stepping out onto the porch, he caught her attention, and she spun to face him, her eyes startled, her nostrils flaring.

The comb fell from her mouth and he snatched it midair. "I can't figure out how you can braid your hair behind your head. You can't see what you're doing."

Her lids were both open, the swelling so far gone that only a bit of puffiness remained beneath the damaged eye, and for the first time he gazed fully into the blue depths. He cringed at the bloodshot look of her, ached for the bruising that had faded over the past days to hues of yellow and pale green…yet at the same time admired the delicate lines of brow and cheek as she tilted her head to look at him.

"I've been doin' it for years. My fingers just know what to do, I guess." She pulled the long braid over her shoulder and continued forming the three strands until there was only a short tail undone. "Tear me off a strip from this belt, will you?" she asked, lifting the makeshift sash she wore, extending it in his direction with two fingers.

He took it from her hand and did as she asked, then handed her the piece of material. She wound it rapidly around the pigtail and tied it with a flourish, then bent in his direction. "I had a talk with your Sophie," she whispered.

He grinned in reply. "I know. She told me."

"Is it all right with her if I stay on here?" Her look toward the kitchen door was anxious. "She was real nice to me, Beau, but I don't want to be in her way."

"You won't." He handed her the comb, recognizing it as his own. "Where's the comb you used before?" he asked.

"It wasn't very good. It only had a few teeth in it, and Sophie threw it out," she admitted. "She told me I could use yours. She didn't think you'd mind."

"No, I don't, but you need your own. I'll get you a new one, and a brush, too, when I go to town tomorrow." Something more feminine, he decided, than the plain black specimen he used. Perhaps a hand mirror, too, and some talcum powder in a tin. It gave him a jolt of pleasure to think of buying her such intimate items, envisioning the delight in her eyes when he presented his gifts.

"I'll earn them out," she said quickly. "I need to be figuring up what all I owe you already."

Unwilling to injure her pride, he nodded agreement, then reached to tug teasingly at the end of her pigtail. Her wince did not escape him and he hesitated. "I won't ever hurt you, Maggie. I've told you that before. When you gonna start believing it?"

Her face was downcast and he fit his palm under her chin, lifting it to his view. She bit at her lip and he shook his head at the movement. "Don't do that. You'll make that lip sore again, and it's just starting to heal up good."

"I'm sorry," she said. "Old habits die hard. My mama always used to say that and I guess I know now what she meant. I know you're a good man, but whenever I see a hand come at me or someone movin' quicklike, my heart pounds real funny and I want to run."

His own heart twinged with pain at her words and he nodded his understanding. "Let's go in to supper, Maggie. The men are coming up from the barn, and Sophie's got supper on the table." His hand touched her shoulder and rested there. "I fed your dog in the barn when we brought the last load of hay in. Those pups look pretty healthy. They're moving around real well."

She shifted and moved beneath his fingers and they tightened a bit, holding her in place. His voice was low, his words gentle. "I'm not going to stop touching you, honey. It's like handling a skittish colt. They just have to get used to it, and I suspect it's going to be the same way with you."

"Maybe," she said quietly, turning from him and opening the screened door. "I thank you kindly for tending to Maisie," she murmured.

He bowed his head. "My pleasure, ma'am."

"How would you like to look at a couple of my books, Maggie?" Beau stood in the doorway and Maggie dried her hands on a towel, turning to face him. "Take them into the parlor," he told her. "I'll be out here in the bathtub and you'd best have something to do for a while."

"Do they have pictures in them?" she asked, laying the towel aside and eyeing his offering. Her heart beat rapidly as she considered his suggestion. No one had ever given her the chance to sit and spend time with a book. The thought of having nothing else to do but look at the pages of words she could not read, trying to decipher the letters she could not name was more than she could fathom.

"Pictures?" He frowned and opened the volume he held. "A few," he said. "There's some maps and some pictures of towns in this one, mostly places in Europe." He held out the slender volume, and she took it carefully, turning it over in her hands. "Now, this one…" he said, offering a second book, a soft-cover publication, larger than the first "…is a lady's fashion book that was my mother's. It's been around awhile, but I thought you might like to see the pictures of clothing and jewelry in it."

She felt a lump rise in her throat as she prepared to make the admission that would surely strip her of any respect she might have gained over the past days. "And that's about all I can do, anyway. I can't read, you know." Her fingers tightened on the book she held, as if the contents might seep through the cover and into her mind. *If only it was that easy.* She closed her eyes against the quick tears that threatened to fall.

Never had she felt so unworthy, so ignorant.

And then his hands covered hers, enclosing her own fingers within his grasp. One broad palm lay atop hers, the other beneath, and between them the books were sandwiched. She stood stock-still, overwhelmed by the warmth of his skin, the silent understanding he offered, and finally by the words he spoke.

''I know that, Maggie. I saw you looking at Sophie's cookbook the other day. I don't know why you never had any schooling, but maybe we can do something about it.'' He waited and she opened her eyes, her gaze captured by the hands that enclosed hers with a firm touch.

''I'm stupid, Beau. My pa said I'll never amount to nothing.''

He inhaled sharply and his grip on her tightened. ''Don't you ever say that again, girl. You're a long way from stupid. You've just never had the opportunity to learn.''

She chanced a glance at his face, finding there only the kindness she'd come to expect at his hand. ''I'd like to look at the pictures, anyway, Beau. Even if I never learn to read the words.'' Her voice faltered. ''I've never had a real book to look at, only parts of my mama's Bible that my pa tore up one day when he was mad at her.''

''Could she read?''

Maggie nodded. ''She read to me and my sisters when Pa wasn't around. That's why he tore the Bible up, when he caught her one day. We found pages of it and Mama pressed them with the sadiron and hid them.'' She smiled a bit at the memory. ''We never did know which pages followed which, but there was some good stuff left, and Mama knew a lot of it by heart anyway.''

Beau cleared his throat and Maggie frowned. ''I'll bet you're tired of hearin' my problems.'' She tried to step back, but he held her fast.

''No, you're wrong there,'' he said quietly. ''For now, though, I want you to go into the parlor and settle down on the sofa. I've lit a lamp for you to see by and you need to stay there until I have my bath. All right?''

All right? It couldn't get much righter, she thought, than to have nothing else to do but sit in a fancy parlor and pretend she was a real lady. She nodded, more than willing to do as he said, and Beau released her hands, stepping aside to make way for her. She held the books to her breast and walked to the wide parlor doors, then into the cozy room where a lamp blazed beside the piece of furniture Beau called a sofa.

She sat gingerly on the seat, sliding on the slippery fabric, then leaned back a bit and placed her feet side by side, books in her lap. The room was just as she'd seen it last, when she'd moved every last piece of furniture and swept with the carpet sweeper Beau had placed in her hands. Such luxury was not to be believed, she'd decided, using the tool carefully, amazed at the way it collected bits of dust and held them in a clever compartment until she tipped it to be emptied.

She'd moved each small item on the table and desk, dusting carefully with a soft rag he'd provided her with, and now she took inventory of each picture and object he treasured. To be given leave to just sit in such a place was beyond anything she'd ever heard of. Her fingers tested the fabric beside her, sliding over the sleek seat and then, with a sigh, she leaned against the high, curved back of the sofa.

A foolish grin curved her lips and she shivered as she thought of what her pa would say if he could see her now.

But, thanks to Beau Jackson, that wasn't going to happen. Not right this minute, anyway, maybe not even tomorrow or the next day. Beyond that she could not imagine, for in the past days, she'd learned to only hope and plan for one day at a time, lest her happiness in this place come to a sudden, crashing stop—and she be thrown once more into the miserable hell she'd known for nineteen years.

Chapter Five

The window was high in the wall, with shutters that closed it from the inside. Maggie stood in the doorway of the storage room, wondering for a moment why Beau had placed the opening so close to the ceiling. The other windows in this house were only a foot or so above the floors, yet this one was so high she'd have to step up on her tiptoes to see outdoors.

And then his reasoning for doing such a thing invaded her mind and she was swamped with a deep sense of appreciation for his thoughtfulness. For, if she couldn't see out, then it made sense that no one from the outside could see into her room. She could leave it open at night for air if she wanted to, or during the day to provide light without fear of being watched.

He'd known, he must have realized her need for privacy, and had acted accordingly. She smiled at this example of the man's thoughtfulness and entered the small room. Reaching up, she pushed the shutters into place, then opened them wide, pleased at the difference.

"Is it all right?" Beau asked from behind her, and she turned to face him.

"It's more than just all right," she told him. She knew

her smile gave away her pleasure, and no more was necessary, but somehow she had to touch him, had to reinforce
her thankfulness for his work on her behalf. She crossed to
where he stood, one hand resting against the doorjamb, the
other shoved into his trouser's pocket.

Without thinking, she reached to touch him, her fingers
resting on his chest. "I want to thank you, Beau. I'd never
have thought of puttin' it so high on the wall, and I was
thinkin' it would bother me to have it open at night. Now
I don't have to worry none that somebody could look in at
me."

He grinned. "There's bushes outside right up tight to the
house, so unless someone wanted to get a ladder I figure
you're out of sight of anybody walking by." He slid the
hand from his pocket and captured her fingers in a movement so rapid she barely had time to squeak a protest.
"Hush," he told her quietly. "I'm not grabbing at you,
Maggie. I just like it that you touched me all on your own."
His smile was quick. "I think I'm making progress with
my skittish filly."

She felt a blush rise to cover her cheeks. "I didn't mean
to be forward," she whispered. "I didn't think." Her fingers curled within his grasp and she felt the calluses that
ridged his palm.

"Now, Maggie," he began, his eyes twinkling as though
he enjoyed her embarrassment. "If you were to kiss me,
that might be considered as being a bit forward. But certainly just touching my shirt doesn't qualify."

Obviously the man didn't know that she could feel the
heat of his body through the shirt she'd grazed with her
fingertips, nor did he understand that she'd never before
laid her hand on a man. The thought of kissing him was so
far beyond the meanderings she'd indulged in, it was nigh
onto mind-boggling. Even the image of her lips touching

any part of his skin brought fresh heat to the blush she knew was even now firmly in place.

And then he lifted her hand from his shirtfront and raised it to his lips. They were warm and dry against her knuckles and his gaze met hers as he held her hand there, his mouth pressing against her flesh. His lips moved then, whispering words against her fingers, causing a tingle to rise from the bottom of her spine, bringing a soft shiver into being.

"I'm pleased to do something for you, Maggie girl. I know you won't give me a kiss in thanks, and I don't expect you to."

She snatched her hand from his grasp and buried it within the folds of her skirt. "Then why did you..." She could not continue, could not speak the word he whispered so readily.

"Why did I kiss your hand? Maybe to thank you for doing the cooking and cleaning and working in the garden and taking care of my cow." As he spoke he held up one finger, then two, three, then four, until he'd enumerated the reasons he'd listed. "If I were paying you wages, I'd be deeply in your debt, you know."

"You don't owe me nuthin', Beau Jackson!" she declared. "That shoe's on the other foot."

"Ah, but I disagree with you there," he said solemnly. "So, when I went to town the other day I brought back some things for you to wear, instead of paying you cash money."

She was perplexed. "You already gave me the dress I'm supposed to wear at the table when we eat supper. What else are you talkin' about?" For he'd indeed brought her a blue checked gingham dress, with buttons all down the front and a sash that tied in the back. She'd made a bow and then looked in the mirror he'd nailed into place on the wall for her benefit and her mouth had fallen open in shock.

Never had a garment fit her before. Once she'd tied that sash, her waist was outlined and her top and bottom looked all curvy and she'd flushed bright red, her gaze taken with the sight of her own form.

"I got you some pants that should fit better than those of Pony's and some shirts. We'll call the account square, seeing as I haven't paid you for your work here." He picked up a parcel from a nearby chair and handed it to her.

Maggie hefted it in her hands. "Feels pretty heavy for a pair of pants and a couple of shirts."

Beau had the grace to look sheepish. "I had the store-keeper put in a pair of boots for you, too. Those you've been wearing are too big. It's a wonder they haven't given you blisters already."

They had, Maggie wanted to say, but then thought better of it. Pony's cast-offs had rubbed her heel raw the first day, and she'd been dabbing the spot with carbolic salve every night and putting bits of clean rag on it every day.

"I thank you," she said instead, trying to fathom the amount of money Beau had spent. Certainly more than she'd earned in her time here.

He leaned forward and his lips were warm against her forehead. As though he'd branded her with a hot iron, she felt the skin tingle and as he stepped back, she was certain Sophie would notice the evidence of his impulsive behavior. Surely a mark must remain, so vivid was the memory of that masculine mouth against her skin.

"That's twice, Maggie." His smile was crooked and his eyes crinkled at the corners.

"Twice what?" Sophie's voice from the kitchen doorway was enough to send Maggie's heart into double time. What if the woman had seen Beau making monkeyshines with her? Sophie'd be thinking that Beau was going soft in the head, or maybe that Maggie had invited the kiss.

"Twice that Maggie thanked me for cutting the window in the wall for her." Beau turned smoothly and faced his housekeeper. His grin well in place, he protected Maggie with his bulk. The girl had looked thunderstruck at the sound of Sophie's question, her hands rising to cover her cheeks, her eyes wide and startled.

"Well, it was good of you, Beau. I thought she must be stifling in that little cubbyhole with no air comin' in or out. Course the nights are gettin' cool now with fall comin' on, but a body still needs fresh air, I always say." Sophie's homily brought a grin to Beau's lips.

"I'll get window glass in town and frame it in right," he told Sophie. "I don't want snow coming in through the cracks around the shutters next month."

"You think we'll have snow so early on?" Sophie looked dubious.

"Pony says the caterpillars are wearing heavy coats. Seems like we've had snow before the end of October some years."

"Well, I hope you don't believe everything Pony tells you," Sophie retorted. "He's tried to convince me that women actually dress up in spangles and show their legs and then stand up on the backs of horses while they're goin' full-tilt around in a circle."

"You didn't believe him?" Beau asked, smothering a chuckle at Sophie's look of horror.

"Well, I wouldn't, either," Maggie said from behind him. "Why would anybody make such a fool of herself that way?"

"Folks pay a bundle to see circus performers," Beau said, moving to allow Maggie passage from her room. His sharp eye surveyed her quickly. She'd recovered from the blush and now stepped to Sophie's side, clearly aligning herself with the other woman.

"You've seen such a thing?" she asked Beau, her mouth pursing as if she judged his character by the forthcoming answer.

"I've been to a circus," he admitted, thinking privately that such an expedition was the least of his ventures into the world of pleasure.

"Were the women wearin'—" Sophie broke off, shaking her head. "Never mind, I don't want to know." Her sniff was accompanied by a straightening of her spine and she turned to Maggie. "We've got better things to do than talk about such vulgarities, girl. There's supper to put on the table." She turned from Beau, but Maggie hesitated.

Her gaze flirted with his for a moment as though memories barred her from such intimate contact. "Beau." The single syllable was whispered almost beneath her breath, and he felt the vibration of its tone deep within his breast. *Damn.* The girl was getting to him in a way he hadn't foreseen. And even as he hardened his heart against her appeal, that most vital of all organs betrayed him.

"Thank you for..." Her hesitation was long, as if she enumerated the list in her mind, and then she clenched her jaw, allowing her blue eyes to clash with the depths of his own dark gaze. "I'd appreciate the window glass. I know it'll cost you dear. Pa always said it wasn't needful to cover windows so's you could see out of them. We only had shutters in the house, and glass only in the kitchen, so Mama wouldn't waste kerosene in the lanterns."

She was so needy, this waif who had invaded his heart and home. Perhaps her appeal was only that he felt pride in being able to help her, give her that which she had so greatly lacked in her growing-up years. And with that thought to sustain him, he offered a smile of benevolence.

"I can afford window glass," he told her. "I'll see to it that you 'earn it out,' as you say." *And thereby keep her here,* his heart sang, beating a triumphant rhythm against his ribs.

Maggie nodded, agreeing to his terms, her glance flickering across his face, her eyes in that moment losing the trace of fear she wore like an old coat that could not be laid aside.

Someday, he thought, he would strip that look forever from her. One day, she would lift her head and survey the world around her with eyes that no longer sought the shadows for what might linger there.

He could wait. His patience was long and his cause might very well be his salvation.

Maggie would not believe him now, should he reveal his soul. He would not ask of her what he needed, while she felt so deeply in his debt. When she came to him, it would be for her own reasons.

When she learned to love…he would be waiting.

The small wooden image was on her pillow. Maggie lowered the candle to better see its form and a smile touched her lips. A cat. Beau had carved her a replica of Cat, with only one foreleg to hold it erect, one lop ear held at an angle from her head, the other upright.

She reached for it and held it within her palm, so small it could almost be concealed in the hollow of her hand. Settling on the edge of her narrow bed, she placed the candle carefully atop the table beside her and touched the small figure with care. All told, it was the length of her index finger, and in such minute detail she could almost see the expression in Cat's eyes, that narrowed gleam of cynicism that revealed the wounding of her trust.

Beau must have gazed long and hard at the critter to so

fully understand her, Maggie decided, smoothing the lines where his knife had carved details almost too small to be believed. That he had a talent for such things was not so much a surprise, as the fact that he would take the time to form a piece of wood into a thing of beauty for the benefit of Maggie O'Neill.

She perched the cat on her table, and bent to remove her boots and the stockings she wore. Another gift from *his* hands, she thought, stripping them from her feet to lay aside for the morning. Three pair, he'd bought her, and she who had not had the luxury of wearing such items in her whole life, had only held them in her hands, without the sense to utter words of thanks.

It seemed that every time she encountered Beau lately, it was for her benefit. He was a generous man. She stood and unbuttoned her dress, folding it carefully as she placed it on her chair. Beneath its bodice was her shift, a colorless piece of cotton, made from a feed sack two, maybe three, years ago, each stitch taken by candlelight as Verna O'Neill formed the garment for her daughter.

A veteran of numberless washings, it threatened to give way, should she tug it from place, and she wondered if Beau had any feed sacks he might give her, to be used in the making of another. She could lay out the old one and cut another to the same pattern. She'd seen her mother do it, had watched as she used her prized possession, a pair of scissors that had come with her on her wedding day in a sewing basket from back east.

Probably the only reason Pa hadn't tossed it into the fire was because Verna used her skills with needle and thread to mend his clothing and make that which her daughters wore. Except for the overalls her Pa had passed to her, Maggie had known only dresses from feed sacks in her whole life.

The revelation of clothing such as she had only dreamed of, within the pages of Beau's book, lingered in her mind as she took off her petticoat, that strange garment, fastened around her waist with ties, that Sophie had offered for her use. Why she needed another skirt beneath her dress was a puzzle. Sophie had said it was so, and Maggie was willing to accept her word.

She had to admit, the soft fabric and the row of lace around the hem was a delight to the eyes and touch. Added to the pure luxury of a dress that was store-bought, complete with a row of pearl buttons down the front, it gave her a sense of feminine pride she had never known. A woman. She felt like a real woman, with a body that fit into the dress that was made to accommodate a woman's round parts.

Rising, she picked up the brush Beau had brought her, then released the tail of her braid and began the task of brushing her hair. It was a joyous thing, this grooming she reveled in every night. Alone in the haven he'd offered, she stood before the mirror he'd provided. Beneath the shift, she found evidence of her form, noted the lifting of her breasts as she pulled the brush through her heavy locks. She was still lean and muscular, yet in the past couple of weeks, she'd noticed a difference, a filling out of her hips, a softening of her frame.

Probably due to the regular meals she was eating. At Beau Jackson's table, she reminded herself. She was so deep in his debt, she'd never be able to crawl out. Sophie gave her chores to do every living day, and she'd become almost good at the kneading of bread, more than capable of churning the butter and knowing just the moment it was ready to be ladled out and worked with the flat paddle in the big wooden bowl.

The chickens had taken to laying their eggs in the clean

straw she provided instead of every-which-where in the coop. They gathered around her feet in a satisfying fashion every morning when she fed them, clucking and pecking at the corn and grain scattered for their benefit. She'd learned to get them out of the henhouse and busy with their breakfast before she gathered the eggs. They gave them up more readily to her hand that way. Feeling beneath their puffed-up feathers had earned her more than one painful peck from a hen's beak.

She placed her brush with care on the chair, then blew out the candle. The sudden dark enclosed her in an embrace that in another time and place might have been frightening. Here it was a comforting thing, and yet she yearned for the moonlight that she knew waited outside the window. With anticipation she turned to the shutters she'd closed earlier, and her fingers slipped the fastening loose, spreading them wide to either side of the window.

Stars hung low from the night sky and the moon, though not in sight, lent its glow to the scene she viewed from her window. And it was hers, hers alone. Probably one of the only things she'd ever possessed that brought such pleasure simply by *being*. She stepped closely to the wall and stood on her tiptoes, her eyes just above the bottom of the rough opening.

At the barn door a figure stood, one shoulder leaning against the doorjamb, one hand shoved into a deep pocket. A broad-rimmed hat shadowed his face, but the man was unmistakably Shay. As she watched, he turned his head, and she knew, as surely as she was Maggie O'Neill, that he saw her there, noted her presence, aware that she looked out at him.

She sensed no fear at his company. As though there were only the two of them sharing the beauty of the night, they remained motionless, and then he lifted one hand, his index finger nudging the brim of his hat. It was a silent greeting, and she lifted her hand, holding it motionless for a moment, before she stepped back from the opening in her wall.

"Maggie!" Her name was a shout, the call an urgent command, and Maggie stood, putting aside the churn in an instant.

"Land sakes, girl. You'd better go see what he wants," Sophie said, turning from the stove.

But her words were spoken to an empty room, for Maggie was on the porch and only a wave of her hand acknowledged Sophie's edict. She jumped to the ground, thankful that she'd donned her boots early on, and her strides were long as she ran toward the barn. Beau stood in the doorway and he held the door open for her entry.

"One of the yearling colts stepped in a piece of barbed wire," he said tersely. "His leg's pretty cut up."

Maggie halted before him, turning to gape at him just inside the barn. "You want me to—"

Beau halted her query. "Rad was going to look at it, but Pony said not. He told me to call you out here. He seems to think you're a good hand at doctoring." His mouth twitched. "Can't say I disagree with him, myself."

Maggie shivered. To be entrusted with one of the prized yearlings was not just an honor, but a responsibility. One she could only hope to be worthy of. But if Beau thought she could help, she'd move heaven and earth to live up to his trust.

"Where's the yearling?" She turned, looking toward the far end of the barn, where that door stood open to allow daylight inside. Even as she spoke, Pony led the limping colt into view, a rope attached to his loose halter. The white stocking that shaped the animal's slender foreleg was bloody, the red stains apparent even from this distance, and

Maggie breathed a sigh of regret that such a noble creature should be so wounded.

"Soap and warm water," she said beneath her breath. "Then carbolic salve and some cobwebs against the wounds."

"Right," Beau replied, turning back to the house, only to pause midway across the yard. "Maggie?" he called, hands on hips as he hollered her name. "Did you say cobwebs?"

His voice was loud, his look incredulous and she grinned as she nodded, then called aloud, lest he not see the inclination of her head. "Check up above, Beau. I'll warrant there's plenty in the hayloft."

He turned, hastening to the house and she went to meet Pony and the yearling colt.

That such fragile-seeming legs could hold this handsome creature erect was one of God's miracles, Maggie had long since decided. Pony held the halter as she examined the damaged skin, washed the blood away and inspected the punctures and slashes the colt had suffered. He was patient, only flinching once as Maggie worked on the open wounds, as her constant stream of words had the desired effect.

"Hold this for me, Pony," she said, placing a pad of clean material around the colt's leg, careful not to disturb the placing of gray cobwebs. It held gobs of salve, each designed to cover the angry sites where wire had pierced through the animal's hide. The pieces of old sheet, freshly torn into strips by Sophie were then wound carefully in place, holding the dressing firmly.

Pony did as she asked, squatting beside her, his hands agile, his whispers to the horse almost an echo of hers. "I've heard of using cobwebs on wounds before," he said softly. "Never tried it myself."

Maggie tied a final knot in the white fabric and rubbed

her hands the length of the colt's leg, careful not to exert pressure on the wounds. "It works, is all I know. I heard it from an old Indian who lived off in the woods for some little while. He was a good hand at healing. Told me a few things."

She glanced up then, recognizing another presence beside her. Shay held the halter, and as she rose, he stepped back. "Thought you needed a hand," he said quietly. He lifted one wide palm to the colt's neck and placed it there, leaning forward to speak softly into the animal's ear. Then turned and walked away.

Pony led the colt to the front stall in the barn, walking slowly, speaking softly to the animal as they went. "I'll give this young'un some grain and enough hay to do him for the day," he said over his shoulder.

From beside her, Beau picked up the lantern and blew out the flame. They were in the shadows once more, and Maggie blinked at the disappearance of the light. She'd noted its presence, thankful for the additional light by which to work, aware now that Beau must have provided it for her benefit. But for those long minutes, the yearling had taken up her attention, and she'd been enclosed in a world that included only herself and the animal she sought to help.

"Thanks, Maggie," Beau said, his eyes on the bandages she'd put in place. "I have to admit, I felt a little foolish gathering up cobwebs in the loft, but I'm not about to turn aside any help offered." He lowered himself with one knee on the floor. "I've been standing here racking my brain, trying to remember where I'd heard such a thing before."

"Did you remember?" She turned to him, balanced on the balls of her feet, aware of the ache in her calves. She'd been in the awkward position for almost half an hour, and the muscles she'd strained began to protest.

He nodded. "It was during the war. I was in a field hospital and supplies were in short supply."

"You were wounded?" she asked quickly, and then subsided as he continued.

"Only a nasty hole in my upper arm. I was one of the lucky ones." He reached up to rub at a spot just below his shoulder, and his mouth drew down, his eyes growing dull with remembered pain.

It was a look Maggie was familiar with, one her mother had worn often, and she felt her heart lurch as she touched his fingers. "I'm glad. I'm glad you weren't hurt worse, I mean. I bet your family was happy to see you come home in one piece."

"They didn't survive," he said, rising abruptly, leaving her off balance with his sudden movement. She landed on her bottom, her feet thrusting to one side as she fell, and she rose quickly, feeling the blood rush to her cheeks.

"I'm sorry," she said stiffly, brushing at her trousers, where hay and straw clung to the fabric. Unable to look at him, embarrassed by her impulsive words that had angered him, she turned away. She limped as her leg protested the sudden movement, and then broke into an awkward trot, aware of Pony's stare as she passed the stall where he tended the yearling colt.

Outside, she leaned for a moment against the side of the barn, bending to squeeze the muscles in her calf that had seized up. A charley horse, her mother had called such things, and a little rubbing at the culprit usually solved the problem nicely. Nothing was going to solve the problem of a runny nose and reddened eyes though, she thought as her tears fell to dampen the dirt at her feet.

"Maggie." He stood beside her, his boots only inches from her own, and she looked stubbornly downward where small circles in the dust gave evidence of her distress.

"Maggie, I'm sorry. I didn't mean to snap at you. And I sure didn't mean to knock you over that way."

"You didn't," she said sullenly. "I lost my balance. I told you I was sorry. I know I ask too many questions. My pa told me that a long time ago."

"I didn't make you fall over on purpose." He squatted beside her and looked upward into her face. His hand went to his back pocket, withdrawing a clean handkerchief. "Here…"

Like a white flag, it lay between them on his outstretched palm, and she focused her gaze on it. No one had ever apologized to her in her whole life. And now this man who owned every piece of clothing she wore, who had provided her with bed and board and shown her only kindness, had crossed that line.

She reached for the cloth he held and wiped her nose, then opened it and rubbed at her damp eyes. "I don't cry," she announced, clearing her throat. "I just had something in my eye."

"You were limping," he reminded her.

"Just a charley horse. I'm fine." The handkerchief twisted between her fingers and she looked away from his crouching figure. "Get up, Beau. You make me feel hateful, getting upset with you that way."

"It wasn't that you asked the question, Maggie. It was that giving the answer caused me pain, and I wanted to run from it."

She waited as he stood erect, aware that Pony watched from the barn door only a few feet away. The need to know was uppermost in her mind, but she would not expose him to her curiosity. If he wanted to talk about it, he knew where to find her. "I'll wash the handkerchief," she said, tucking it in her back pocket. "Thank you."

Pony slid into the shadows as she turned to the house

and Beau lengthened his stride to catch up with her. "What did I catch you in the midst of?" he asked. "When I called you to the barn, I mean."

"I was about done with the churning. I'll warrant Sophie has it finished by now."

"Maggie, wait," he said as she climbed to the porch. "I wanted to tell you that I moved Maisie and her pups to the woodshed."

"Why?" Turning to face him, she caught him searching her features, and then his hand reached for her arm, and he drew her back down the steps. "Come out and take a look," he said. His voice lowered. "You need to splash off your face a little, or I'll have Sophie on my neck. Anybody'd think you've been crying."

Maggie halted before the pump and lowered the handle twice, bringing forth a stream of water. She filled her hands and splashed her face, blinking her eyes and shaking her head as the wet, cold water refreshed her. Her teeth clenched as she looked up at Beau. "I told you, I don't cry."

"All right." He grasped her hand, and her wet fingers slid in his grasp. "Come on. Your dog's been missing you." He grinned down at her. "I've got a surprise for you. The pups' eyes are wide open."

Chapter Six

Beau had gone beyond her expectations and brought home a ready-made window, with two panes that slid independently of each other. She tested out the contraption, easing the bottom one flat against the upper, allowing fresh air to enter her room, and then turned to him.

"I must seem like a loony to you," she said, unable to hide her glee. "I just never seen such a thing before I came here. And now to have one for my very own is…" She hesitated, lost for words to describe her pleasure.

His grin matched hers and he stuck his hands into his front pockets and rocked back on his heels. "You make it such fun, Maggie. I haven't had such a good time in years."

"What?" she asked. "Watchin' me act the fool over such a thing as a window?" She reached up and slid the bottom pane into place, then smiled smugly, her hands unmoving against the sanded surface of the frame. "Long as I'm here, this is my very own window, Beau. Just let me enjoy it."

She felt the heat of his body as he stepped closer, his breath warm against her ear. "I'm taking as much joy from it as you," he told her, and she closed her eyes, wishing his hands would clasp her shoulders, that his long fingers would warm her flesh through the shirt she wore. And then shook her head at the foolishness of her thoughts.

"Don't deny me the sharing of your pleasure," he said, and she hastened to explain herself.

"No…no, that's not what I meant. I was only…" How to explain the fanciful ideas he brought to life? There was no hope for it, and she shook her head again. "I was just thinkin' about something else. I know it makes you happy to do things for folks."

If she turned, he would be close enough to touch, and that was a thought both tempting and yet fraught with…not fear, but something akin to it. His hands had only touched her with gentle care, and yet, there was that moment of doubt, that cringing of her soul when he stood too close. As he stood now.

"Maggie?" She felt the loss of his body heat as he backed away, heard the touch of his boots against the wooden floor. And finally felt safe in turning to face him. His brow was furrowed, his eyes troubled. "I don't keep a count, Maggie," he said quietly. "You don't owe me anything. This room needed a window, and if having a frame and sash brings you a bit of cool air or light to see by, then that's payment enough for me. No matter if you're here or not, it will always be your window, because I bought it for you."

Beau blocked the doorway, his shoulders wide, his big hands falling loosely at his sides, and she was struck almost speechless as she looked fully into his face. Too handsome for words, he was, with that straight nose and wide forehead, those dark eyes holding secrets she could not fathom. She'd felt those lips against her skin, her hand and forehead. She knew that men and women kissed, their lips touching, had heard that much from late-night whisperings before Emily and Roberta had gone from home.

They'd murmured other secrets in the dark, strange images coming to mind as she'd listened, about men's hands touching their skin, leaving pleasure in their wake. It had seemed far-fetched then. Now those visions sprang to life as she focused on Beau's long fingers. A flush warmed her breasts and spread upward, her throat and cheeks burning with embarrassment at the thoughts flooding her mind.

"Maggie?" Again he spoke her name and she turned away, confusion rife within her, searching for ordinary words to speak. Words that would conceal the strange yearnings tumbling within her breast.

A vision of the pasture beyond the barn filled her mind and she seized upon the horses that pranced and romped within those fences. "You promised to let me help with the yearlings," she said, amazed that her voice sounded next to normal. Bending, she picked up her boots from the corner of the room, then turned back to face him. "I'll be ready in just a minute."

He hesitated, then nodded, turning away to walk across the kitchen floor.

Maggie watched him move out of sight, then sat on her chair, tugging her boots on, leaning to tie them snugly. He'd promised her a chance at the yearlings and she trembled as she thought of the agile creatures waiting in the near pasture. She'd whisper to them, caress those shiny coats, teach them to follow. Her mind spun with delight as she hastened through the kitchen, snatching up the warm coat Beau had brought her. Her boots clattered across the porch and she sped across the yard.

"Them horses ain't goin' nowhere, missy," Pony said with a grin as she skidded to a halt beside him. "Come on with me and I'll show you how this here thing is done."

By noontime she'd shed her coat, her arms ached from brushing the three colts Pony had assigned to her care, and she was enraptured by the antics of the youthful horses. It seemed that teaching the colts to stand still for her curry comb was the first step in the learning process. She'd done well, she thought, and then had led them in turn around the corral, holding them firmly by the halter, then easing out the length of rope so that they followed at her heels.

Whether they were just good-natured, or she'd managed to teach them anything was a moot question, but lead them she did. And wonder of wonders, they followed, nosing her shoulder or back as the mood took them, playful as the puppies in the woodshed.

"Think you can handle five, Maggie?" Beau asked from the top of the corral fence. He perched there, boot heels caught on a rail, hat tilted back, watching her progress. His mouth held a trace of amusement, the corners tilting upward. "Pony says you've got the touch."

She stopped stock-still and the colt behind her bumped her with his nose, nudging her forward. "He did?" she asked in surprise, reaching back to halt the playful antics. Grasping the halter, she drew the horse to her side, whispering softly as his head bent at her bidding. "There now, you behave, young'un. I'll find you a carrot out of the garden if you're a good boy."

"He thinks you can handle them," Beau said, his watchful gaze measuring the colt's behavior. "It's a big responsibility. These are the best of the lot."

"You're selling off the rest?" she asked, looking toward the pasture where more than two dozen yearlings grazed.

"I've got buyers waiting for my horses," Beau said, with just a touch of pride tinging his words. "These are ready to train. If they want me to work with them, I will, but they'll pay extra."

"Which are you sending to Dodge City?" Maggie asked.

"Three- and four-year-old geldings," he said. "They're ready for the army to use. They're used to a saddle and bridle, but they're only green-broke. We'll round them up in a week or so and send them off. It won't take long for the soldiers to train them." He motioned to the pasture. "Whichever of the yearlings I don't sell, I'll put out to pasture for another year before they get a saddle on their backs."

"I guess I didn't know there was so much to it," Maggie said, reaching absently to rub between the colt's ears. "I just thought when they got big enough, you got on their backs and rode 'em."

"If somebody buys a horse from me, it's already been handled and trained to follow a lead rope, and most likely been ridden. All but the yearlings. They're too young to take that much weight on their backs yet."

Beau slid down from the fence and stepped closer, laughing as the colt kicked up his heels at his approach. "Come on, pretty boy. It's time for Maggie's dinner. We'll put you back where you belong for now." He unlatched the gate and Maggie led the prancing horse toward a smaller enclosure, where almost a dozen other chosen yearlings stood, noses in the grass. She unsnapped the lead rope from his halter and released her charge, laughing aloud as he trotted toward the small herd, head high, his whinny sounding in the chill air.

She snatched her coat from a fence post and slid into it, flipping the tail of her braid from beneath the collar. "I feel kinda guilty, not helping Sophie in the kitchen this morning," she said, walking beside Beau toward the house.

"You're earning your keep, Maggie," he told her. "Sophie was keeping house before you got here. She doesn't mind."

And she apparently didn't, turning to welcome them into the kitchen just moments later. "Wash up quick," Sophie said. "I told the men to come on up for dinner. They'd just as well eat in the house. Pony said they was sick of their own cookin' whilst I was gone last month. I figure I can make enough for all of us now that winter's comin' on. By the time they get that cookstove stoked up for meals, it'll be easier to have them come in here, where it's already warm."

Beau headed for the sink where wash water awaited. "Go ahead," he said to Maggie, motioning to the shallow pan.

She hesitated, and Sophie nodded agreement. "You can help me dish up, Maggie. Take first dibs on the warm water."

It felt heavenly, she decided, splashing the dirt from her hands and face, reaching for the towel Sophie'd placed close at hand. The soap smelled clean, and left her face shiny, the skin taut. A small mirror over the sink reflected her image and she grimaced as she noted the flyaway wisps of hair around her face, clinging damply to her forehead. "I'm a sight," she announced, wishing for her comb.

"You look just fine," Beau said at her elbow. "Move over so I can pour fresh water." She dumped the pan, sloshing it with clean water from the pump, and stepped aside. If Beau thought she was passable, she'd take his word for it.

The meal was hearty, Sophie having cooked her biggest kettle full of beef stew. Fluffy dumplings rested atop the thickened gravy and she ladled out bowls full of savory meat and vegetables, topped with the light dumplings Maggie had yet to learn the knack of preparing. She passed the wide bowls around the table, then placed the last two before her chair and Sophie's own sturdy armchair.

The men ate without speaking, their spoons scraping to retrieve the last scrap from their bowls. Without urging, Sophie rose and took the stewpot to the table, ladling second helpings around. Maggie had never in her life seen such appetites, in her past used to scant rations that seldom allowed for more than a single serving at her mother's table.

Pa had always taken his share and more, first off the bat, making sure he got an ample portion, she remembered. Beau, on the other hand, waited until his men had been served before he held out his own bowl for refilling. He shot a glance her way and lifted a brow.

"Had enough? I'd have thought anybody who'd been dragging three yearling colts around the corral all morning would be ready for more than one helping."

"If there's enough left, I'll have a bit more," she allowed, peering over the edge of the big kettle. She held out her bowl, and Sophie dished up a full ladle. "Thank you," Maggie murmured, lifting a bite of tender dumpling on her fork. "Sure wish I could get the hang of these, Sophie."

"Nothin' to it. You just have to drop them in when the gravy's come to a good boil, then clap the lid on and put the kettle at the back of the stove for twenty minutes or so."

Maggie nodded glumly. "You make it sound so easy."

"Well, I'm not much at barn work," Sophie said cheerfully, returning the kettle to the stove. "I reckon we all have our uses."

The table emptied quickly, once the men were finished, and Maggie stood, gathering bowls in both hands.

"Joe found a hawk with a broken wing," Beau said. "He wondered if you wanted to bother with it, or if he should just put it out of its misery."

"I can take a look," Maggie said quickly. "I've mended

more than one bird's wing. There's a cage out behind the barn." She halted and turned back to the table. "I've got a red fox in there already, but he's about ready to turn loose."

"I saw him," Beau told her. "Pony said you'd rescued him from the trap outside the henhouse." His look was resigned. "Maggie, we can't have foxes running loose. If they get in the coop, they'll wreak havoc with the chickens. The trap's there for a reason."

"Well, if you don't want me fixin' up the fox, why are you givin' me a hawk to tend? He was likely keepin' an eye on your flock of chickens himself."

Beau shrugged. "I don't know. I just hate to see a creature wounded, though I'd have probably got rid of the fox if I'd seen him first. Maybe he'll stay clear of here, once you turn him loose. Once caught in a trap, he'd ought to be wary enough to keep his distance."

"I'll take a look at the hawk," Maggie said, depositing the bowls in the sink and returning to the table for another load.

"Go on ahead," Sophie told her. "I'll finish up in here."

With a grateful look at the housekeeper, Maggie reached for her coat and followed Beau from the house. "You'd rather be outdoors anyway, wouldn't you?" he asked, grinning down at her as she kept pace with his longer stride.

She skipped once to take up the slack in her step, and felt her heart leap as his approval of her made itself apparent. "I can do either," she told him. "I'm pretty good at runnin' that carpet sweeper thing you showed me, and I haven't broken anything in your parlor yet."

He cast her a measuring glance, his gaze thoughtful. Then, halting before the barn door, he held up a hand, bringing her to a halt. "We'll have time after dark to spend at the kitchen table tonight, Maggie," he told her. "I thought maybe I'd show you some other books I've got, see if I can teach you some letters.''

She looked up at him, her eyes taking in the sober look he bestowed, her heart singing as she considered the offer he'd made, so casually, so easily, as if it were of little value. ''I'd be pleased, if you've got the time to waste on me.'' More than pleased, she wanted to say as the idea of making sense out of the squiggles in his books set her thoughts to dancing.

''It won't be a waste,'' he assured her. ''Learning to read is about as important as learning to breathe. Before long, you'll be equally as good at one as the other.'' His quick grin sealed the bargain, and she followed him into the barn, aware that she trod at his heels much like the colts had scampered behind her this morning. And wondered if he was gentling her to his purpose in much the same manner.

The squiggles had names, and definite shapes, she discovered over the next week. Beau told her she was smart, assured her that in no time at all, she'd be reading the books he'd brought from town. Books he'd talked the schoolteacher into giving him, she found, after much prodding.

''Didn't she wonder what you needed 'em for?'' she asked, her hands careful as she turned the pages. ''Does she know I'm here?'' Her eyes widened as the thought made itself known, and she felt a sense of panic as Beau nodded agreement.

''She knows, but she won't tell,'' he assured her. ''She remembers your sisters from years back, when your pa let them come to school for a year or so. She didn't know there were three of you though. I made her take a vow of silence, and she agreed.'' His eyes flashed darkly. ''She doesn't think much of your pa. And she said to tell you that your sisters were getting along fine. She knows the men they married.''

Maggie leaned forward across the table. ''Are they happy? They're not bein' used poorly?''

Beau's forehead creased as he considered her question. ''Used poorly? Do you mean, are their husbands being kind to them?'' At Maggie's nod, he sighed. ''Most men are decent to their wives. I think you can rest easy. Your sisters are fine, certainly much better off than they were at home.''

Maggie sat back in her chair, digesting the news he'd given her. ''Maybe sometime I can see them, let them know I'm all right.'' She shrugged as another thought struck. ''They might not even know I've run off. Maybe they think I'm still livin' at home.''

''We'll talk about it,'' Beau promised. ''I don't want your pa to know you're here, Maggie. I'm not sure what he could do about it, and I don't want to have to face him down with a gun in my hand. He hasn't come nosing around yet, and I'd just as soon keep your whereabouts from him.

''Now let me see your paper. Sophie says you were practicing your letters this afternoon.''

Maggie drew a sheet of paper from beneath her book and offered it for his perusal. Beau glanced at it quickly and then a smile lit his face. ''You learned how to write my name. Did Sophie show you?'' At Maggie's nod, he placed the paper before her. ''You've got the letters right, every one of them. Do you remember them all now?''

''It wasn't so hard,'' she answered. ''I asked Sophie about a couple. I had the straight line on the wrong side of the circles, when I was writin' them small, but once I figured that out and put a name to them, I caught on pretty good.''

And indeed she had, Beau thought, feeling an inordinate

sense of pride as he remembered the lines of letters she'd printed. And beneath them, her name, both printed and then written in cursive, the letters imperfect but legible. But it was the final series of letters on the page that had brought a lump to his throat. She'd painstakingly printed out his name, not only once, but three times, with capital letters to be sure, but in order, and with a flourish that told him she'd done so with a mind to pleasing him.

"Let's take a look at the book now," he said. "I'll tell you the words and you see if the letters make sense to you." He rose and walked around the table, pulling another chair close to where she sat. "I think it will work better if I sit beside you," he told her, careful as he placed one hand on the back of her chair.

She looked up at him, her eyes as startled as those of the fox he'd come upon in the cage behind the barn last week. Maggie'd been a wild creature, to be sure, yet taming nicely, he decided, sliding his chair a bit nearer. His index finger traced a line beneath the first word on the page and he spoke it aloud. "This…"

She whispered it beneath her breath, the sound hissing as she repeated the single syllable. And then looked up at him eagerly. "What does the next word say?"

From the doorway, Sophie caught his glance and he nodded, aware that she left to climb the stairs to the bedrooms above. From a dubious watchfulness, she'd altered her stance over the past weeks, now entrusting him with Maggie. She'd hovered near those first days, and then a tacit understanding had developed between them, as if Sophie sensed his regard for the girl, and approved.

"Beau?" Filled with impatience, Maggie nudged his finger, edging it toward the next word, and he capitulated, grinning at her eagerness.

"…is," he said. And then he read the whole sentence,

slowly, one word at a time, as Maggie listened, absorbing in rapt silence the string of words that would begin to open up a whole new world to her eager mind.

November brought the first snowfall. The pups were kept inside the woodshed by a board across the doorway, high enough so that they could not climb over. Maggie visited them daily, teaching them human touch, tending to their droppings and assuring Maisie of her love. They'd learned quickly how to drink from a pan, leaving Maisie alone for the most part, since table scraps filled their need for solid food. Beau studied the best way to break the news that it was past time to find homes for most of them.

He'd already decided to keep at least one of the litter, since their shepherd ancestry had shown up in the largest of the six. The brown-and-black pup would work well with herding the cows—if he could keep Maggie from making a pet of it. He approached the shed, just as the sun rose over the peach orchard, milk pail in his hand, and swung the shed door open in preparation for feeding the noisy youngsters who were yapping impatiently inside.

The sun's pale rays flooded the interior of the shed and he halted abruptly, his mouth forming a grim line as he beheld the scene before him. A rattler, apparently seeking warmth, had invaded Maisie's territory and met its death between her teeth. It still hung there, bitten almost in half, long dead. But in dying, it had dealt a fatal blow to the female whose only thought was to defend her litter of pups.

Maggie must not see this, Beau decided rapidly, swinging the door shut behind him as he stepped inside the shed. From the single window enough light illuminated the rough interior to provide him with clear vision, and he filled the pups's milk pan quickly, watching as they gathered around to drink their fill. From the wall, he took a gunny sack and carefully deposited Maisie's stiff carcass within its folds. Gingerly, he used a shovel to tuck the snake inside, then tied the top with a length of twine.

From the house, he heard the door close, heard Maggie's voice as she spoke to her cat. Hastily, he opened the shed door and stepped outside, leaving it ajar behind him.

"Did you feed the pups?" she asked, stepping eagerly, leaning to peer within. "Where's Maisie? Did she run off already? She's been leaving them alone a lot lately, now that they don't nurse anymore," Maggie said, bending to rub a round belly as one of the pups rolled to her back.

"Maggie." Beau cleared his throat, surprised at the emotion tinging his voice.

She looked up at him, then stood quickly. "What's wrong?" Her glance encompassed the gunny sack he held and her eyes grew fearful. "What's in the sack?" she asked quietly. "Did something happen, Beau?" Looking back inside the shed, she accounted for the pups and even as he watched, he saw the slight droop of her shoulders, the moment of awareness as she sensed what he would tell her.

"It's Maisie, ain't it?" She braced herself, stiffening as she turned back to him. "What happened, Beau?"

He told her, as quickly and gently as he could—yet it wasn't enough. Even knowing that the dog had died to keep her pups alive was not sufficient solace to comfort the girl standing before him. Her eyes barren of joy, her mouth turned down in sorrow, she wept—harsh, bitter sobs that shook him to his depths.

Beau placed the gunny on the ground, dimly aware of Pony's approach as the man picked up the sack to tend to its disposal. Intent only on giving what comfort he could to the woman before him, he held out his arms and she took the single step required to allow him to enfold her against himself. Her head touched his chest and he enclosed her loosely, lest she not allow the fullness of his embrace. Her shoulders shook and she burrowed against his coat, her sobs muffled in the wool plaid he wore.

He could only hold her, clasping her more closely as she clung, her fingers reaching for him, gripping the front of his coat. And over her head, he watched as the men questioned Pony. Shay glanced up, meeting Beau's gaze, and nodded, his silent message clear. He would tend to the burying of the dog. Within moments, Beau saw Pony and Shay head for the peach orchard, Shay carrying the long shovel.

He turned Maggie from the sight and walked with her to the house. She rubbed at her eyes, muttering beneath her breath, and he pulled his kerchief from around his neck. "Here, it's clean. I just pulled it out of my drawer this morning." She took it and wiped her cheeks, then glanced back at the woodshed.

"Do you think there was another one? Maybe the first rattler's mate?"

"If there was, it's long gone," Beau said. "I'm surprised there was even the one. It's too late in the year for snakes to be out and about. They're pretty much holed up for the winter already."

Maggie nodded in agreement. "You're probably right. It was just bad luck, that's all." Her chin lifted and her mouth firmed. "No sense in getting attached to animals."

He felt the shudder of her grief and tightened his grip on her shoulder. "I forgot the pail of milk," he said quietly. "Will you want to give some to the cat?" He halted and watched as she considered the idea.

"Might as well. She tried chasin' a mouse in the barn yesterday, but ended up fallin' on her face. She's about as worthless as they come, I guess. Not good for much of anything." The gray creature watched from beside the steps, as though aware that Maggie spoke of her, then hobbled to lean against her mistress.

"Worthless, that's all you are," Maggie said roughly, bending to touch the gray fur. She settled on the second step, lifting the cat to her lap. Her head bent, her forehead resting against the animal's gray fur.

Beau turned back to retrieve the milk, Maggie's words in his ears. No matter how true they might be, for indeed the cat was not worth much in the general scheme of things, for now, she was a comfort to the woman who held her. And if for no other reason than that alone, Cat had earned herself a place here.

The soft chords crept beneath her door and invaded the darkness. Maggie sat upright in her bed, tilting her head, as if to better hear the music coming from beyond her room. If he'd planned it, she thought, he couldn't have tempted her more. Yet how was Beau Jackson to know that her heart had ever hungered for the sounds that pleased her ear? Songbirds held within their breasts the ability to charm her from the darkest depths of despair. Their melodies had lured her more than once from her bed at night, out into the darkness where the nightbirds sang.

Tonight she was tempted by another, even more potent lure. For with the harmony of strings and human voice, Beau was calling to her in a way she could not resist.

Sliding her feet to the floor, she wrapped the quilt around her, cocooning herself in the warmth, drawn by the simple melody Beau was singing. Her door opened silently, and the whispering words pierced her heart as he sang of a love lost to the arms of another. She listened, her feet moving quietly across the kitchen floor, down the hallway to the parlor door. There she halted, unwilling to disturb his lament.

One hand gripping the quilt against her bosom, the other holding it up from the floor, she peered around the doorway. He sat on the floor, leaning against the sofa, his head bent as he watched his fingers press the strings. They shifted, producing another chord, then another, his voice blending with each, each tone roughened with emotion.

"'...she's gone, gone far away,'" he sang softly. "'...and I am left to pray...for love to find its way...to me once more...'"

His eyes opened and as if drawn by her presence, he lifted his head, his gaze meshing with hers. "Maggie." His voice was a whisper. "I didn't know if you'd join me." He smiled and her heart wept at the beauty of the man. "I'm glad you came."

Maggie could only nod. Of course, she'd come. As if the man didn't know that music such as he'd made with a piece of wood, six strings and a thumb nail to strum across them, would lure even the fairies from the woods. "I heard you singing," she said, suddenly, foolishly aware that she was next to naked under the quilt, only her threadbare shift covering all her parts.

"I tried to go to sleep, but my eyes wouldn't close," he told her, lifting his hand from the guitar to motion her closer. "Sit by me, Maggie."

"I'm not dressed," she said.

His grin made a small dimple appear in one cheek. "I noticed," he said. "But I'd say you're well-covered."

Reluctantly, she crossed the threshold, thankful for the warmth of the carpet against her bare feet, then settled herself on a chair, allowing the quilt to droop over her toes.

Beau shook his head. "Come over here, sweetheart." He patted the floor beside him, and the dimple lured her from her chosen seat.

"All right," she said agreeably, willing to do as he asked

if he would only place those fingers back on the strings and coax the music from the depths of the curved instrument. His eyes shone their approval as she settled next to him, drawing her knees up so that the quilt tented over her.

"That's better. Now, we'll sing together." His left hand gripped the neck of the guitar, his fingers touching the strings in a pattern of moves that amazed her. His right hand strummed, both thumb and fingers plucking out a melody. And then he sang, a simple melody she remembered from somewhere. Probably one of the few her mother had sung, she decided.

"Do you know this?" he asked, even as his fingers plucked the melody.

She shook her head, unwilling to mar the beauty of his voice by adding her own. "I'd rather listen," she whispered. And she did, as he played a livelier melody, then another, slower, more tender than the first, his voice low, whispering the words.

The chords vibrated in the air as he finished, and then his hand pressed them into silence with his palm. "Would you like to learn how to play?"

She felt a hot warmth invade her cheeks. "I couldn't. I'd never be able to learn, and besides—" She spread her hand wide against the quilt. "My hand's not near as big as yours. My fingers would never stretch."

He spread his hand, matching his fingers against hers. "I think you could do it, Maggie. See? You have long, slender fingers."

The back of her hand was warmed by his palm, and then he curled his long fingers around to contain hers within his grasp. "I'll teach you if you like," he offered. His smile enticed her, his eyes beckoned her and she felt her heart beat increase until it pounded in her ears.

A feeling akin to fear overwhelmed her and she snatched

her hand from his grasp, scooting from his side. "I don't think so," she whispered, aware of the silence of the house, the shadowed depths of the parlor and most of all the clean scent of the man beside her.

"Are you afraid of me, Maggie?" he asked, his words speaking of sadness, his eyes searching her face. "Don't you know I wouldn't do anything to hurt you?"

"I shouldn't be in here with you, all alone."

"Sophie's upstairs," he reminded her. And then he smiled again, and his voice held the trace of amusement she was so familiar with. "She'd skin me alive if I did anything to frighten you." He lifted the guitar and placed it in her lap. "Here, I'll press the strings," he said. "You just strum with your right hand."

Placing his arm above her shoulders, he leaned closer and gripped the neck of the guitar, his long fingers holding firmly. "Now, strum," he instructed her.

She did, awkwardly at first, using her thumb, listening to each tone as it vibrated at her touch. He shifted his fingers. "Again," he told her. And again she brushed her thumb across the strings, hearing another chord.

From within her being, a sunburst of joy spewed forth, and she felt her mouth curve upward, heard the chuckle she could not contain. "See? You can do it," he said. His fingers moved again and without urging, she strummed, feeling the rhythm as he formed new chords. His voice joined in and he whispered words of a river running to the sea. And then he halted, and his hand that had hovered near, dropped to her shoulder, and his fingers squeezed.

"Will you let me teach you the fingering, Maggie?"

The room was silent, and she considered the offer.

"We could work at it a couple of evenings every week," he said, his voice casual, as though it mattered not, one way or the other. "After your reading lesson, maybe."

"You do too much for me," she said. "I won't ever be able to pay you back. This isn't something I can earn out, Beau."

His fingers tightened and then as if he thought better of it, he lifted his arm from her shoulder and rose to his feet, leaving the guitar in her lap. Walking to the window, he pushed the lace curtain to one side and looked upward to where only darkness beckoned.

"I'm not asking anything of you, Maggie. Only your company. Let me be your friend, will you?"

Her hand caressed the satin finish of his guitar, and her eyes stung with unbidden emotion. She, who rarely felt the urge to weep, had twice today been overcome by a rush of hot tears. The first time with a desperate surge of sorrow. Now, with a feeling akin to sheer joy.

Beau Jackson wanted to be her friend.

Chapter Seven

The blue scarf hung over her coat on the hook by the back door. Maggie lifted it, aware of Sophie's gaze resting on her. The yarn was warm against her hands, the color like that of sky at twilight, when the sun is gone and the last of daylight lingers.

"I thought it was the same color as your eyes," Sophie said. "You needed something to keep your neck warm." Her voice was gruff, and she turned away to tend the stove, but not before Maggie noted the softening of the woman's features.

"I never noticed that my eyes were any particular color," she said, "but I thank you for taking the time to make it for me."

"Didn't take long," Sophie said dismissively. "You'd better wind it around your collar and tie it tight. That wind's rising. You don't want to be down with a case of the quinsy."

Maggie lifted her coat from the hook and slid into it. "Sophie?" Scarf in hand, she hesitated, then plunged ahead. "Do you think you could show me how to knit?"

"I'd say you got enough learnin' goin' on already," Sophie told her, turning with spoon in hand. "What with sitting at the table every night with your head in a book, and then sittin' in the parlor, messing with Beau's guitar, I don't know that you've got time for cramming much more into that head of yours.''

"My mama used to make mitts for us when we were little, and sometimes socks for my pa." Maggie told her. "I was thinking maybe I could make something for Beau."

Sophie's mouth twitched. "Maybe you'd ought to start with something simple. Scarves are about the easiest thing to knit. You just keep goin' till you get it long enough and then end it. Socks take a bit more know-how, what with turnin' the heel and all.''

"A scarf would be fine," Maggie said. "Is it costly to buy the yarn? Maybe I could sell one of the pups to somebody and have enough money.''

"Well, that's a thought," Sophie allowed. "There's always folks looking for a dog. Maybe Beau would know of someone. He's probably gonna be thinking about finding places for them anyway. They're climbing out of the woodshed. There's no keepin' them penned up anymore.''

Maggie felt gloom clutch at her. "I hate to lose them. But I know it's costly to feed animals that don't earn their keep.''

"I wouldn't be surprised if Beau's planning on hanging on to one of them," Sophie said.

The cloud over her head vanished as Maggie clutched at the straw of hope Sophie offered. "I'll bet they'd be good at herdin'. That shepherd dog Maisie got tangled up with was a good cattle dog." Her fingers flew, pushing her coat buttons into place, her mind already plotting. The new scarf was warm against her throat as she wound it beneath her collar, and she flipped the ends over her back.

"Here, let me tie that for you," Sophie said, clucking her tongue at Maggie's haste. Her hands swept the length of the scarf into a loose knot and she turned Maggie to face her. "I was right. Matches your eyes just like I thought it would."

"Cross your fingers, Sophie. It won't be near as hard to see those pups go if Beau keeps one. I'll bet he'd like the biggest one. He looks most like the shepherd dog."

"You go on out there and talk to Beau," Sophie told her. "And then feed those chickens, and bring me in the eggs."

"Yes, ma'am." Maggie stepped onto the porch, drawing the door closed behind her. The wind was sharp this morning, the sky tinged with winter's gray, as though snow clouds hovered near. She pulled her hat tighter, drawing it across her brow, and headed across the yard. The woodshed door stood open and an old door lay on its side across the opening, effectively penning the pups inside.

Hearing her approach, they began to bark, and several heads appeared over the top of the barricade, tongues lolling and ears twitching as the pups begged her attention. Maggie bent to touch one head, then another. "What's all the noise for?" she said, laughing at their antics. They stood on back legs, their front paws sliding against the barrier, vying for position, their tongues busily swiping at her hand.

"Which one do you like best, Maggie?" From behind her, Beau's voice offered a new distraction and the puppies yipped their approval of their latest visitor.

Maggie stood erect, turning to face him. "It's hard to decide, ain't it? They're all cute as the dickens."

"They have to find new homes, Maggie," he said. "We don't need six dogs here."

Now that sounded hopeful, she thought. "Do you think we could keep one?" And wouldn't that be a job, choosing one of them, when all six made her feel like breakfast mush every time she sat in their midst.

Beau nodded. "I thought I'd ask you if I can have the black-and-tan male. Pony seems to think he'd be easy enough to train. He'd like to take him out to the barn and get him used to the animals."

"You're askin' me?"

"They're your dogs."

"You're the one's been feedin' them and givin' them a place to stay," Maggie said stubbornly. "I don't feel like I've got the right to deny you anything, Beau. Least of all a mongrel pup."

"Well, that's decided then," he said, stepping closer to the shed door. Bending low, he cradled one round belly in his hands and lifted the squirming creature to his chest. "How'd you like to be a cattle dog, Buster?" Both front paws against Beau's shirtfront, the pup leaned toward Beau to lap his approval of the idea. Beau's head tilted back, out of reach of the eager tongue and he laughed aloud.

"I think he's taken with the idea, Maggie."

She grinned, her task accomplished with no effort on her part. "And here I was going to ask you about keeping one of them," she told Beau.

"For yourself?" he asked, lowering the pup to the ground and watching as it squatted to relieve itself.

Hope rose within her as she met his gaze. "Not exactly. I was just hopin' you'd keep one here for a watchdog or maybe to herd cattle. If you like this one the best, that's fine with me."

"Maybe we should keep two of them, Maggie. Having a guard dog for the house wouldn't be a bad idea, now that I think of it."

"I'd take care of it," she offered. "Maybe I could build

a coop up by the porch. I'm pretty handy with nailin' boards together."

The pup, feeling neglected by the looks of things, stood on his hind legs and pawed at Beau's pant leg. "Down, boy," Beau said firmly, and Maggie grinned as the pup sat abruptly and watched with hopeful eyes.

"Pick out the one you want, Maggie," Beau told her. "I'll check around and see if anybody's in need of a dog, and we'll see if we can find homes for the rest."

She was overwhelmed with the simplicity of it all. There'd been no hassle or bargaining to be done, no need to worry about a man's anger or moods. Life with Beau was a far cry from what she'd known over the past years. "Some days I feel like I've died and gone to heaven," she said quietly.

Beau shot her a look that searched her face, and then softened as his eyes met hers. "This is a far cry from heaven, Maggie. The trouble with you is that you've never lived any place where folks liked each other, and tried to make life enjoyable."

"I just know that livin' here is like being in a dream. I thank you for bein' kind to me, and for doin' all you do." Emotion welled within her and words spurted forth. "I just feel like huggin' you," she blurted. And that was probably enough to scare him off if anything ever would, she thought.

"You can if you want to," he said, his grin wide. "I've thought about hugging you a few times myself. In fact," he said, reaching to brush a strand of hair from her cheek, "I'd really like to kiss you, if you wouldn't mind."

"You want to kiss *me?*" she asked incredulously. And then laughed aloud. "Nobody ever kissed me in my life, excepting for my mama."

He leaned closer, bending his head and she felt her eyes

widen as his face neared. His mouth was open just the slightest bit and then it touched hers, his lips moving, pressing gently. Her eyes closed and she inhaled deeply, her indrawn breath a sigh.

"Maggie?" His hands clasped her shoulders and she opened her eyes to gaze at his face, barely able to contain herself. He'd kissed her, right on the mouth, and that such a thing could cause her heart to stammer and cut up the way hers was, was not to be believed. If this was a sample of what Emily and Roberta had been whispering about, it was no wonder they'd run off with those two fellas.

"I think I like this kissin' stuff," she said, her tongue touching her upper lip.

"I think I do, too." He released her from his grip and stepped back. "I don't believe we want the men to be watching though, do we?"

Her head spun to the left and she scanned the open barn door. "They'll think I'm carryin' on with you," she said. And then tilted her chin with a hint of defiance. "You can kiss me any time you want to. And if it pleasures you to be doin' it, that's just fine with me. I don't know how it felt to you, but I thought it was about the warmest feeling I ever had."

"Is that so?" His eyes glittered and she thought he might speak, but, as if he changed his mind, he looked aside, then down at the pup. "Buster's looking for some attention," he said, bending to rub the dark head. The pup whined with delight, then pawed again at Beau's boots, his mouth wide in a grin. "There's only one thing about this dog," Beau told her. "You can't make a pet out of him. Choose the one you want for the house, and do all the pampering you want, but you have to leave Buster alone. If he's going to be a cattle dog, he's got to learn that he's not a pet."

Maggie nodded. "I guess I understand that. He probably

won't care, will he? He'll be happy doin' what his kind does, workin' with the men.'' She bent over the barrier to where the rest of the litter romped and her hand fell unerringly on a brown female with white legs and chest. Her hand curved around the soft belly, and she lifted the wriggling creature to her breast.

"I've kinda taken a fancy to this little one, anyway. I don't know how good a guard dog she'll be, but I'd like to have her for my own, if that's all right with you.''

Beau nodded. "I told you to take your choice. I'm going to have Joe put up a pen for the rest, so we can keep them corralled until we find places for them. You'll need to get some wood from the barn. I'll give you a hand with a dog coop.''

The chosen dog at his heels, Beau headed for the barn, and Maggie made a path to the coop where a flock of hens awaited their breakfast. The pup stood outside the chicken yard while Maggie scattered feed, then went inside to gather eggs. Her hat was called into service, and she filled it with the bounty from Beau's flock.

The dog waited by the gate as Maggie slipped through the opening, careful lest the adventuresome hens followed. "I think I'll call you Rascal," she said, glancing down at the pup romping around her feet. "You better stay out of the way, so I don't trip over you.''

"Looks like you got yourself a dog," Sophie said from the open door.

"Beau said I could keep her for my own," Maggie told her, both hands holding the hat brim as she climbed the steps. "I forgot a basket for the eggs, and my hat's full." She looked back at the pup, whose front paws were propped on the bottom stair. "Stay right there, Rascal. I'll be back.''

"Rascal?" Sophie shook her head. "Give me those eggs,

and pen that dog up before you go out to the barn. You don't want her to get stepped on first thing.''

Beau watched the small herd of horses set off, Joe, Rad and Pony riding on either side and at the rear of the procession. Loading the animals into box cars at the rail line might be costly, but the time saved, not to mention the fact that it only took two men to accomplish unloading and corralling them once they reached Dodge City, made it worthwhile. Pony would return to the ranch, once the horses were on their way, and Joe and Rad would handle the rest of the job.

Selling his animals to the army made sense, Beau told Maggie. The colonel he'd served under during the war made every effort to put his soldiers on prime horseflesh, and Beau's stock filled the bill. And with any luck, Joe and Rad would return in three days, bringing enough money to pay off the rest of the mortgage on Beau's ranch.

The dinner table held plates for four, and Maggie missed the hubbub of talk and laughter she'd become accustomed to. Shay, never much for speaking his mind, ate abundantly of Sophie's cooking, murmured a word of thanks and left the house silently. Beau, preoccupied with the threat of snow, kept a weather eye out the window as he ate, and Maggie was left to clear the table as Sophie trotted out to the clotheslines, fearful of the clothes being blown away. The wind from the west almost snatched the sheets from her hands as she unpinned them, and Maggie ran out to help, setting the dishes aside.

"Looks like Beau was right," Sophie said breathlessly. "We're gonna have a storm."

Both carrying armloads of clothing, they went back to the house. "You want me to put the irons on the stove?" Maggie asked, shaking the shirts and folding them. "The wrinkles are pretty near blown away. They just need some touch-up.''

Sophie nodded. ''They're still damp enough to iron. We won't need to sprinkle them, that's for sure. You can do the sheets first, to get the chill off and dry the hems.''

Between them, the two women made short work of the laundry and Maggie carried the results of their labor up the stairs. Beau's room, at the far end of the house, was her first stop, and she placed sheets and pillowcases on his mattress. His shirts, folded and pressed went into his dresser, and she lingered there, taken with the sight of small clothes and neatly ironed kerchiefs. Her fingers smoothed their surfaces and she rearranged the contents, making room for the shirts she carried.

And then turned to face the bed. The place where Beau slept every night, his head on the very pillow she lifted to press against her breasts. She held it beneath her chin, reaching for a pillowcase, then slid the plump pillow into place, repeating the action with the second of the pair. Placing them squarely on a straight chair, she turned again to the bed, snapping a sheet in the air, then watching it float to the mattress. Ma had taught her the trick of square corners, and Maggie pulled the sheet taut, then tucked it carefully. The top sheet followed and she viewed the results with a grin.

Who'd have thought she'd be right here in a man's bedroom, doing the chores a wife would do? And enjoying it, she reminded herself. When Beau Jackson finally found himself a woman to marry, she'd do well to appreciate the man, Maggie thought, fluffing the feather pillows before she put them into place. There weren't many as good-hearted as the man who slept in this bed. She lifted his quilt and held it to her face, glancing at the door, lest Sophie catch her at her foolishness. Closing her eyes, she rubbed the fabric against her cheek and inhaled the faint scent he'd left behind.

And then with a muffled chuckle, spread the coverlet over the bed and tucked it in place.

He was a neat man, she decided, hesitating by his dresser to straighten the black comb and brush he used. His extra boots stood neatly, side by side against the wall, beneath hooks that held his trousers. A book lay open on the bedside table and Maggie bent low to examine it. A slender volume, it bore a name on its cover she had not seen before.

"Char-less," she murmured, her finger tracing the letters. "Dick-ens." She placed it where she'd found it, repeating the words. "Sure is a funny name for a book," she muttered. And then bent low to examine it again. Another pair of words beneath the first were even more difficult to make out, and she shook her head.

It would not do to ask about it. Beau would think she'd been snooping. And so she had, she admitted, taking one last look around the room as she hesitated in the doorway.

"You about done up there?" Sophie called from the foot of the stairs. "Never saw anybody make such a production out of puttin' sheets on a bed."

Maggie's feet skimmed the stairs as she heeded the words. "I'm not as good at it as you, probably," she said jauntily. "But I'm learnin'."

Sophie waited, another load of clothing in her arms. "You can trot right back up there and leave this stuff in my room," she told Maggie. "I'll do my bed later. I think Beau wants you in the barn. He was headin' this way a minute ago."

Maggie did as bidden, filled with the importance of being needed. Beau's confidence in her had grown over the past weeks, and with three men gone, it was not surprising that her presence was required outdoors. Within minutes, she was donning her boots and coat. From the kitchen, Beau's voice called her name.

"I'm coming," she answered. "Sophie said she thought you needed me."

"Shay's building a lean-to for the mares in the pasture," he told her. "There's not much shelter out there, and not enough room in the barn for all of them. I want you to help me haul some hay for them. If it snows tonight, those horses'll have a dickens of a time finding grass."

"Dickens." Maggie halted in her tracks. "That's the word on your book." Pleased that she had recognized it, she grinned at Beau. "I saw it by your bed when I was puttin' on your sheets."

He turned to her. "You made my bed?" His cheekbones wore a ruddy glow as he spoke, and Maggie could only nod in reply. Snatching her new blue scarf from the hook by the door, he held it in her direction and she reached for it, surprised when his fingers did not release their grip. Instead, he tugged her nearer and she did his silent bidding.

"Wasn't I supposed to?" she asked. "Sophie sent me up there." Her fingers tangled in the scarf, and then they were covered by his hands. His were cold against her warm skin, and she shivered. "I won't go in your room anymore if you don't want me to."

He shook his head. "No, that's fine. You do whatever Sophie tells you." He lifted the scarf and her hands were released. The length of knitted wool was draped around her throat and she stood before him, mesmerized by the glow of his dark eyes.

"What does Char-less mean?" she asked, searching for words to speak, aware of his hands against her skin as he arranged the blue scarf in place.

He frowned, his fingers stilled by the word she spoke. "'Char-less'?"

"It was on the cover of your book," she said. "Right above the Dickens part."

His mouth curved in a smile. "That's the author's name. Charles Dickens." He cocked his head to one side. "You really recognized those words?"

Maggie nodded. "I said the letters in my head, like you told me to. I just couldn't figure out the first part." She repeated the name he'd spoken. "Charles Dickens."

"Would you like to hear the story, Maggie?" he asked, turning her to the door, his hand on her shoulder. "I'll read it to you, starting tonight, if you like. By the time the winter's over, I'll warrant you'll be able to read it yourself, at the rate you're going."

She shook her head. "I'll never be that smart. I'm doin' good to write my name and be makin' all those rows of numbers."

He opened the door and waited for her to step out onto the porch. "Don't put yourself down. You're smart. The problem is you never had a chance to learn before." They trudged to the barn, side by side and Beau stepped in front of her, to open the wide door.

"Maggie." His arm stretched before her, effectively halting her progress and she looked up into his face, where a smudge of whiskers told her he had not shaved since yesterday. "When I climb in my bed tonight, I'll be thinking of you, and appreciating those nice clean sheets."

"Sophie washed them," she blurted, unwilling to take credit where it was not due her. "I only pressed out the hems and made the bed."

"You're a big help here. I want you to know that," he said quietly. "I think we overwork you some days, what with helping Sophie and doing barn work and taking care of the—"

"Hush, Beau Jackson," she said sharply. "You don't

ever need to thank me for anything. I'm so deep in your debt, I'll never haul myself out. I've never had it so good in my whole life.'' Flustered at his appreciation, she pushed past him and snatched up a pitchfork from the wall. "I'll go up in the loft and pitch hay out the back window. You can pile it on the wagon.''

He laughed aloud, following in her wake. "Yes, ma'am. Whatever you say.''

Halfway up the ladder, she halted, closing her eyes as she considered the words she'd spoken with such haste. "I don't mean to be tellin' you what to do,'' she said, backing down slowly. "I was just—''

His hands were warm against her waist, his grip firm through the layers of clothing she wore. "Just stay put,'' he said. "I know what you were just—'' He allowed the pause to vibrate between them, and then he tugged her backward and she fell against him. His hands clutched her shoulders and he turned her, his arms enclosing her in a loose embrace. "I'm happy you're here, Maggie.'' His frown seemed at odds with his words, and she held her breath as his eyes met hers. "That's not what I wanted to say,'' he murmured, the frown lines smoothing as his head bent to her.

"Are you gonna kiss me again?'' she asked, her lips tingling at the prospect.

"Is that all right?'' he asked, his lips touching her mouth in the briefest of caresses.

She nodded. Not for anything in the world would she deny him, and even as his mouth pressed against hers again, she lifted to her toes, the better to accomplish this kissing he'd begun. His hands slid to her waist and he held her more closely, his lips firm and warm, opening a bit as he brushed them across her mouth in a lazy, yet somehow eager touch. He turned his head a bit and she found her cheek pressed against his shoulder as he captured her against his body.

And still those firm lips danced across her mouth, a series of tiny, nibbling kisses setting a flame burning deep within her body. She clung to him, her arms sliding up his chest, one wrapping around his back, the other clasping his neck. His mouth moved, pressing deliberate kisses against her cheeks, across her forehead and even on the tip of her nose.

Maggie chuckled, the sound welling from her depths, unable to halt the expression of pure joy. "You're makin' me tingle all over," she whispered, finding his ear nearby as she spoke. His cheek pressed hers and the whiskers he'd ignored this morning rubbed against her more tender skin. Yet even that was no deterrent, and she clung to him with a desperate need she could only express with kisses of her own. That they fell against his ear and the slope of his throat was accidental. Her mouth formed itself to his flesh and she took liberties such as she had only imagined.

His indrawn breath signaled her, as did the release of his grip on her body. "Maggie, girl," he whispered, his voice deep and resonant. "I'm sorry."

She tilted her head, searching for a glimpse of those dark eyes that held such mysteries. Even now, half open, they possessed a burning intensity that both urged her closer and at the same time warned her of an unknown danger.

"Don't be sorry, Beau. I told you I like your kissin' me. If it pleasures you, I don't mind." And if the truth be known, she'd garnered more pleasure for herself than she'd expected. It wouldn't do to blurt that out, she decided. He'd think she was wanton, a sin Pa had declared both Emily and Roberta guilty of. His rantings had included even more name-calling once he got to going at it, and those words stuck in her memory.

"I'm not a slut, am I, Beau?" she asked, fetching one of Pa's favorite expressions to mind.

Beau's hands latched onto her shoulders and he shook her in his grasp, only once but with a fierceness she had not expected of him. "Don't you ever say that word again, Maggie," he told her. "That word does not apply to you. Where did you hear it?"

"My pa—" she began and he cut her explanation short.

"Your pa was wrong to speak it in your presence," Beau said sharply. His hands rubbed her shoulders as if he rued his roughness. "Forget all the things he ever said to you. You're as innocent as the day you were born, and I've taken advantage of you." He stepped back. "Now, go on up there and pitch down some hay. We'll talk about this later."

Oliver Twist was the name of the book. And before the evening was over, Maggie was deeply involved in the story of the young boy who lived in an orphanage. She sighed as Beau closed the book, leaving a scrap of paper to mark the stopping place he'd chosen.

"I never heard such a story before," she said. "Do you really think I'll be able to read such things someday?"

Beau's eyes rested on her eager face. Like a baby bird, she gobbled up the scraps of learning he fed, as eagerly as the fluffy robins who were hatched in the maple trees outside his kitchen took food from their parents' beaks in the springtime. And like those same baby birds, she was ever ready for more, her thirst for knowledge urging him to provide the sustenance her eager mind demanded.

"One of these days, you'll be reading as well as any student in the schoolroom. Probably better," he amended.

Maggie looked doubtful, and he ached to banish her uncertainties. "I can't even talk proper," she said ruefully.

"I keep thinkin' I should say my words different, the way you do, and then I forget."

"Would you like me to teach you?" he asked, unwilling to be thought critical, and yet agreeable should she be serious in her endeavor.

"Oh, yes," she whispered. "I been tryin' hard not to say *ain't* anymore. You never say it, do you? And there's some other things, like the cusswords Pa always said. I never hear you hollerin' at the men or swearin' with God's name." She nodded wisely, as if she considered such a thing to be beyond the pale. "My ma always said that there's a place in the Bible that forbids men to say swearwords." Her mouth twisted in a wry manner as she glanced up at him. "I don't think my pa ever read a word of that book."

"Maggie, my mother had a Bible, and I've kept it since she died. It's over there in the bookcase." He glanced at the glass-fronted cabinet near the window. "Would you like to have it for your own?"

"Oh, Beau," she whispered, shaking her head. "I couldn't take such a thing from you." Her eyes cast a longing glance to where three rows of books resided, and her hands clenched in her lap. "That's a treasure, to have something from your mother."

He stood, placing the book he held in her lap. The glass door lifted upward and he reached for the leather-bound Bible he'd found at his mother's bedside. That his mother had been long dead made the book even more precious, and yet he'd not opened its pages since that day.

"When I returned home from the war, my folks were dead, Maggie. My brothers lost their lives in battles right close to home, and my father died with a Southern bullet in his back. A nearby neighbor told me that my mother passed on the very next day. Her heart just quit beating. I think she couldn't face life without my father." He cleared his throat, aware of the lump he'd kept at bay for four years, refusing his grief to flow ever again, once that first torrent of tears had unmanned him.

"For some reason, the soldiers left the house standing, just taken the horses and animals from the barn to feed the army and give the men new mounts. Most of the things in this room are from my mother's parlor." He looked around at the chairs he'd brought with him, the couch Maggie sat upon and the tables he'd loaded with care upon a farm wagon. "I think she'd like you to have this," he said, holding the well-worn book in one hand as he lowered the glass door into place.

Beside Maggie once more, he placed it in her hands, watching as she traced the gold lettering on the front. "This second word says *Bible,* don't it?" she asked.

"*Doesn't* it," he said, correcting her gently. "And yes, it does. The first word is *Holy.* I'm not really sure why they call it that, but I think it's because it's known as the word of God."

"Wouldn't it be prime to go to a real church sometime?" she asked wistfully, her fingers carefully opening the cover to reveal the first page.

That such a wish was within his power to grant humbled Beau. "We can do that if you want to," he told her. "Maybe not right now, but soon." And before that could come to pass, he would have to find a way to protect the girl from the threat of her father's wrath, should the man realize she'd taken shelter here.

"I'm gonna put this away," Maggie said, rising with the Bible clutched to her breast. She turned at the doorway. "I can't think of any words to tell you how beholden I am to you. This makes me feel like my Mama is close by."

Beau followed her down the hallway to the kitchen, then watched as she crossed to the storeroom. The light from the kitchen lantern spread past her threshold and as he paused in the doorway, she bent to strike a match, lighting her candle. It flared, and she was illuminated in its glow, her hair gleaming darkly, her face lit from within with a joy he felt somewhat responsible for.

"I'm gonna keep it right here on my table," she announced, placing it just so, then moving it a bit, so that it was catercorner. Her fingers brushed a stray bit of dust from the leather cover and she looked up at him, her eagerness a boon to his spirit.

"Now can I do something for you?" she asked, an impish grin lighting her face. "Just to thank you properly?" And before he could reply, she stepped forward and tilted her head, pressing her mouth against his. "Is that all right?" She blinked, and an anxious look flooded her expressive features.

Was that all right? His heart beat in his throat as he looked down at her. The yearning to lift her in his arms and carry her up to his bedroom was strong. And only the presence of Sophie overhead offered the deterrent keeping him from such folly. He'd never known such a flood of love could fill him for another human being. The year he'd yearned over the fickle Sally Hudson was in the past. That his childhood sweetheart could so casually marry another even as Beau fought in a war not of his choosing, had been a blow he'd thought never to recover from.

Yet he had, although he'd not allowed his wary heart to fasten affection elsewhere until now. There'd been that fleeting attraction to Rachel McPherson, but he'd rapidly quashed that emotion, lest it develop into a heartache he might not recover from. Now there was Maggie, and his yearning for the waif he'd taken under his wing was almost more than his masculine self could keep in check.

He found himself wanting her, not only in his arms, but

in his bed, and that could not be. Not until the girl knew her own worth and was able to recognize the growing attraction between them. He'd seen hints of it in her gaze, in the sidelong glances she cast in his direction, in the look of pleasure she'd made no attempt to conceal as she accepted his gift just moments ago.

Now, she'd kissed him. Unbidden, she'd pressed her mouth against his, and he'd ached to deepen the caress. "It's all right for you to kiss me any time you want to," he said, his hands at her waist. "But only if it gives you pleasure, Maggie."

Her eyes sparkled and she nodded her head. "Just lookin' at you gives me pleasure." A blush rose from her throat to tinge her cheeks, and she lifted her palms to press them against the heat. "I shouldn't say that, should I?"

Beau kissed the backs of her hands, one after the other, then pressed his mouth against her forehead. "You bring me joy," he said quietly. "One of these days, you'll know just how much." He watched as her hands fell to her sides, then clasped at her waist. Her eyes questioned him, seeking enlightenment.

"I need you here, in my home, Maggie," he said. "I need your smile and your help, and your company." *But, most of all, I need you to love me.*

Chapter Eight

Being shorthanded meant more work for Shay and Beau, and Maggie did her best to hide her glee as Beau drafted her to help. "I hate to leave you with all the work in the house," she told Sophie, dragging on her boots as she readied for the outdoors.

Sophie cast her a speaking glance. "Don't give me that stuff, child. Your heart's out there with those horses. You can't fool an old lady like me."

Maggie hid her grin, bending her head as she tied her boot laces. "Sure beats dustin' all those knickknacks in the parlor. And I've got the pen to build for Rascal today. Beau said maybe we'd go to town and see about selling the others." She paused, her hands tangled in the laces. "Do you think my pa will find out if I show up in Green Rapids?"

"That's something none of us knows the answer to," Sophie said. "You won't find out till you get there, and maybe not even then. Was your pa a one for runnin' to town all the time?"

Maggie considered that, then shook her head. "Only once every couple of weeks or so." A weight lifted from her shoulders. "Chances are he'll never find out. Besides, Beau will know what to do, won't he? Even if Pa should be there and see me." Her confidence bolstered by her own words, she double knotted her laces and stood, reaching for her coat.

"I made you some mittens, the last couple of evenings," Sophie said gruffly, reaching into her enormous apron pocket. "Thought you'd better keep your hands warm, lest you get frostbite."

Maggie took the gift, speechless at such generosity. "I thought the scarf was a fine present," she said, drawing on the dark blue mitts. "This is way beyond, Sophie." She held them up before her, examining the stitches, and her mouth drew down in a doubtful grimace. "I'm not sure I'll ever be able to knit so well."

"If you get a chance today, go on in the store and pick out a color yarn for a scarf for Beau," Sophie told her. "We'll get you started on it. Don't worry about the money. Just tell Conrad Carson I said to put it on my bill. You can pay me after you sell those pups and I'll take care of it."

"Are you sure?" She stood in front of the door, not liking to be so indebted, but the prospect of actually beginning a scarf for Beau weighed heavily, and she nodded as Sophie waved away her query.

Rascal met her at the steps, tail wagging, tongue lolling as she scampered about. A new piece of rope attached to a length of leather adorned her neck, and Maggie bent to examine the arrangement. Someone had pierced the leather strap to the proper length, then set a brad in place, before tying the pup to the porch railing. Maggie rubbed at the shiny head. "You better stay here and guard the house for now. I've got a heap of work to do in the barn."

Mournful howls followed her as she turned away, and she grinned as the pup expressed her displeasure. "That dog's not happy without you," Beau said from inside the barn. Pitchfork heaped high, he paused to glance past Maggie to where the pup lifted her head to the sky, and let her disappointment be known. The straw, heavily weighted with manure landed in the wheelbarrow, and Beau bent to his task.

"You want me to do that?" Maggie asked, even as her heart yearned toward the corral where the yearlings awaited attention.

Beau grinned. "You don't really want to, do you?"

"I will," she said stubbornly. "You only have to tell me."

"Go on out back. There's five horses out there waiting for you." He bent low, lifting another forkful, then aimed it at the barrow. "Get out of my way," he scolded.

She turned away, aware of his teasing, then looked back over her shoulder to see him watching her. "Thank you for the collar you put on Rascal," she said. "And the piece of new rope."

Beau shrugged. "It wasn't me. Must have been Shay."

Shay? Maggie considered that thought as she walked the length of the barn and out into the sunshine. Enough snow to cover the ground had fallen yesterday. This morning the sun was making inroads on it, but the dirt in the corral was firm enough. Working in the mud would not have been her first choice. Beyond the fence, the mares fed, some of them gathered around the trough Shay and Beau had built for them. They'd forsaken the lean-to once the sun rose and the wind died down. Now they wandered between patches of grass sticking up through the snow and the hay provided for them.

Carrying the lead line and currycomb, Maggie stepped over the corral fence, speaking softly to the young horses who watched her. "Come on over here," she coaxed, reaching for the halter of the nearest animal. He whinnied and tossed his head, kicking up his heels, as if to thwart her plans. She hung on, lifted from her feet for a moment as the colt's mane flew through the air, and his front feet left the ground.

"Now that's about enough, you rascal," she said firmly, holding the halter next to his jaw and tugging his head down. With sudden acquiescence, he lowered his nose to her chest, nudging in a playful manner. Maggie laughed aloud, her knuckles rubbing against his head. She whispered in his ear, foolishness that pleased the young animal. Perhaps it was just the tone of her voice that had the effect. She knew only that soft whispers and a gentle touch had more value than the whipping into shape her pa had been so fond of.

The thought of the horse she'd tended to back home gave her pause, and her mouth drew tight as she considered the abuse that patient animal lived with. Her shoulders straightened and she held the halter firmly as she began the task of cleaning and grooming. A long shiver traveled the length of the yearling's back, and Maggie laughed aloud, her strokes long and firm as she worked.

"You like that, don't you?" she murmured, bending to work at the sleek sides and down the horse's flank. A velvet nose nudged her and she turned back, wrapping an arm around his neck, rubbing her face against the coarse hair. "Well, I surely like you, too," she said, making her way around to the other side.

"You're good at that," Shay said from behind her.

Maggie looked over her shoulder. "It's easy enough to like animals," she told him. "All you gotta do is treat them kindly and they'll pretty much bend to your will." She turned the currycomb, working at the yearling's mane. "I thank you for the collar you made my pup. Do I owe you for the new piece of rope?"

Shay was silent, and Maggie looked up, fearful that she'd

made a misstep. His eyes were on her, and his usual somber look prevailed. "Some things in life come without a price tag, ma'am. I only thought to keep the pup away from the barn, lest he gets stepped on."

And that was the longest conversation she'd ever had with the man, Maggie thought, as Shay turned away and walked back into the barn. She lengthened the lead line a bit, and walked to the center of the corral, urging the colt to follow. Letting the rope run through her hand, she paced him, allowing him to trot, then as he broke into a gamboling canter, she tugged him into submission, easing him to the pace she had set. He followed her, traveling in a wide circle, his ears pricked forward, an urgency in his gait. Maggie gave him his head and he loped easily, circling the corral, his long legs reaching and stretching.

"He's coming right along, isn't he?" From the top of the fence, Beau watched and Maggie's mind was snatched from the colt to the man who spoke. Behind him, the sun shone brightly and she squinted as she met his gaze.

"You gonna keep him? He'd make a dandy horse for you. He's a tall one."

"I don't know," Beau said. "Cord McPherson's on the lookout for a couple of yearlings for Rachel's brothers. He'd like them to train their own horses. I thought this one might fit the bill. He seems smart and good-natured."

Maggie nodded. The horse was all of that and more. That was the trouble with animals. You got all attached and then had to give them up. And she'd sworn just days ago not to travel that road again.

She tightened the lead rope, bringing the colt closer, halting his carefree pace. He lifted his head and whinnied, loudly and long, and she grinned at his exuberance. Easing to a walk, he nudged her and snorted, and she obliged, patting and praising him as she turned him into the pasture.

"I reckon that one and the black would be good for a couple of young'uns," she told Beau. "I'll spend some time with both of them, get them tamed down good."

Beau nodded, sliding from the fence. "We'll stop and tell Cord on the way to town afterwhile."

Clad in a pair of her new trousers, her head covered by the wide-brimmed hat he'd bought her and resplendent with her new scarf and mittens, Maggie climbed onto the wagon seat. Beau offered his hand, but she waved it away, scorning the need for help. He'd have to talk to her one day about allowing men to be courteous, he decided, snapping the reins over the backs of his team.

For now, he'd settle back and enjoy the sight of Maggie on her first outing since her arrival at his ranch. She glowed. There was no other word to describe the gleam of dark blue eyes as she scanned the road ahead. No other phrase could adequately define the bloom of rosy cheeks and lips that refused to be sober.

Lips he'd kissed three times, he reminded himself. Even as he was sorely tempted to bend and taste their pink flesh at this moment. She was becoming more of a temptation with each day. There was no way around it. He'd become eager to woo this wary female to his will.

"You got your gun with you?" she asked, peering behind her to the floor of the wagon.

"I never leave home without my shotgun," he told her. "You worried about something?"

She turned to meet his gaze. "What if we come across my pa? Should I just skedaddle? I don't want you gettin' into a hassle for my sake."

"I promised to look after you," he reminded her. "I told you I'd keep you safe, Maggie. Do you doubt me already, when we haven't even seen hide nor hair of your father?"

"No, I guess not." She heaved a deep sigh and settled a bit closer to his side. "Maybe I just needed remindin', is all."

"Let's have a lesson while we're riding," he suggested. He'd keep her mind off the wretch who'd made her life miserable, one way or another. "I've wanted to give you a couple of pointers, just something to think about."

"Have at it," she said. "I been tryin' to remember everything you told me, but I know I forget sometimes."

"I want you to think about some of the words you say," he began. "Instead of saying *tryin'*, I'd like you to pronounce the whole word. Say, *trying*, Maggie."

Her eyes widened. "I never thought about it, I reckon. You always talk so fine, and maybe it's 'cause you put such a fine ending on words." She touched her upper lip with her tongue and then pursed her lips. *"Trying."* Emphasizing the final syllable, she said it again.

"That'll work with all them words that end thataway, won't it?"

Beau nodded, wondering if he dared correct the sentence she'd just blurted out. No, one step at a time would be enough, he decided, unwilling to put a damper on her joyous expression as she considered the idea he'd planted in her head.

Cord McPherson's place was a short trip down the road, and Maggie stilled as they drove up the long lane, her gaze rapt as she viewed the big farmhouse and the assortment of outbuildings. "This is surely a beautiful place," she whispered. "Is this really where the bread lady lives?"

"Her name's Rachel," Beau reminded her. "You'll like her."

As if beckoned by his words, the back door opened and a dark-haired woman stepped onto the porch, lifting a hand to her forehead as she watched their approach. "Good afternoon," she called, and then lifted her skirts to descend the steps to the yard. "You must be Maggie." Her smile was bright, and Maggie felt reassured.

"Sure am," she said. "Beau brought me callin'—*calling*." Her haste in correcting the pronunciation brought a wide grin to Beau's mouth, and he jumped down from the wagon, reaching up to offer her his hand.

Her frown, and the quick shake of her head denied his help, but he persisted. "Let me help you down, Maggie." Perhaps it was the note of warning in his voice, or else the stubborn look he knew must be squaring his jaw. Whichever prompting did the trick, Maggie placed her gloved hand in his and allowed him to assist her from the wagon.

"Did I do that right?" she whispered in his ear as he lifted her by the waist to the ground.

"You did fine," he answered, then turned with her to face his neighbor. "I'm going out to talk to Cord," he told Rachel. "Maggie's real fond of tea. Maybe you can have a cup with her and get acquainted."

Rachel's eyes lit with pleasure as she claimed Maggie's hand, drawing her toward the porch. "You just take all the time you like out in the barn," she told Beau. "I've been lonesome for another woman to talk to for days."

"Well, what did you think of her?" Beau asked, once more on the road to town after a half hour of dickering with Cord McPherson. The fact that two young boys were hanging on every word spoken by the two men only added to the fun. They'd arrived at a bargain, on the premise that Cord and Rachel's brothers approved of the yearlings chosen. And of that there was no doubt in Beau's mind. Another week with Maggie would assure the delivery of two tractable colts to the McPherson farm. And the deposit of a tidy sum in Beau's bank account.

Maggie chose her words carefully. "I think she's right pretty. And she makes a fine pan of cinnamon rolls. I never had any better in my life." She thought for a moment. "Matter of fact, I only had cinnamon rolls one time, when the man in town gave a pinch of cinnamon and nutmeg and a couple of other things I can't remember to my mama at Christmastime one year. He put the stuff in a little bit of cotton material and tied it with a string, and told her it was a happy Christmas present."

She sighed. "It sure was fine to taste that flavor again. I almost forgot how good it was." Her smile flashed widely as another thought struck her. "I remembered real good, Beau. I said all my words slow and made them sound like you told me."

"I'm proud of you," he said. And found to his surprise that he was, more than he'd thought possible. She'd learned so much over the past weeks, from cooking to writing letters and words and reading the results, painstakingly slow perhaps, but with a determination he could only admire.

He slid his arm around her waist, and she looked up, surprise alive in her gaze, but not a trace of fear that he could see. "I'm sure Rachel was pleased to know you," he said. Allowing his gaze to sweep her length, he formed a decision, one he realized was already half in place, and had been for the past several days.

"I'd like to buy you another dress, so that when we go calling next time, you can feel like a lady in Rachel's kitchen."

"I'm not a lady," she stated, her glow diminished by his words. "I'm just Maggie O'Neill, and bein'—*being* a lady is not for the likes of me."

"I think you'll turn out to be a fine lady, one of these days," Beau assured her, willing her to smile once more. "In fact, you're well on your way. By the time you learn how to read the books in my parlor, and catch on to adding and subtracting the numbers, no one will ever believe you weren't born to be a female from top to bottom.''

"Is that what you want?" Her eyes clouded with doubt, and her hands gripped tightly in her lap.

"I want you to be happy. If learning how to wear a dress and be womanly isn't what will accomplish that, then we'll just forget the whole thing. If you'd rather work like a man and shovel manure, I'll let you.''

"Ain't—" She paused, worrying her lip between her teeth. "Isn't there some way I can do both? And still have you liking me?"

He closed his eyes, and his arm tightened around her. Drawing the reins taut, he drew his team to a halt in the middle of the road. "Maggie, I like you more than you know. That's not the issue here. You can help with the horses in your britches and wear a dress for supper at night, and that's all fine and good." He turned to face her, and his hand rested on her shoulder, the other turning her on the seat.

"Are you gonna kiss me?" she asked, looking at him from the corner of her eye, turning her head toward the patient horses.

"Not if you don't want me to." And he wouldn't, he determined. Never would he force his attentions on her.

"Oh, I don't mind. You know, I kinda like it. I already told you that. It's just that it makes me all wobbly inside and I get red-faced and I don't know what to do. I'm not very good at kissing back."

He bent his head and she closed her eyes, turning her face for his appraisal. "Tell me how to do it, Beau," she whispered. "I want to do it right for you."

"Just do as I do, and we'll be fine." His heart wrenched within his chest as he heard her words, knowing she would allow him to do as he would, and his hands grew warm as he thought of the places they yearned to touch. He kissed her then, and his lips opened, savoring the taste of her. She followed his lead, and a quick intake of breath signaled her delight.

"You taste like licorice," she whispered.

"Cord gave me a piece in the barn. Rachel's brothers are partial to it, and he keeps a cache out there for them." Their mouths were but a breath apart as they spoke, their lips brushing, tantalizing him with her sweetness.

"You had sugar in your tea, didn't you?" he asked, his tongue gentle as it stroked the inside of her top lip.

She nodded, gasping a bit.

It seemed she would not deny him, and his trousers fit more snugly as he shifted in the seat. Just once, he thought, just once he would touch her, allow his hand to fill with the fullness of her breast. His fingers tightened at her shoulder, then slid to clasp her ribs, and she obliged, slipping her arm around his neck.

Her coat was heavy, but the unmistakable, firm shape of a woman's breast met his seeking palm, and she gasped again, inhaling sharply. "Nobody ever touched me there," she whispered, tilting her head back, her eyes open to meet his gaze.

"I thought as much," Beau whispered. "I'd like to touch you without your coat in the way, honey."

"Are you goin' to—"

"*Going.*" Beau spoke the word, prompting her compliance.

"Are you? Gonna—"

"*Going,*" he repeated. "Say it, Maggie."

Her voice whispered the word obediently. "Going."

"No," he told her. "I'm not going to do anything else. What I'd like to do and what I feel is right for both of us are two different things, I fear.'' His hand left the curve of her breast and returned to her shoulder. ''One of these days we're going to talk about this again. For now, we'll just go on into town and get our errands run.'' He bent for a loud, smacking kiss directly on her lips, and she reciprocated.

Picking up the reins, he set the team into motion. ''Would you like to get married one of these days?'' he asked in what he hoped was a casual manner.

Maggie huddled next to him. ''I don't know. Maybe it would be worth it to get the kissing and such. I just don't think I'd like the other part. I heard my mama crying too many nights when Pa was busy giving her bruises and making their bed bang against the wall.''

His heart lurched within his chest as he heard her blurted disclosure. ''It isn't supposed to be that way, Maggie. Men and women—'' How could he explain to this woman-child that loving could be fine and good and filled with the greatest joy given to mankind? ''We'll talk about it again,'' he promised. And in the meantime, he'd better come up with words that would express his mind without sending her into a tizzy of embarrassment.

The store was a wonderment to her. Beau saw it in the gleam of her eyes as they walked in the wide doorway. Conrad's doors were of heavy oak, with gleaming beveled-glass windows inset, and Maggie paused to examine the cuts that gathered the light and shone prisms of color on the floor of his establishment. If the aromas of leather goods and apples piled in peck baskets, mingling with spices and the smell of wood smoke were heavy to Beau's mind, they seemed to have the opposite effect on the woman who clung to his arm.

She looked eagerly at first one display, then another, her eyes avid as she scanned the apples, then traveled to the bolts of colorful yardgoods that decorated the counter.

"He's surely got a passel of treasures, don't he?" she whispered.

"Doesn't," Beau whispered back, and Maggie grinned.

"Doesn't he?" she repeated, her eyes shiny with delight.

"Go ahead and look around," Beau told her. "I'm going to talk to a couple of the men by the stove. Let's see if I can find a buyer for the puppies."

Even the threat of losing her beloved pups was not enough to deter her apparently, for she nodded and stepped away from his side, and Beau watched as she slipped her mittens off, tucking them into her pockets, in order to touch with careful fingers the array of fabric.

Once more Maggie felt as though she'd gone to heaven, that mysterious place her mama'd assured her existed beyond the sun and moon, to which good folks would somehow be transported from the earth upon their death. If such a place really did exist, it would surely be no more inviting than the four walls surrounding her now, she decided.

A basket of eggs sat on the counter, and she looked at them disdainfully. The ones from Beau's chicken coop were larger, most of them double-yolked at that. She moved on to where a display of ladies' boots took her fancy, not that she needed such things. With small heels and buttons marching up the side, they were far too fine to be subjected to chicken poop and corral dust.

Ah, there. She sighed. There in glass bins on tall shelves, were bits and pieces of fine fabric, with snatches of lace visible in the folds, and she wondered, clenching her fingers into fists, what it would be like to possess such finery.

"May I show you something?" a young woman asked, smiling a greeting, even as she cast a surreptitious glance at Maggie's attire.

"What's all the stuff in those boxes?" Maggie whispered, leaning across the counter, nodding at the display.

"Ladies' undergarments," the woman answered. "You know, like petticoats and chemises and such."

"Like a shift, you mean?"

The woman nodded. "It's about the same thing as a chemise, I think."

"Do they cost dearly?" She knew her tone was wistful and Maggie cleared her throat. "Never mind, I need other things." She turned her head, searching the shelves for what she sought. "Do you have any yarn for knitting stuff? You know, like scarves and such?"

"Certainly, right down here." Leading the way down the counter, the woman lifted a box from below, opening the lid to uncover a variety of yarn, all neatly separated in skeins.

"How much does it take to make a scarf?" Maggie asked softly. "If it's not too much, Miss Sophie, out at Beau Jackson's ranch, where I'm working, said I should get some." She bent closer. "It's for a scarf for him." She nodded briefly to where Beau stood beside three other men in front of the pot-bellied stove across the room.

"I think he'd look well in brown," the woman said, taking two skeins from the box. "Did Sophie want it on her bill?"

Maggie could only nod, amazed at the ease of the transaction. "Wrap it up, please, would you? In a piece of paper or something?" Capable hands made short work of the task, and Maggie reached for her purchase. "Thank you," she said, tucking the package inside her coat. Sparing one last glance at the tempting garments behind the counter, she turned to where Beau was deep in conversation.

As if he felt her regard, he looked up. "Maggie, come get the list Sophie made out and let Cora get things together for us."

She nodded, walking to where he waited, and took the

list from his hand. Head bent, unwilling to meet the gaze of his companions, she stepped back to the counter and offered the brown paper to Cora.

"Your name's Maggie?" Cora asked, perusing the scribbled words. "Did you write this? Is this brown sugar you want, or the fine granulated?"

"I don't know," Maggie admitted, peering to see the words Sophie had printed. "Sophie made out the list. I know we have white sugar on the table, and I think there's a plenty of it in the bin yet. Must be she means brown." *Sugar,* she decided, must be the word on the top line. It began with that snakey-looking letter, the one that sounded like it looked. And it was the same word as was on the big sack of sugar Sophie had in the pantry. She felt a jolt of delight as she recognized the letters, yearning to turn to Beau and tell him of her discovery.

"Well, everything else is plain enough," Cora said, reaching for a bottle on the shelf behind her. "There's pails of lard over there, if you want to get one," she told Maggie. "And why don't you pick out one of those baskets of apples for her."

Feeling a sense of importance she was most unfamiliar with, Maggie did as she was bidden, then looked up as Beau took the basket from her hand.

"I'll take that," he said. He bent low to speak directly into her ear. "Charlie wants one of the pups, and Herm Dorchester said he'd like a pair of them. His dogs ate bad meat and died last month."

A pang struck Maggie as she nodded her agreement. It was what they'd come to town for, at least part of the reason. As long as the animals were given good homes, she would have no complaint, miss them though she might. Anyway, she couldn't fault Beau for accomplishing his goal, and if he gave her a bit of what money the pups brought, she'd have enough to pay Sophie for the yarn. And then, she thought, given the chance, she might even consider replacing her worn-out shift with one of those lacy, fancy-looking things the lady, Cora, had called a chemise. And wasn't that a slinky-sounding thing to be wearing under her clothes.

"Will they come out and get the pups?" she asked Beau, following him to the counter.

"Tomorrow," he said, drawing money from his pocket for the supplies Cora was readying for them.

"I've got an extra cardboard box you can have to carry this in," she offered, and at Beau's nod of thanks, she reached beneath the counter and placed the container beside his purchases. "It'll most all fit," she told him, stacking the items inside.

"Are you all set, Maggie?" Beau picked up the box and placed it atop his shoulder, reaching for the basket with his free hand. "Open the door for me, will you?" he asked, nodding a goodbye to the men who watched their departure.

"Did you recognize any of those fellas?" he asked Maggie as he stowed the supplies in the wagon. She sat on the seat waiting for him, and her gaze swung back to the store window. One of the three men watched, and then, as she met his gaze, he turned back to the stove.

"No," she said. "I never paid any mind to anybody the couple of times I came to town. And Pa didn't have much company on the farm. Just once in a while somebody stopped by to pick up a jug from him."

Beau's eyebrow rose quizzically. "A jug? Your pa made moonshine?"

Maggie nodded. "He said it was the best cash crop he had."

Chapter Nine

"You don't do much drinking, do you, Beau?" Sitting beside him on the sofa, Maggie watched as he fingered the strings of his guitar, playing an elusive melody. He looked up at her and shook his head. "I didn't think so," she said. "At least I never smelled any booze on you."

"Does your pa drink a lot of the stuff he sells?" Beau asked, certain already of her answer.

"He's his own best customer." She brushed at her skirt, smoothing the fabric and picking at a bit of thread. "I've been thinking maybe I'd try to see my mama, find out if she's all right."

Beau's hands flattened against the guitar, stilling the music. "Do you think that's a good idea?" The thought of Maggie coming face to face with Edgar O'Neill, and perhaps falling victim to his fists again made his heart clench in his chest, prompting his offer. "Shall I go with you?"

"No, I'd just sneak on the place while he's up at his still. He makes a trip into the woods out back of the barn every couple of days."

"I don't like to have you run the risk of him finding you there," Beau told her.

Her hands clenched in the fabric of her skirt and her head bowed as she spoke. "I guess I need to do this."

It was not in him to forbid her the visit, but he could sure as hell discourage it, Beau decided. "How you going to get there? And how do you know your father won't punish your mother if he finds out?"

Her eyes were bleak when she met his gaze. "I don't know. And I know that sounds foolish, that I would walk back into that house after what all I put up with there. But, the fact is, I keep thinking about my mama."

"I can't stop you, Maggie. I won't even try, I guess," he admitted. "But would you wait till Joe and Rad get back? They'll be here by day after tomorrow."

She tilted her chin and shot him a disdainful look. "Do you think I'd leave you in the lurch, short-handed as you are right now? I guess you don't know me very well, Beau Jackson."

Well, that gave him another day or so to change her mind. "I guess I know you about as well as anyone else, sweetheart. I know you're loyal, especially to your mother. I suppose I wasn't sure that loyalty extended to me."

Her look softened and she leaned closer, lifting her hand to brush her palm against his cheek. "I'm about as loyal as that old hound I brought with me. I'd do most anything in the world for you. I never liked anybody in my life the way I like you."

"Have you ever loved anyone, Maggie? Besides your mother and maybe your sisters?"

"I don't feel that way about you, Beau," she told him sharply. "That's a different kind of thing altogether. Lovin' my mama just came natural."

Sorely tempted to correct her, he whispered the word. "*Loving,* Maggie. Loving. I don't feel the same way about you that I felt about my mother and father. It's still love, but it's a man and woman thing.''

Her mouth formed the word he'd spoken. ''Loving.'' It emerged in a whisper and she repeated it. ''You're talking about loving me? In that man and woman kinda way?'' She drew back from him. ''I thought you just liked me, like a friend. That's what you told me, that you wanted to be my friend.''

He nodded. ''I do. I thought we were friends. But that doesn't mean we can't be more than that one day.''

''What day're you talkin' about?'' she asked suspiciously, her careful pronunciation forgotten. ''Is this about the way you were touchin' my bosom when we were goin' to town?''

He'd might as well sink or swim, he decided. ''I'm talking about asking you to marry me.'' There, it was in the open, and for a moment, he feared he'd frightened her beyond measure.

Her eyes refused to meet his, her hands clenched into fists and she shot to her feet. ''You don't have to do that. I don't want you feelin' sorry for me, enough so's you think you have to marry me.'' Her shoulders slumped as she turned from him.

''I wouldn't marry anyone out of pity,'' he told her. ''I thought I loved a girl once, and almost married her, but she found someone else while I was in the army. And then after a while, when I came to Kansas and bought this place, I saw a woman I might have loved, but she was already taken. And I don't poach, Maggie.''

She'd turned back as he spoke, her gaze intent on him. ''No, I don't think you'd ever be lookin'—looking at a married woman. But I'll warrant there's plenty of women hereabouts who'd be happy to have you come calling.''

"Maybe," he agreed. "But I'd only marry a woman if I loved her."

"Are you telling me…" She shook her head. "Nah, you're pulling my leg."

It took every bit of willpower he owned to sit still, but he would do nothing at this point to scare her off. "I wouldn't lie to you. I love you. I want you to marry me. I want to take care of you and have babies with you."

She bit at her lip. "We're talking about doing that man and woman thing, aren't we?" A visible shiver possessed her and she hugged herself, as if the room had lost its warmth. "I don't know if I can do that. It's not that I'm afraid. I just don't like the idea of having a man owning me."

"No man owns another human being, Maggie. Not anymore, at least not in this country." He stood then, and she dropped her arms to her sides, her cheeks flushing as he approached. "That's one of the reasons there was a war, so that people could be free. I don't think that should only apply to the Negroes who were slaves, but to women, as well. I might own my horses and my cow and even the pup you gave me, but I'll never own the woman I marry."

"If I didn't want to do all that stuff, I wouldn't have to?" she asked, her eyes suspiciously damp.

"I'd never make you do anything you didn't want to," he vowed. "I'd try to persuade you, maybe," he allowed, with a grin that refused to be stifled, "but I'll never force you to sleep in my bed."

"Can I think about it?" she asked, turning toward the window.

"Are you crying? Did I say something to…"

"No." She shook her head, and her voice trembled. "I just never thought anybody like you would say all those things to me. I didn't want to get married off just to get away from my pa, like Emily and Roberta did.'' She spun to face him, and his heart ached for the tears that she shed. ''I don't even know if they're happy. And I don't want to marry up with you and then find out I made a mistake and be stuck with it.''

He could resist no longer, and if she fled from his touch, he would have to go back to the beginning and woo her anew. His arms enclosed her and with a firm touch, he drew her into his embrace. She stiffened and he closed his eyes, willing her to soften to his caress. His hands against her back, he bent to press his lips in the curve of her neck, where the open collar of her dress exposed the soft skin of her throat.

Maggie's breath hissed past his ear and he hesitated. ''I like the kissing stuff, Beau. Maybe I'd like the rest of it.'' Her hands crept up to clench the fabric of his shirt and she tilted her head a bit, offering him a scant few inches of bared flesh. ''My mama said it was wrong to crawl into a man's bed, lessen you was married to him.''

''Your mama was right,'' he agreed in a husky whisper. His tongue tasted the flavor of her throat and found there the scent of woman, of Maggie. ''Would you like me to talk to the preacher in town?''

''Maybe I don't love you,'' she warned him. ''But it surely feels fine when you kiss on me like this. And I guess I can't think of anybody else I'd rather live with than you and Sophie.''

Her hands moved to touch his hair and he felt the tension leave her body, sensed the softening of her flesh as she leaned more fully against him. ''Would you kiss me on the mouth, Beau?''

Would I? Like a thirsty man being offered a cup of water, he accepted her invitation. His lips pressed gently, carefully, moving with caution, finally catching hold of hers in a teasing manner. With teeth and tongue, he explored the tender flesh, patient as she allowed the intimacy, encouraged as her own lips responded. She opened to him, touching him with the tip of her tongue, hesitant and yet eager.

"I never thought before, you know, when I heard Emily and Roberta talking about it...that kissing would be like this." Her whisper was breathless, and she leaned back to look fully into his face. "You're making me feel all hot and tingly in some strange places. And every time this happens, I like it better."

His right hand left her back, only to slide against her ribs and across her breast, to where black buttons held her dress in place. His fingers were agile, and the buttonholes gave way easily. Maggie's head tilted downward as she watched his progress. Beneath the dress, her breasts were covered, though the fabric was threadbare. No buttons allowed entry there, only the fragile material of a well-washed undergarment.

"What if I tear this thing?" he asked, amusement vying with impatience.

"It's the only shift I've got," she said. "My other fell apart, and I been washing this one out in my basin every night and hanging it to dry over my chair."

"Well," he said, impatience winning out, "I guess I'd better buy you a couple of new ones, hadn't I?" His fingers shredded the fabric with little effort, exposing the skin beneath. Her breasts were round and firm, and his memory of their fullness became reality as he slipped his hand against bare skin, his fingers flexing gently.

She shivered, and as he watched, her eyes closed, a faint flush creeping up from the treasure he cradled, to blossom in her cheeks. "I surely like what you're doing to me."

Her words were choked, and her head tilted back, exposing the long line of skin from her throat to her breasts.

"You'll like this, too." His body urging him to completion, he bent his head, his mouth open against her pale skin, where the sun had not shone its rays. His lips captured the small bit of flesh that lured him, and he touched it with the edges of his teeth, then drew it into his mouth, suckling gently.

She moaned and her body convulsed against him, moving in a rhythm he could not mistake. His hand slid from her waist to press against the firm rounding of her bottom and he paced her erratic wiggling with the firm thrust of his hips. And then held her fast, warned by the intensity of his own arousal. In another moment he'd have her on the floor, skirts up around her waist and his trousers undone.

"Maggie...Maggie." Sounding like a rusty hinge, his voice called her name, and she shuddered, drawing in deep, shivering breaths.

"I'm thinkin' I like this more than I oughta," she said after a moment. Her hands fell from his head and she levered herself against his shoulders. He released her, his eyes unwilling to lose sight of the breast he'd held within his mouth. Her skin glowed with the gleam of pearls he'd seen in a jewelry store once, and the dark crest puckered tighter as he watched.

"I think we'd better get married right away," he said, his words harsh. "Whether you love me or not, I don't think you'll turn me away, Maggie."

Her fingers were clumsy as she buttoned her dress, and he watched silently, aware that his control had been tested to its limit. "I'm going into my room now," she said, her voice holding a tremor that matched that of her hands. "You're a powerful man, Beau. You must've done lots of this sort of stuff. You sure know how to make me all wobbly and shaky inside. And I need to think about this without your hands on me.''

She turned from him, then looked back from the doorway, her wistful smile as unknowing a temptation as ever existed. ''Play me a song, Beau. One of those pretty ones about loving and such.''

Bending, he picked up his guitar, and nodded his assent. Even as she walked from the room and down the hallway toward the kitchen, his fingers touched the strings and formed a chord. His right hand picked out a melody and his voice was low and husky as he sang words of finding a love beneath the limbs of a weeping willow, in the arms of a blue-eyed woman.

Maggie's footsteps moved slowly across the kitchen floor and his keen hearing picked up the sound of the storage room door as its hinges squeaked open.

It did not close again, and he sang for her, his voice not much more than a whisper, as his heart soared within him.

Rad and Joe rode into the yard before dinner the next day, their horses lathered, both men leaping from their saddles. From the corral, Maggie heard their raised voices, and that of Beau as he shot angry queries at the pair of men. Something was wrong. The colt tugged at the lead rope and whinnied loudly, tossing his head and kicking his heels.

Maggie wrestled with the horse, speaking softly, even as she strained to hear. ''You're just fine,'' she cooed, holding tightly to his halter. ''All that racket doesn't mean diddly squat. There's just you and me here, boy. Now settle down. You hear me?'' Her hands worked at the yearling's head, rubbing and assuring the fey creature of his safety. Above all else, young horses needed a sure and steady hand, and Maggie determined not to allow the fuss beyond the barn to influence her tending to this animal.

She led him through his paces, talking in a low voice, reassuring him constantly, and then, when he'd performed to her leading, she relented and loosed him into the pasture. "Now, what on earth do you suppose all that was about?" she asked beneath her breath as she hurried through the barn.

In the yard, near the porch, five men gathered in a huddle, Beau at its center. "You lost me somewhere!" His words vibrated in the air as he faced Rad, head-on. "You had the money, and now you don't. What the hell are you trying to pull?"

Maggie slowed her steps, unwilling to interfere, then turned back before Beau could see her. Somehow, Rad had lost the money from the horses, and that fact made her heart ache for Beau. What his plans were for that income didn't matter. He didn't seem to be headed for the poorhouse that she could tell. But he no doubt had a place for such a considerable amount of cash.

And now those plans had come to naught. She stepped back inside the barn and drew her coat tightly around herself. The men shifted position, and Joe Armstrong seemed to be the center of attention. Maggie watched as his head shook slowly, and then he spoke, shrugging his shoulders and shoving his hands deep into his pockets. "All I know is he had the money with him when he was playin' poker, and when I saw him next, it was gone."

"You lost my cash at a damned poker table?" Beau roared.

A look of disdain swept Rad's face and his laugh was harsh. Breaking away, he stalked toward his horse, mounting with an agile movement. "I don't give a damn what you believe, Jackson." His voice was savage with intensity, and the horse reared as Rad turned it in a tight circle. "I'm headin' out,'' he yelled. "You can find yourself another cowboy."

"That's my horse you're riding," Beau called.

"I'll leave it at the livery stable. It's nothin' but a nag anyway."

Beau swore, hands on hips, his voice a grating sound that sent a chill through Maggie. Shay reached for him, one hand gripping Beau's shoulder, and spoke words Maggie could not hear. She watched in horror as Rad rode toward town, cringing as he prodded his mount into a wild gallop.

And then Beau headed for the barn at a trot, sweeping his hat from his head. Behind him, Shay shook his head at Joe, and both men followed at a run. Maggie stepped back into a corner, and it was a measure of Beau's anger that he walked past her, unseeing. His stallion's halter was changed for a bridle, and within minutes, the horse was saddled.

"Wait up, boss," Joe said, bringing a fresh horse from a stall. "I'll ride with you."

"You've got two minutes," Beau warned him, the words harsh and biting. Then he turned to the back of the barn, where sunlight shed its rays across the floor.

"Maggie!" The sound of his voice shouting her name brought her from her corner and she moved quickly to where he stood.

"I'm here."

"Take care of Joe's horse. He needs to be unsaddled and dried off. Don't let him eat or drink till you get him cooled down."

"I'll take care of it," she told him, and fled from the barn to where the weary horse stood near the house. His sides were heaving and lather was flecked white on his flanks. It was obvious that he'd been sorely used and Maggie took his reins and led him back toward the barn. She slid his saddle to the ground, tipping it on end, then led the gelding around the yard, holding the bridle near his head, speaking softly as she walked with him.

In less time than she'd have thought possible, Beau rode from the barn, ducking his head as his stud headed out the door, Joe fast on his heels. Maggie watched, worry gnawing at her. She'd not thought Beau capable of such fury. And yet, if she had heard it right, Rad had somehow lost the money from the shipment of horses.

"He's not mad at you, missy. He wouldn't have raised his voice to you if he'd been thinkin'." Shay stood before her, his gaze dark with anger as Maggie slowed her pace. "Rad's got himself in a peck of trouble. It looks like he lost the money in a card game, and Beau's after his hide."

"I know he was upset," she said, her gaze meeting his. "He was counting on that money." She looked after the men, the only sign of their passage a cloud of dust moving in their wake. "He doesn't have his gun, does he?"

"He won't need a gun." Shay turned away and Maggie shivered at the menace revealed in those few words. *He won't need a gun.*

It was after dark when the two men returned, riding to the barn, where Pony met them. Maggie watched from her window, reassured as Beau slid to the ground and spoke for a moment with Joe before he turned to the house. They'd come back on their own, with no sheriff in obvious pursuit, and neither man seemed to bear bruises from a fight. She stepped back from the window pane and sat on the side of her bed. How Rad could be dishonest was beyond her ability to conceive. Beau had trusted the man. And perhaps that was the worst of it. Placing your trust and having it betrayed was more hurtful than a beating any day of the week.

In the kitchen, beyond her door, Sophie's low tones

blended with those of Beau's. He sounded weary, Maggie decided, his voice a growling rumble. The clang of the coffeepot on the iron stove and the scrape of a chair against the kitchen floor told her that Beau had been persuaded to sit and perhaps eat the supper Sophie'd kept in the warming oven.

"Is she awake?" His words penetrated, and Maggie rose, moving quietly toward her door. His chair moved against the floor again, and then soft footsteps neared.

"Maggie?" His voice low, so as not to awaken her should she be asleep, he called her name.

"I'm here." Turning the knob, she opened her door and faced him. His eyes were bleak, and she mourned the hurt he'd suffered. "Did you find him?"

Beau shook his head. "He must have turned into the woods somewhere. He wasn't at the livery stable and neither Joe nor I saw any tracks leading off across country, anywhere near town. It wouldn't have been hard to lose us. We were both dead set on getting to town. Didn't even think about him cutting off and taking cover anywhere near here."

"Did he steal your money, Beau?"

"You better believe it," he said, his words bitter, his eyes narrowing with a hint of anger. "Joe said he'd left Rad in a bar, playing poker, and when he showed up at the hotel in the middle of the night, he spun a tale about two men jumping him on the street. Joe knew better. Rad didn't have a mark on him. Hell, his clothes weren't even rumpled."

"Did he lose it all?" Maggie couldn't imagine placing such a sum of money on a gambling table, then walking away and leaving it there.

"I don't know," Beau said harshly. "Maybe he set some aside to line his pockets with. All I know is that they came home empty-handed. And that bas—'' He halted, the word unspoken. ''He was lying to me. As sure as I'm standing here, that man lied to my face, and was madder than hell when I wouldn't believe him.''

''Do you think he'll steal your horse?'' Rad might have called the gelding he rode a nag, but Maggie knew better. Every cow pony on the place was hand-picked by Beau for his string. They were the chosen ones, the cream of the crop, and not a second-rate animal among them.

''If he does, he's facing a hanging when he gets caught.'' Beau's jaw firmed. ''And if I get my hands on him first, there won't be enough left to tie a rope on.''

Maggie shivered at the menace expressed by his chill tone, and she touched his arm. ''Don't dirty your hands, Beau. He's not worth it.''

He looked down at her slender fingers against the rough cotton of his shirt, then met her gaze again. His mouth curved with a humorless smile. ''Come sit with me. I need some company.''

She looked past him at the empty kitchen. ''I thought I heard Sophie out here.''

''I sent her to bed.'' He turned his arm and clasped her fingers. ''I owe you an apology.''

Maggie shook her head. ''No, you don't. Telling me what to do is your right, Beau Jackson. I work here.''

''I was madder than hell and I shouted at you, Maggie. You didn't deserve that.''

''My feelings aren't that tender,'' she told him. ''I've been hollered at before.'' She looked past him to where his plate waited his attention. ''Your supper's getting cold. Did Joe eat anything?''

''He got a bite in town.'' His eyes lit suddenly, chasing the gloom from his face. ''I almost forgot something. You wait right here,'' he told her, grabbing his coat and shoving his arms into it quickly. She shivered as he opened the door, allowing a cold draft to envelope her. And then he was gone, the door closing behind him.

Maggie walked to the window, watching him cross the yard, his form a dark shadow against the scattering of snow. He vanished inside the barn, where a lantern glowed, and then in only seconds reappeared, sliding the big door shut. His stride was long as he neared, and he looked up to where she watched, his face a pale blur, his grin allowing a slash of white teeth to gleam in the moonlight.

She turned from the window as he stepped into the kitchen, shedding his coat quickly. A wrapped package in one hand, he approached her. "I got you something at the general store." And hadn't Conrad Carson had a grin a mile wide as Beau had counted out the cash for his purchase. "Cora wasn't there," he said. "So I couldn't ask her which one you liked, and the store owner liked them all, so he wasn't any help. Old Conrad was about to burst when I bought it. He had all he could do not to ask me who I was buying such a thing for."

Maggie eyed the paper-wrapped bundle he held, her heart beating double time. "It's for me?" she asked, knowing even as he placed it in her hand that he'd kept his promise. What else would all his hemming and hawing be about? Her fingers fumbled with the string and Beau made an impatient sound in his throat, his hand slipping into his pocket to withdraw his knife.

"Here, let me cut that for you," he said, sliding the knife beneath the multiple strands, slicing through them firmly. "Now open it up."

Maggie unwrapped the parcel slowly, her cheeks burning as she envisioned the contents, recalling the fine fabric and lacy edges she'd seen in the glass case. The final wrapping fell away and she held a double handful of undergarments, the smooth material soft against her fingers.

"Oh, my word, Beau!" Her whisper was almost reverent as she allowed one chemise to unfold.

"Do you like them?" he asked, reaching to touch the bodice where small pearl buttons lay in a row.

She felt her eyes burn with unshed tears and her lashes blinked rapidly. "You said you was gonna replace my shift, not buy me some kinda fancy stuff like this."

His long index finger lifted her chin and his dark eyes narrowed as tears slid down her cheeks. "When I saw these, I didn't look any further, honey. Maybe Carson has some plain ones like your shift, but I wanted you to have lace and bitty little buttons."

"He'll think I'm a kept woman," Maggie whispered, and then wondered what else she could possibly be considered. Beau had indeed *kept* her for the past weeks, if that meant providing her with everything she ate and drank and wore on her back.

"He doesn't even know who I bought them for," Beau told her.

"Well, Cora saw me with you in the store." Her fingers warmed by the delicate garments she held, she lifted them to brush her face against the white fabric.

"I don't care, Maggie." Firm as the floor he stood upon, his words were a statement she could not mistake. Beau owed explanations to no one, and his intentions were honorable. "I'm planning on talking you into a wedding before long."

The memory of his hands on her skin and his mouth nuzzling her breast filled her mind. That he would unbutton those fine, dainty buttons she held in her grasp was almost a certainty. Heat such as she'd only experienced in the past few days enveloped her and she wondered that she could withstand such yearning. Beau had said he would not force her to sleep in his bed, and she believed him.

But coax her, he would. Of that she had no doubt. And it would not be in her to refuse him whatever he asked. Not only because she owed him, but because her body hungered for him. Her skin tingled at his touch, her breasts were tight and aching even now, and heaven only knew what would happen once he tossed back the covers and invited her into that big bed on the second floor.

If only she could talk to Roberta and Emily. Maybe they could tell her what she should know, once she was face-to-face with a man with needs, expecting her to do all the womanly things a wife was supposed to know about. But finding her way to wherever they lived in Green Rapids was beyond her. She wouldn't even know who to ask, and besides, going into town alone was not to be considered.

That left Mama, she decided. Not that she'd ever managed to do anything to keep Pa happy, Maggie thought glumly. But at least she could clear up some of the mystery attached to this man and woman thing. Asking Beau was out of the question. He already knew she was ignorant in more ways than one. No sense in spitting the words out, telling him she was dumb as a post about this.

Tomorrow, she decided. Tomorrow she'd skin out of here after the morning chores were done and go take a look-see at her pa's still, find out if he was there. And if he was, she'd high-tail it to the house and spend a few minutes with Mama. Her heart yearned for a glimpse of the woman who'd birthed her, and she felt a sudden pang of loneliness.

"Maggie?" Beau's voice brought her eyes open and she smiled at him. "Come sit with me."

"All right," she agreed. "Just let me put these away first." In moments she'd folded the two chemises with care, placing them on her bed until she could find a proper place for them to be stored. Her stockings and drawers were folded on the chair, and somehow the rough feed sack fabric looked even more faded and worn, compared to the dainty garments Beau had given her tonight.

The nails she'd pounded into the wall held her pants and shirts. Now she'd have to put a shelf beside them, where her wealth of underwear could be stored. Never before had she been so rich, with changes of work clothes and even two dresses to her name.

Looking back from the doorway, her gaze scanned the room, resting on the curtains Sophie had hung only yesterday, then dancing back to the bed where two lacy, feminine garments measured the kindness of Beau Jackson.

Chapter Ten

Never had the chores gone so slowly. And today of all days, Beau had asked her to milk the cow. Very kindly, to be sure, but it had taken all of her good manners to smile nicely and agree. Sophie had even looked at her askance, no doubt wondering what was setting such fire under her this morning.

If they only knew. Maggie leaned her forehead against the cow's flank, her fingers nimble as they stripped the last of the milk from the animal's udder. "There you go, Bess," she murmured, dodging the creature's long tail as it swished in her direction. The bucket was light as she swung it from the floor. Everything was lit with a shiny glow this morning, she decided.

Strange that the prospect of a visit with her mother should bring about so much happiness in her soul. Especially considering that she'd left home determined never to darken that miserable doorway again.

The door to the springhouse stood open and Maggie carried the milk inside. She placed it on the bench and reached for a clean cloth, covering the pail carefully, lest bugs or dust spoil the milk.

"You all done with chores, Maggie?" Beau called from outside the door.

"Just about," she answered, hoping against hope that he wouldn't come up with a whole slew of work for her to tackle this morning.

"I just wanted to let you know we're heading out to the far pastures to check on the rest of the cattle and make sure we've got all the yearlings and nursing mares up close to the barn."

She breathed a sigh of relief. He'd be long gone when she set out for her visit with Mama. First she had to come up with a story for Sophie, and that would be tough. Telling tales went against the grain. But it couldn't be helped. Not if she wanted to spend a few minutes with Mama today. And from the look on Beau's face, she wouldn't have many more days before he carried through on his threat.

Or was it a promise? Either way, she was headed for a wedding. And for the life of her, she couldn't find a thing to be mournful about when she considered the idea.

"I'll be going back to the house in a few minutes," she told Beau. "I just want to spend a few minutes with the pups." She left the springhouse, closing the door behind herself. "You got any place in mind for the last one?" she asked.

"I was thinking about asking Cord McPherson if Rachel's brothers would like to have him. They've got a cattle dog, but it's getting on in age. Either way, they might be looking for a new dog." He cast a glance at Maggie and grinned. "It wouldn't be far away. You could check up on it every once in a while."

"Maybe when you deliver the yearlings to Cord, he could take a look at the pup. Kinda let them see how smart he is."

"You want to go along with me?" Beau asked, then

grinned at her quick nod. "Maybe you'll have news to tell Rachel by then."

"News? What news?"

Beau sighed deeply. "We're going to get married, Maggie. Surely you'll want Rachel to know about it from you."

"She won't care on my account," Maggie told him. "She'll probably think you got roped into it some way or another."

His hand swept up to cradle her cheek. "Don't you understand anything at all, Maggie O'Neill? I'm marrying you because I want to, and don't you forget that for one little skinny minute."

"Well, you're not gonna do it today," she replied smartly. "You've got stock to tend to before the snow blows in."

Beau looked at the western sky where gray clouds hung low. "And probably before the sun sets," he agreed. He pulled his hat lower over his forehead, then reached for his gloves, tugging them from his back pocket. "Put your scarf on when you go out to the barn later," he told her. "That wind's coming up, and Sophie'll skin you alive if you get a case of the quinsy."

"I wonder why she hasn't made you one?" Maggie said.

"Can't figure that out," he agreed. "It's probably in the works though." He bent to her and pressed his mouth against hers, his kiss brief, but thorough. "Stay close to the house today, Maggie. I don't want to have to worry about you."

She smiled, hoping he'd be satisfied with that small assurance, unwilling to nod or agree in words with his edict. Not when she planned on skedaddling down the road just as soon as he was out of sight.

"Mama?" The house was quiet, not even a whisper of smoke coming from the chimney as Maggie approached from the front. She slid from her mount and tied the mare to the front porch railing. Guilt had been her companion during the past hour. First because she'd borrowed a horse from Beau's stable, and then because she'd snuck away without letting Sophie know where she was heading.

With a vague wave of her hand, she'd gone out of the house, Sophie likely assuming she would be in the corral with the yearlings. The woman trusted her and though she hadn't lied aloud, she'd let her actions speak for her. Then, saddling the mare, she'd whispered an apology to the absent Beau, her hands working quickly as she readied the animal for the trip.

It had taken more than an hour to find the trail to her pa's still, and she'd had to hide the mare while she crept closer afoot. The scent of his brew gave notice of his whereabouts and she'd hidden inside a grove of trees, until she was certain that Pa was there, and likely to be busy for a while longer. It was slow going, making her way back toward the mare, and then finally riding hell-bent for the farmhouse.

Now, even though the day was cold and she knew from experience that the house was drafty, there seemed to be no fire lit in the kitchen stove. Maggie's heart trembled in her chest as she considered what might be wrong. And then she threw caution to the winds, leaping onto the front porch, and opening the unlocked door with a twist of the handle.

"Mama?" she called again, more loudly this time. "Where are you, Mama?"

A faint sound from a bedroom at the back of the house was her answer, and Maggie ran from the parlor, through the cold kitchen and into the small bedroom her parents shared. On the bed, her mother's frail form huddled beneath a quilt, one hand lifted to signal Maggie of her awareness.

"What are you doin' here, girl?" Verna O'Neill's voice asked frantically. "Your pa will throttle you if he finds you here."

"What's wrong with you?" Maggie cried, falling to her knees beside the bed. "Did he beat you again, Mama?" She reached for her mother's outstretched hand, holding the chilled member between her own wool-covered fingers. Even through the heavy knitted mitts, Maggie sensed the cold that gripped her mother's frame.

"I'll light the fire," Maggie said quickly. "Is there wood in the kitchen?"

Verna shook her head. "No, don't do that, daughter. If your pa comes in…" As if the thought were too much to give voice to, she shook her head. "Go on back to wherever you've been, Mag. Don't let him get you."

"He won't find me, Mama. He's out by the still. I checked first. He's got a whole slew of jugs and he hasn't even started filling them." She rose and pulled her warm mittens off, slipping them over her mother's fingers. "These'll keep you warm, Mama," she whispered, her eyes scanning the worn face, noting the dried blood that stained her mother's mouth and cheek.

"I'll be right back," she promised, backing from the tiny room. In the kitchen, she opened the stove and set kindling ablaze, then added small chunks of wood, until a fire warmed her hands. Placing the lid in place, she backed from the room, intent on getting her mother into the warmth.

"Let me help you into the kitchen," she said, approaching the bed. Her mother rose on one elbow, nodding agreement, then slid her bare feet onto the floor. Maggie helped her rise, unable to still her fears as she realized that the woman's body had become even more frail in the past weeks.

"Haven't you been eating, Mama?" she asked, draping the quilt over her mother's shoulders.

"I'm not very hungry these days," Verna answered, holding fast to Maggie's hand. Together they walked into the kitchen, Maggie's arm around her mother's waist, until she could lower her into a chair near the stove. Verna huddled there, shivering, tucking her feet inside the folds of the quilt.

"Let me heat up the coffee for you," Maggie said, sliding the coffeepot to the front of the stove.

Verna shook her head. "It's from yesterday. When your pa got up and found out I hadn't cooked his breakfast, he just left without puttin' wood in the stove."

"When did he do this to you?" Maggie asked, her fingers gentle as she touched her mother's face.

"Yesterday." The word was mumbled as Verna drew the quilt up over the bottom of her face, as if she could hide the evidence of Edgar O'Neill's abuse.

"Will you come with me?" Maggie asked, already knowing the answer she would get. "I know a place you can stay, where Pa won't be able to find you."

"Just get me a piece of bread to eat outta the cupboard and get yourself outta here," Verna told her. "He'll be back before long, and he'll kill you if he sees you here."

"He'll never touch me again," Maggie vowed, her head erect as she glanced toward the barn. And then smothered the pain that rose within her as she recalled her last encounter with the man. "I just wanted to see you, Mama. I'm going to be married."

Verna's eyes widened. "Who to? Somebody from hereabouts?" The quilt fell to her chin and she straightened in the chair. "Somebody got you in the family way, girl?"

"No, Mama. He's never touched me. Beau wouldn't do that." And then she covered her mouth with her hand as she realized she'd spoken the name she'd vowed not to say aloud in this house.

"Beau?" Verna repeated it. "Beau Jackson? That fella that lives beyond the McPherson's ranch? You're gonna marry up with him?" Her eyes lit with satisfaction as she considered the idea. "Yer pa would have a screamin' fit if he knew that. It ain't bad enough that Emily and Roberta got away. He's been hollerin' for weeks about you skinnin' out the way you did, and how he needs you here to take care of the horse."

"What's wrong with the horse?" Maggie asked quickly. "What did Pa do to him?"

Verna shook her head and shivered again. "You know yer Pa. Said the damn horse balked on him and he laid it low with an ax handle. Split it right to the bone across the withers. Now it's infected and he's afraid the critter's gonna die on him."

Maggie bundled her coat up to the throat and walked to the back door. "I want to take you home with me, Mama. If you'll put some clothes on, I'll come back in and get you. But I won't be long. You'll have to hurry." She stepped out onto the porch and hastened across the yard to where the barn door stood partway open.

The gelding stood in the first stall, one hind foot lifted above the manure he stood in. The stench of fouled straw and unkempt animals assailed her nostrils and she made her way gingerly to the horse's head, untying his halter from the stall. She backed with him into the aisle and then out the door, filling her lungs with fresh air as she passed through the portal.

"Come on, boy. We'll take you home and get you fixed up," she murmured to the horse, leading him across the yard and up to the back porch. Affixing his lead rope to the porch railing, she stepped inside the back door, only to halt as her mother turned her head.

"You're not ready, Mama," Maggie said quietly, knowing as she spoke that her mother would not leave this place.

"You go on, Mag." Verna took the mittens from her hands and held them out to Maggie. "Take these with you. If your Pa sees them, he'll know someone was here." She looked at the blue wool and back up at her daughter. "Somebody must think a lot of you to make these for you."

Maggie nodded, taking the mittens and sliding her own hands into their warmth. "I have to hurry, Mama. I don't want to take a chance on seeing Pa."

"Don't come back, Mag," her mother warned. "Don't let him have another chance at you. He'll kill you, girl. He means it."

Maggie shuddered and backed from the house, then led the horse around to the front where the mare waited. She lifted herself into the saddle, and without a backward look, headed for the road, matching the mare's pace to the slower gait of the abused animal who followed.

"Where the hell did that decrepit nag come from?" Beau burst in the back door, his gaze moving unerringly to Maggie. She squared her shoulders and faced him. "Tell me you didn't bring that horse into my barn," Beau thundered.

"I can't tell you that," she answered. "I did put him in the barn, and made a poultice for him and then put salve on his withers. On top of that," she blurted, "I stole him."

"You *stole* that pitiful bag of bones? Hell, girl, if you were going to steal a horse, you could at least have made it one worth dragging home. That miserable thing doesn't look like he'll make it till morning."

Maggie's eyes darted to the window and she hurried to gaze through the pane. "Is he down? He was on his feet when I left him."

"He's still up," Beau told her. "But, probably not for long. Pony thinks he's in a pretty bad way. You can't see him from here. I had Pony put him in the back where it's warmer."

"Well, this girl's not going back out there till she gets some food in her," Sophie put in, from her spot in front of the stove. "She just dragged in here a few minutes ago, about poohed-out. And not a thing to eat since breakfast."

"Well, there's plenty of food in the house," Beau blustered, stepping closer to Maggie. "There's no excuse for not eating," he said, his tone softer. "Where'd you get the horse?" And even as he asked the question, he knew the answer. "You went to see your mother, didn't you? And the horse was in the barn, and you couldn't stand the thought of your pa taking out his hatefulness on a dumb animal."

Her eyes widened. "How did you know?" she whispered, tilting her head back to search his eyes. "Are you going to put him..." She shook her head. "No, of course you're not. You wouldn't have let Pony move him to a warmer spot if you were gonna put him out in the cold." Her lips twitched and a sad smile came into being. "You're not as tough as you'd like me to think, Beau Jackson."

"I'll be tougher than you could ever imagine if I have to face down your father over that pathetic excuse for a horse," he told her firmly. And then, as she nodded her head in agreement, he wrapped his arms around her waist and tugged her closer. Across the room, Sophie snorted loudly, and Beau cast a warning look in her direction.

He felt chilled, overwhelmed with thoughts of what might have happened to this woman he loved had her father discovered her presence in his house. Anger threatened to overwhelm him, not only for Maggie and the danger she'd placed herself in today, but that there was any danger at all. A young woman should be able to visit her mother without fear of the consequences.

"We'll look after the horse," Beau said, swallowing the hatred he felt for the miserable excuse for a man who'd so foully abused the animal sheltered even now in his barn.

"I had to bring him here," Maggie whispered. "You can't imagine the stall he was standing in, and the filth I washed off him before I put him out back."

The presence of her wrapped in his arms brought calm to his storm-tossed emotions, reassuring him that she was safe here beneath his roof. "Do you think he'll make it, Maggie?" Beau asked, bending to kiss her forehead. His goal was a bit lower, somewhere between her nose and chin, but the presence of Sophie in the room made him choose a safer target.

"Maybe. I don't know." Her fingers trailed across his coat, loosening his buttons and spreading wide the lapels. Then she nuzzled against the vee of his open-collared shirt. "I had to do it, Beau. I couldn't make my mama come along, but that old gelding just followed right behind me, like he knew he was going to a better place."

"You saw your mama." Beau's hand were moving gently across her back, measuring the narrow width, then clasping her tightly.

She nodded. "The house was cold and I built a fire and made her go into the kitchen to get warm. She said she had to stay and cook for him." A hopeless note permeated her voice and Beau winced at the sorrow that filled her words. The urge to carry her from the kitchen, find a place of privacy and console her with whatever means available was powerful. Lifting her in his arms was tempting, the lure of his bed was almost more than he could resist. And yet he obeyed his better instincts.

"Sit down and eat something, Maggie," he said, turning her to the table, shooting a glance at Sophie. She did as he asked, and he drew up a second chair beside her. A bowl appeared before her, and Sophie placed a spoon beside it.

"Good vegetable stew, all but the dumplings," she said. "You can have some more of it in an hour, when supper's ready. Eat that for now."

Maggie picked up the spoon, a child obeying orders, Beau thought, as she obediently lifted steaming vegetables to her mouth. "Don't burn yourself," he warned. "It's too hot." And she was too tired to care, he decided, leaning closer to blow on the spoon.

She flushed, and he was relieved to see color on her cheeks. "Thank you," she murmured, her smile lopsided as she tilted her head to watch him.

"Blow it yourself," he told her, sitting back, his grin coming easier now. "Just eat it, one way or the other." And then watched her as she devoured the bowlful of food.

The night was long, with Pony at her side, ministering with her to the horse she'd rescued. "He ain't hardly worth the trouble," Pony muttered, handing her a steaming poultice.

"I know it," she admitted. "But what else can we do? Just let him die, without anybody caring?"

"Reckon not," Pony said, his hands working slowly, brushing and grooming the animal's hindquarters. "Don't know how anyone can treat a horse so bad. Probably hasn't been cleaned up in weeks."

"More like months," she admitted. "Knowing my pa the way I do, I'd say he just used and abused this poor thing. He's real handy at doing that." She lifted the poultice and turned it, then covered the horse's withers with a blanket, holding in the heat.

"You might's well sit down for a while," Pony told her. "If this is gonna work, we'll know pretty soon. Seems like that thing's drained pretty good."

"I'm afraid if we leave him, he'll be down, and then we'll never get him on his feet." Maggie's hands rubbed at the gelding's head and she spoke softly into the twitching ears.

"It's almost morning," Beau said, from the aisle. "There's new snow. We'll need to feed horses, Pony."

"What we need to do is get this girl to bed, boss," Pony told him. "She's about tuckered out."

"You've been up all night, too," Maggie said, as if determined not to be hustled off to the house. "I'm going in for breakfast pretty soon. Just another half hour or so, and I'll put drawing salve on him and bandage it over."

"What do you think?" Beau asked. The horse looked a little perkier, he decided, and he'd been eating some hay from Maggie's hand the past little while. "Did you give him any oats or corn?"

"I thought we'd try some mash," she said. "If you don't mind." She turned to face Beau, and the gelding's head lifted, his nose nudging Maggie's shoulder.

"He likes you petting on him," Beau told her. And he couldn't blame the animal. He'd give a lot to have Maggie's hands work a little magic in his direction. "Why don't you finish up here for a while, Maggie," Beau urged her. "Get a blanket over him and come on up to the house."

"Go on ahead," Pony said. "Beau can bring me some grub, and I'll pitch hay down to the wagon."

Her feet dragged, shuffling through the snow, and Beau's arm was welcome, gripping her waist through the folds of her coat. "I'm tired," she admitted, yawning as she watched the pink shards of sunlight on the eastern sky.

"Sophie said she was going to heat water for a bath," Beau told her. "You'll feel better if you can soak those muscles."

In minutes he'd stripped her of her coat, then aimed her at the sink, where Sophie had laid out soap and a clean washrag. Bending her head over the basin, Maggie washed slowly, and with obvious relish, cleaning the grime from hands and arms. Beau was reminded of the first time she'd been in this kitchen, scrubbing an accumulation of dirt and then turning to him defiantly, her small face bruised and battered, one eye shut and swollen and her lips and mouth damaged by a man's fist.

He'd loved her then, he realized. He'd felt the need to cherish and protect her, his masculine urges centered on healing the fey creature who'd entered his life. And in the giving of what small gifts she would allow, he'd learned to appreciate the vibrant woman who inhabited the slender body of a girl. Not a taker, his Maggie. Used to hard work, she'd made a place for herself here, earned his respect that first day. And in the weeks following had filled the aching hollow in his heart.

Gone was the pain of love lost, in those long-ago days back home. Forever vanished was the attraction he'd felt for Rachel McPherson, leaving in its wake a friendship he valued. Here now was Maggie O'Neill.

"What're you looking at?" she asked, her eyes seeking his as she turned from the sink. "Didn't I get all the dirt off my face?"

"Yeah, you did. You look fine, sweetheart." Bemused by the warmth her presence generated in his heart, he lifted a hand to brush damp hair from her forehead. And then, because he could not resist, he kissed the spot, ignoring the smell of horse and barn and medicine that permeated her clothing. His mouth cherished her, moving from forehead to cheek to lips, neither seeking a response nor expecting one, only enjoying the smooth, clear skin and the pink, soft lips of the woman he loved.

"You make me lose my breath sometimes," she whispered, her eyes closing.

"I'm planning on doing a lot of that. Pretty soon, in fact." His hands drew her closer and she leaned against him, limp with weariness after the long night. He'd give her today to recuperate and catch up on her sleep. By tomorrow, if he had his way, she'd be in his bed.

She'd lost a whole day, Maggie realized. Feet on the floor, she looked up at her window, amazed to find that the sun was well above the horizon, if the blazing warmth coming through the glass panes was anything to go by. The golden rays were focused on her bed and she stretched widely, yawning as she tested sore muscles in her arms and legs. Caring for sick animals always took a lot out of her, and adding cold weather and a night without sleep, she'd found herself too weary for words.

Beau had roused her at suppertime to make sure she ate, and then tucked her back into the narrow bed afterward. She closed her eyes, the memory of his hands against her body bringing a flush to her cheeks. He'd knelt there, right where her feet were even now resting on the braided rug, bending over her bed, kissing her with gentle care and whispering to her.

Her eyes popped open. What had he said? *We're getting married tomorrow, sweetheart.*

Tomorrow? That meant today. And that thought brought her to her feet, only then noticing that her door stood open wide, allowing heat from the kitchen stove to warm her.

"About time you woke up," Sophie said from across the kitchen. "Thought you were going to sleep another day away."

"I'm up," Maggie told her quickly. "Where's Beau?"

"Gone out to the barn. He'll be back shortly for breakfast. He was waitin' for you to get up before he ate."

Maggie pushed her legs into clean trousers and reached for a shirt. She'd slept in underwear, more of Pony's cast-offs, long-legged, fleece-lined drawers, well worn, but warm. Her undershirt was new, and her own, softest cotton knit, eliminating the need for her new chemise beneath it. Her plaid flannel shirt buttoned, she sat to pull stockings in place. A quick once-over with her hairbrush took care of snarls, and she went into the kitchen with her long hair loose, a heavy, dark fall reaching below her waist.

A cup of coffee waited on the table and she murmured her thanks, lifting it to inhale the pungent aroma. "Thank you, Sophie." The heat from the cookstove was welcome and Maggie backed close to bask in the warmth. This was about as close to heaven as she'd ever been. She'd thought before that Beau's home was paradise to her needy soul, but now, with the memory of his kisses and the words he'd spoken, she had moved on to another realm.

She was going to be Mrs. Beau Jackson, a married lady.

From the yard, a shout shattered her reverie, and a gunshot blasted the window across the room. Sophie whirled, grabbing Maggie and hurling them both to the kitchen floor. Coffee cascaded across the stove, hissing as it splattered and bounced in droplets, evaporating on the hot iron surface.

"What happened?" Maggie whispered, edging beneath the heavy table. A blast of cold air from the broken windowpanes sent shivers through her, vibrating in her voice.

"Some idiot took a shot at the house," Sophie answered

angrily. "Can't imagine that Rad would show his face here." She lifted her head to peer across the room, just as another shot rang out and a man's voice called a challenge.

"You got my girl in there, Jackson! I want her out here right now. I'm takin' her home where she belongs."

Maggie buried her face against the floor, a rush of fear flooding her body. *"Beau!"* Her throat constricted as she called his name, and the single syllable was a pleading whisper.

"Don't worry none," Sophie said staunchly. "Beau's not about to give you over to that rotten piece of humanity, girl. I'm gettin' the shotgun from the pantry." On her haunches, Sophie made her way to the open doorway where the food was stored on wide shelves. She lifted herself inside the narrow room, and as Maggie watched, the woman's capable hands opened the shotgun, then closed it with a harsh, metallic sound.

"It's loaded," Sophie said firmly. "And I know how to shoot the thing."

From the yard, a commotion she could not decipher battered Maggie's ears—the sounds of men's voices raised in anger, two shots from handguns and the raging fury of a drunken man merged into a ruckus the likes of which she'd never heard.

"Get your sorry butt off my property," Beau called, his words harsh and penetrating.

"That's Beau, out by the barn," Sophie reported from her spot in the pantry. "He's got a gun, must be Pony's pistol."

Edgar O'Neill shouted curses, the words familiar to Maggie, and she trembled anew.

"Your pa's havin' a fit out there," Sophie said. "His poor horse is frantic, with the old man sawin' at his mouth. He'll be lucky if he don't get dumped."

"Come on out of there, girl," Edgar called again. "I'll shoot Beau Jackson where he stands if'n you don't come on home with me."

"You stay put, Maggie. You hear me?" Beau's anger was apparent, his words steely with purpose. And beneath the table, Maggie trembled all the more.

If Beau took a bullet because of her, she'd never forgive herself. She rose to her hands and knees and crept carefully to the window, edging past broken shards of glass, ignoring the cuts she could not escape.

"You stay back," Sophie ordered, moving from the shelter of the pantry to crouch near the window. "Don't even think about goin' out there, Maggie. Beau'll handle this."

And he did. Maggie lifted to her knees and watched as Beau leveled his gun at Edgar, then shot with precision, the first bullet claiming the drunken man's hat, the second blasting the long gun from his hand. With a howl of pain, Edgar wheeled his horse in a half circle and bent low over the animal's neck.

"I'll be back," he shouted, lurching in the saddle as the frightened horse galloped from the yard.

"And we'll be ready for you," Sophie muttered, rising to her feet. "Get off that floor," she told Maggie. "You're bleedin' in half a dozen places. Don't be brushin' off your clothes, just slip those pants down your legs and step out of 'em."

Maggie stood, eyeing her hands critically. Blood dripped from several cuts, but none of them seemed to have slivers of glass imbedded. "I'm fine," she said. "I just need to wash good and get some salve on them."

The door opened, slamming against the wall as Beau burst into the kitchen. "Are you all right?" His eyes were narrowed, dark with anger and focused on Maggie. He scanned her quickly, his gaze dropping to the floor around her, where sunlight glittered on the broken glass. "Step away from there, Maggie."

She laughed, a brittle sound that held a trace of confusion. "Y'all need to decide between you what I'm supposed to do. Sophie wants me to take off my pants and you want me to..." She looked away from Beau, then back, her fright vanishing as relief swamped her senses. Tears threatened and she blinked them away.

"Maggie." He could only speak her name, his heart racing as he thought of what might have been, as once more she was exposed to danger. "Sophie's right. Undo your pants. I can see glass sticking to them. We'll rinse them off in a bucket and hang them out to dry."

"You want me to undress in front of you?" she asked unbelievingly.

"That's what I said, and while you're at it be careful where you walk. You don't even have your boots on." Beau turned his back on her, stepping into her room to snatch a quilt from the bed. She'd undone the pants and was lowering them gingerly down her legs, bending to step from them when he turned back to the kitchen.

With care, she moved to the table and Sophie pulled a chair out. "Let Beau wrap that quilt around you," she said, and then lent a hand as he enveloped Maggie in the warmth of patchwork and flannel.

"I'll clean up this mess," Sophie told him. "You get this girl some coffee." Reaching for her broom, Sophie made short work of the task, and Beau settled beside Maggie, helping her fit her hands around a thick china mug.

"I'm getting it all bloody," she said, her voice sounding hollow. Her fingers gripped the cup and she lifted it to her mouth to sip at the hot brew. She settled it back on the table and turned her hands palm up for inspection. Sophie placed a clean, wet cloth across them and wiped at the small cuts. Fresh blood welled to the surface, but it was obvious that the cuts were minor.

"We'll just wrap them for a while," Sophie said, tearing a piece of worn sheet into long strips, then winding them over Maggie's hands. Layers of soft fabric beneath the strips formed pressure against the wounds, and in moments Sophie had wiped off the soiled cup and pronounced Maggie a candidate for breakfast.

Pony was on the porch, pounding a piece of wood over the broken window, and Beau stood to light the lantern over the table. Except for the visible traces of her father's madness, all was back to normal, and Maggie nestled deeper into the quilt. She was safe, and Beau knew a moment's relief as color returned to her pale cheeks. She had to know that she was protected by those around her, who cared that she be secure within these walls. And yet, Beau sensed that she had succumbed to a sense of guilt that she had brought trouble to Beau's ranch. That her presence here had put him and his household in danger.

"I'm sorry, Beau," she said quietly, speaking the words he'd expected from her lips. "I should never have gone to see my mama. I might have known that Pa would make her tell where I was." She met his gaze and her chin firmed. "I mentioned your name without even thinking, and I'm sure it didn't take Pa long to find out everything Mama knew."

His hand rose to caress her cheek. "It was going to happen sooner or later. It just makes our trip to town today more important than ever."

"Town?" Maggie's confusion was obvious. "Today?"

"We're getting married this afternoon," he told her. "Soon as we eat some breakfast, and you get dressed. I'll get cleaned up, and then we're taking the buggy to town to see the preacher."

Chapter Eleven

The Reverend Bryant met them at the door to the parsonage, welcoming them warmly. "You must be Maggie O'Neill," he said, taking Maggie's hand in his. He held it with a firm grip, his eyes searching her face.

What he found there seemed to please him, for he smiled kindly upon her, calling over his shoulder to the woman who watched from the parlor doorway. "Willie, come and meet Miss O'Neill. She's the young lady who's been working at the Jackson ranch."

"I'm Wilhelmina Bryant," the preacher's wife announced, casting a reproving glance at her husband. Apparently *Willie* was not a name to be used in public. "Won't the two of you come on in?"

Beau swept his hat from his head and nodded, escorting Maggie through the small foyer to the doors of the parsonage parlor. Pictures and small mementos gave notice of long years of marriage, scattered over tables and on shelves. The mantel held a gilt-framed picture of two much younger people, resplendent in their wedding clothes, and recognizable as the Reverend and Mrs. Bryant. Maggie smiled as she scanned the room. Someone surely did a powerful amount of dusting to keep everything so shiny, she decided.

Beau's hand on her back applied pressure, and she glanced up at him. He looked more solemn than she'd ever seen him before. His fingers nudged her then and he nodded at the sofa. She obeyed, sitting gingerly on the edge of the cushion, as Wilhelmina lowered herself into a matching chair. Looking decidedly uncomfortable, Beau remained standing, hat in hand.

"Reverend Bryant, I told you last week that we were planning a wedding," he began, and Maggie's eyes widened at the words. When on earth he'd done that was a puzzlement to her. "We've decided to take the step today...if you have the time to perform the ceremony."

Reverend Bryant nodded judiciously, his eyes twinkling. "Performing marriage ceremonies is the most enjoyable part of my ministry. I'd say you've found a fine young woman to be your bride, Mr. Jackson."

"I think so," Beau agreed. He glanced down at Maggie, then back at the preacher. "I have to tell you that we've got a reason to rush this along. Maggie's father is a man of uncertain temperament."

Uncertain temperament, indeed, Maggie thought.

"He's decided that Maggie should return to the family farm, and I can't allow that to happen," Beau continued. "I've wanted to make her my bride for several weeks, so this isn't a spur of the moment gesture. I'm determined to protect her and I can do that best if she's my wife."

"Well, I think we have good reason to perform a ceremony, then," the Reverend Bryant said agreeably. He turned to Maggie and offered his hand. "Come along, young lady, and we'll turn you into a married woman right here and now." Wilhelmina rose and stepped to Maggie's side. "Willie, here, will be your witness."

Bemused by the course of events, Maggie did as she was directed, standing beside Beau, listening to the solemn words of the wedding ceremony. If her voice was less than firm, it seemed to make no matter, for Beau's was both loud and clear as he spoke the words of the marriage service. He would not take his vows lightly. If she knew nothing else, Maggie was sure of that.

Then, at the minister's urging, Maggie made promises to take care of the man beside her, and she repeated the words gladly. Tending to Beau's needs would be a joy. Richer and poorer wasn't a problem, either. She'd been as poor as she could imagine all of her life. Anything Beau had to offer was far and above what she was used to.

And then her voice faltered a bit as she vowed to love and obey. It seemed hardly right to speak about love when she wasn't even sure what the word entailed, when it came to a marriage. But doing as Beau asked would certainly be small potatoes compared to the orders she'd taken from Edgar O'Neill all her livelong days.

There was a final, long pause as Wilhelmina blew her nose loudly into a lacy handkerchief. And then the Reverend Bryant gave Beau his final instruction, his words delivered with a wide smile. "You may kiss your bride."

Maggie hadn't been aware that getting married involved a kiss right in front of the preacher, but Beau seemed to find no fault with the idea. He bent to her, one hand at her waist, the other beneath her chin. His eyes met hers, and his look of solemnity became a tender smile, transforming him from sober bridegroom to the man she'd come to know over the past weeks.

The kiss was perfect, a brush of lips, then a whisper of breath as he spoke her name, a wistful sound that tangled around her heart and warmed her insides like hot tea on a cold afternoon.

"Well, now," the Reverend Bryant said, as proudly as if he'd instigated this whole procedure. "I'm sure my wife can find some refreshments in the kitchen. We'll just sit down for a visit."

The visit lasted longer than either Beau or Maggie had planned, and it was past dinnertime when they left the parsonage, Wilhelmina's cooking too inviting to refuse and the minister's stories too delightful to miss. "We need to stop by the general store," Beau said as he helped Maggie into the buggy. Bemused by his assistance, she straightened her skirts, still unused to the courtesies he seemed to take for granted.

"Sophie gave me a list of things to get," Beau said, lifting the reins. "Shouldn't take long. And then, it's time to carry you over the threshold, Mrs. Jackson."

Maggie stifled a chuckle. "Why would you want to do that?" she asked. "I been walking for about eighteen years now. Seems like I can make it over your doorsill all by myself."

Beau grinned, his eyes narrowing as he swept her with an admiring look. "You're going to be a bride today, Maggie. Carrying you over the threshold is a custom we're not going to ignore. And then we're going to move you and all your belongings upstairs to my room."

"I'll be sleeping in your bed?" And why that idea should send shivers of delight up her spine was something to consider. The thought of sharing a bedroom, let alone the bed itself, with a man, had never held any appeal for her. Yet, when Beau's eyes warmed her with a look that promised much, she could not refuse him.

She only wished that Emily and Roberta were handy. There were a few things she'd sure like to ask them.

The general store was busy, with folks coming and going through the double, glass-pane doors. Cord McPherson stepped across the threshold as Beau lifted Maggie from the buggy, and he raised a hand in greeting.

"Beau. Good to see you. I'd heard you were in town."

Beau's brow lifted. "Word gets around fast. Anybody tell you why we spent an hour at the parsonage?"

Cord's face brightened. "There's some speculation goin' on inside. Lorena said she saw you gettin' out of your buggy with a pretty girl." His gaze lit and lingered on Maggie. "She was right on the button there." A glint of contemplation measured the couple before him. "Don't tell me you got married."

"All right, McPherson," Beau answered. "I won't tell you." His hand rested firmly at Maggie's waist and she was warmed by his support. Cord McPherson was enjoying this, she'd wager.

"Well, I'd offer to kiss the bride, but I doubt Rachel would like that idea," Cord said. "She'll sure be pleased as punch to hear the news though. You'll have to bring Maggie back by to visit. Rachel took a real shine to her." He glanced back at the doorway. "You'll be exposin' yourselves to a hive of busybodies in there, you know."

"Might as well be now as later," Beau said. "Thanks for the invitation. I'll bring Maggie by before long."

Cord stepped aside and then paused. "Introduce Maggie to Lorena. She's buyin' flannel for diapers." He bent closer to Maggie. "My brother, Jake, is about to bust his buttons, with Lorena expecting most any day."

Inside the Emporium, Maggie found herself the focus of attention, with several pairs of curious eyes turned in her direction. A tall, blond woman turned from the counter, her skirts covering an obvious pregnancy. She smiled broadly and stepped toward Maggie, hands outstretched.

"You must be Maggie. Rachel told me about you, and I've been wanted to see you for myself." Looking ruefully down at her expanded waistline, she sighed. "I don't seem to do much roaming around the countryside these days. Jake keeps me pretty close to home.''

"Are you Lorena?" It had to be, Maggie thought. Pregnant and apparently married to the man named Jake, it could be no other. The friendly smile was welcome and Maggie took Lorena's hands. They were smooth to the touch, a direct contrast to her own callused fingers and palms.

And yet, Lorena took no apparent notice, drawing Maggie with her toward the counter where Cora was busily measuring flannel from a bolt. "I'm going to have a baby," Lorena confided quietly.

Maggie nodded solemnly. "I noticed." Try as she might, she couldn't keep from smiling, and was pleased when Lorena laughed aloud.

"It's hard to keep it a secret at this stage. But I really don't care. Jake is so happy and I'm tickled to death." Lorena glanced around and whispered, "Poor Beau. He's wishing he could drag you out of here and head for home, I'll warrant."

Maggie peered past Lorena, her gaze settling on Beau who was looking more than a little uncomfortable. Three men were cutting up at his expense, and she felt a pang of sympathy as Beau dodged their remarks.

"Am I right? Did you just get married?" Lorena asked in a low tone. "I thought as much when I saw his buggy at the parsonage, and then Cord said Beau was really sweet on you."

"How'd *he* know?" Maggie asked quickly. "I'll bet Beau hasn't been passing out that news to just anybody."

Lorena shrugged. "Rachel told me the other day that she wouldn't be surprised if Beau married you." She pressed her lips together and then sighed. "I've heard about your daddy, Maggie. I know your sisters, and they haven't been shy about letting folks know where they came from.''

''You know Emily and Roberta?'' Maggie's heart leaped with joy as she spoke her sisters' names. ''Can you tell me where they live? I haven't seen either of them in…'' She paused. ''It's been longer than forever, I swear,'' she said sadly. And then in a rush, her questions flew fast and furiously. Lorena waved her hand, hushing the flood of words.

''They're both living here in town, almost next door to each other. And they're fine, truly they are. Just worried about you. They heard that you'd left home, but no one knew where you'd gone.'' She grinned widely and bent closer to speak softly. ''Do you think Beau would take you by to see them before you go back home? They'll be so glad to hear that he married you.''

Maggie swallowed hard, fighting a sudden rush of tears. Seeing her sisters would be a dream come true. ''I'll ask Beau if we can stop. They'll know how I feel, always looking over my shoulder lest Pa shows up, and now to know he can't touch me. I think that's why Beau married me.''

Lorena muffled a laugh behind her hand. ''*I* think you've got a lot to learn. Beau had other reasons than that. A man doesn't take wedding vows unless…''

''Maggie?'' Beau was at her back, and Lorena's words came to an abrupt halt.

Whatever Lorena thought would have to wait for another time, Maggie knew. For now she was anxious to coax Beau into finding directions to Emily's and Roberta's homes. ''I'm ready,'' she announced, turning to face him.

''Soon as Cora gets a chance to fill this order, we need to be on our way home,'' he told her. ''I have to stop at the livery stable to check on my horse.'' His mouth firmed and a frown marred the fine lines of his brow. ''Rad made the mistake of bragging around town that he'd made a fool of me. I doubt he had the decency to leave my horse behind, but I'll give it a shot anyway." He stepped closer to the counter, list in hand, waiting his turn.

"Then he did steal your money?" Maggie's heart sank as Beau nodded.

"Looks that way, from what he said. He skinned out before the sheriff could get hold of him."

Cora, her hands occupied with folding the enormous length of flannel she'd cut for Lorena, glanced up at Maggie, nodding efficiently. "I'm pretty near done with Miz McPherson here. I'll get to you right away."

Right away turned out to be almost half an hour, and Beau's watch had been peered at several times before the busy clerk began adding up his purchases. "Lorena told me where your sisters live," he told Maggie in a low tone. "We'll make a quick stop."

Maggie clenched his arm, the urge to hug him almost beyond belief. This had been a day she'd remember forever. Not only because she'd taken a husband, but because her sisters were nearby.

Beau placed his hand atop hers, his touch a caress, as though he cared little for the onlookers. "There's not much room to put all this stuff in the front of the buggy. You'll have to sit close to me," he whispered in Maggie's ear as Cora filled two boxes with tins of fruit and bags of dry goods.

With Conrad Carson lending a hand, the supplies were loaded and Beau lifted Maggie to the seat. Untying the lead line from the hitching post in front of the store, he caught sight of the sheriff marching across the street, his face set in a scowl.

"Beau Jackson! I need to talk to you." Tom Clemons

was a big man, well put together, and the frown he wore promised trouble.

"What can I do for you?" Beau asked, looking beyond the lawman, to where a small crowd gathered.

"Is the woman with you named Maggie O'Neill?"

"No, sir, she's not. She's my wife, Maggie Jackson." A note of pride in his voice stiffened Maggie's spine as she listened to the exchange.

"Well, if she's the daughter of Edgar O'Neill, I'm afraid I've got bad news for her. Her pa's in town, and he's claimin' she stole his horse." His gaze was stern as he turned it on Maggie. "Is that true, young lady?"

"I reckon you could say so," she agreed. "That poor creature was about half dead from him flogging it with an ax handle. He split it wide open across the withers and then let the open sore get all putrified."

He winced and shook his head. "My sympathy is with the horse, ma'am, but it makes no matter what shape the animal was in. It was still his animal. And if you took it from his barn, I'd have to say you stole it."

Beau cut in sharply. "Maybe if you took a look at the horse, you'd think differently, Sheriff. Maggie's been knocking herself out, trying to keep the creature on his feet. He'd probably be dead by now if she'd left him where he was."

Sheriff Clemons shook his head. "Makes no matter, son. If she took the horse, she's in trouble." He walked to the side of the buggy, lifting his hand to Maggie. "I'm afraid I'll have to arrest you, ma'am. Stealin' horses is a serious offence."

She drew back from his big, callused hand, her eyes seeking Beau. "Can he do this?" she asked, her voice choking in her throat.

Beau's hands clenched at his sides as he nodded. "Afraid

so, honey. We'll have to go along to the jailhouse and get this straightened out." His look was grim as he shook his head at Sheriff Clemons. "I'll bring my wife over. There's no need to arrest her here."

Tom Clemons looked relieved. "That'll work fine. Bring your buggy along and we'll tie it out back." He stepped aside as Beau grasped his mare's bridle, leading the horse across the street to where the curious townsfolk gathered. The cluster of men moved from the front of the jailhouse, and in their midst, Maggie caught sight of her father. His thumbs were caught up in his suspenders, and he shot her a look of pure hatred, his lips twisting in a sneer.

"Beau." It was a whisper, but his head nodded. "Don't let him…" She could not speak further, only tremble as Edgar's look of triumph sent her to the depths of despair.

It was only the strength of Beau's arm around her that allowed her to walk into the sheriff's office. Tom drew a chair forward and she sank into it, her heart racing, perspiration dotting her forehead, and a violent need to vomit forcing her to seek a private corner. She put one hand over her mouth, and sought Beau's attention, attempting to rise from the chair.

"Whoa, there," the sheriff said quickly. With a single, efficient move, he slid the wastebasket from beside his desk, directly in front of Maggie. "You just heave in there, young lady."

It was just in time, and within seconds Maggie's dinner was deposited atop an assortment of trash in the metal basket. Her groan was muffled by Beau's handkerchief as he thrust it against her mouth, and she held it there, embarrassed beyond measure.

"I'll take this out back and wash it under the pump," Sheriff Clemons said, whisking away the evidence of Maggie's distress. "You folks just sit tight."

Beau knelt beside her and Maggie's head drooped, resting against his shoulder. "I can't believe I did that," she whispered.

"I can," Beau told her, his hands holding her close. He brushed stray locks of hair from her brow, and his hands were cool and welcome against her hot skin. "Take it easy, honey. It's going to be all right. We'll get this all straightened out."

"She's gonna hang, is what's gonna happen," said Edgar, his body blocking the sunlight from the room as he stood in the doorway. "She'll learn not to steal from her pa."

Beau growled, a feral, primitive sound, and in one sweeping movement, he put Maggie aside and rose to his feet. Edgar stepped back, stumbling over his boots as he attempted to escape the man who lunged at him.

"I'll have you put in jail, too," Edgar yelled, spittle running from his mouth as he backed onto the sidewalk.

"You just go right ahead," Beau told him, reaching to lift the man from his feet. One hand buried in Edgar's shirtfront, Beau had him dangling inches off the wooden walkway, and around them a group of men crowded closer. Edgar was big, but Beau's anger seemed to lend strength to his muscular arms, and as Maggie watched, her father was pressed against an upright post, wide-eyed and sputtering.

"Beau Jackson, you put that man down." The sheriff's boots thumped the floor loudly as he tore past Maggie.

"He's gonna kill me, Sheriff!" Edgar gasped, his eyes bulging from the pressure of Beau's grasp knuckling into his throat.

"I don't think so." The sheriff skidded to a stop behind Beau, and his hands gripped wide shoulders with punishing force. "Just lower him nice and easy, Jackson. We ain't havin' any mayhem takin' place today."

Beau's hands released Edgar's shirt and the hapless, gasping man slid down the post to collapse at Beau's feet. He stepped back, and the sheriff released him from his grip. Edgar coughed and choked and Maggie buried her face in her hands, unwilling to look upon her father's face any longer.

She'd managed to get Beau in a peck of trouble, not to mention facing a hanging herself. There was no way in the world things could get any worse.

"You men all head on out of here," the sheriff shouted. "We don't need all this commotion goin' on. And you come on in my office, Beau."

The two men watched as the lingering crowd drifted away. Then the office door closed behind them as they joined Maggie once more. "What were you thinkin' of, Beau?" Tom asked. "I don't need you in a cell, too. It's bad enough I have to hold your wife till I get to the bottom of this."

"Can you put her in my custody?" Beau asked, his gaze pinning Maggie to the chair. *There goes my wedding night,* he thought glumly.

"Horse stealin' is a mighty serious thing, you know that."

"Are you going to hang me?" Maggie asked. Beau muttered a word beneath his breath, and then crossed the floor, squatting beside her chair.

"You're not going to hang, sweetheart. I just barely got married to you. Do you think I'm ready to bury you?" It was an effort, but he managed a grin and was rewarded by her smile.

"Can we pay for the horse?" she asked. "Would my pa leave us alone if I borrowed money to give him?"

Beau snorted. "That pathetic creature isn't worth two

bits. And no, you're not going to borrow money for any-thing.''

''You might want to listen to her, Beau,'' the sheriff advised. ''If you pay for the horse, maybe we can have Edgar drop the charges.''

The door burst open, banging against the wall and Mag-gie's father stood on the threshold. He'd tucked his shirt haphazardly into his trousers, and his ruddy complexion no longer reflected the ordeal he'd gone through. Yet, there was an insane glow that warned Beau of more trouble to come. ''If you think for one minute I'll let her off the hook, you got another think comin', Sheriff. I heard you from outside the window, and there ain't any amount of money that'll pay for my horse. She's gonna pay for this.''

Tom sent a disgusted look in Edgar's direction. ''Don't be tellin' me how to do my job, O'Neill. You and me are gonna take a look at your animal come tomorrow morning. I'll meet you at Beau Jackson's place right after breakfast. And in case you don't get up early, I'm talkin' about no later than nine o'clock.''

''What are we goin' there for?'' Edgar sputtered. ''I just want my horse back. I kin go out there today and get it.''

''Not on your life,'' Tom returned. ''You'd better not set one foot on Jackson's ranch until tomorrow morning.'' When the door slammed shut behind Edgar, Tom turned to Beau. ''I'm gonna put your wife in a cell, Beau. You might want to get her something to eat from the hotel restaurant. Supper's not much. My wife does pretty well at dinnertime, but a piece of bread is about all she'll get here this time of the day.''

''I'm not leaving her,'' Beau said staunchly. ''If she goes in the cell, I go with her.''

''Suit yourself,'' Tom said genially. ''I'll find you some grub, and bring over an extra blanket.'' Reaching into his desk drawer, he pulled out a ring and sorted through the dangling keys. "Either one of you need to use the necessary before I lock you up?"

"You didn't have to stay here, Beau." Wrapped in a quilt, Maggie sat on the edge of a hard bench, watching as Beau looked out the window.

"Tom needs to cover this," he said absently. "The stove can't put out enough heat to stave off the cold air from outdoors." Beyond him, the sky was scattered with stars, and Maggie wished she were looking out her window in the store room, with her narrow bed waiting.

But if she were at home tonight, she'd be on her way to Beau's bed in the biggest bedroom in the house. In that room where a woman could find shelter in her husband's arms. She'd allowed that thought to bring her to a fine edge of anticipation all afternoon. Until she'd admitted to stealing her father's horse. And for that act, she would not hang her head. Although if her father had his way, her feet would dangle while a rope tightened around her neck.

She shivered at the gruesome thought and hugged herself, seeking warmth from the patchwork quilt. She probably ought to offer it to Beau, let him cover the window with it. But the thought of giving up its comfort didn't appeal to her. Maybe if they put the lamp on the floor, it would shed some heat. Tom Clemons had brought a small table into the cell and placed the lamp there, where it shed a circle of light.

They were isolated in the small room, barricaded by a wall of bars from the freedom beyond the jailhouse, and Beau had chosen this place to spend the night, when by all rights he should have been smack-dab in the middle of his big bed.

He turned to search the cell, his eyes measuring the meager furnishings. "I wonder if we pushed that table through the bars, maybe it would keep the wind from us," he said. He placed the lamp on the floor, pushing it closer to Maggie and she opened the quilt a little, inviting the heat to warm her legs. The table was a bit bigger than the window, but the legs were inset and they fit with barely inches to spare in the barred space.

"It would have been smarter to close the shutters from the outside before I let him lock us in here," Beau muttered. "I just hated to be in the dark."

"Well, it's bound to be a lot warmer now," Maggie told him, pulling her skirts up to her shins.

He lifted the second quilt from the bench and settled next to her, draping it over their shoulders, and tugging her close to his side. "I'll get you warm, sweetheart," he said. "It's not what I had in mind for tonight, but we'll get things straightened out tomorrow and before you know it, we'll forget this whole thing. And if we bring it to mind, we'll laugh about it."

Doubt edged her voice. "You really think so? I can't find much to smile at right now, Beau. I just keep wondering if they can really hang me."

"Sure they can," he said agreeably. "But they're not going to. They haven't hung a woman in this town since last week." His words held subdued laughter and she responded in like fashion, choking back a giggle as her elbow poked his ribs. He gave a satisfying grumble and she looked up at his face.

A grin stretched his mouth, and his eyes twinkled, glittering in the lamplight. "Now that I've got you in a better mood, why don't you give me a kiss, Mrs. Jackson," he murmured, turning her to face him. "In fact, why don't I lie down here and you can cuddle up in front of me and between me and the quilts and that lamp, we'll get you nice and warm.''

"You want us both to lay down on this bench?''

"Sure,'' he agreed. "Just stand up for a minute, and I'll wrap one quilt around me and then you can pull the other one over us both.''

She rose. If Beau said it could be done, she'd give it a try. With the draft from the window blocked, the room was not nearly so cold now anyway. And no one could peer in from outside with the table in place. She watched as Beau draped himself in the quilt, then spread it beside him, his back against the wall. Only inches remained and she shook her head.

"I don't think there's room for me,'' she told him, even as he motioned her to sit beside him. She obeyed and he nudged her to a prone position, his arm beneath her head. Tucking the second quilt around her, she reached to drape it over his shoulder. If she were any bigger, she'd be on the floor, she decided, edging back until her bottom fit snugly against Beau's front.

He groaned, a muffled sound he buried in her hair and went rigid in his arms. "Beau? What did I do?''

His reply was a grunt as he tightened his grip on her, one leg lifting to hold her in place. "You're fine,'' he said after a moment. "We're neither one of us gonna be comfortable tonight, no matter how you slice it.''

"So long as you hold on to me, I'll be fine,'' she assured him, nestling as close as the layers of clothing between them would allow.

"You'll have to lay still, honey,'' he told her. "There's a few things I'd just as soon you didn't know about until tomorrow night, and I'm not sure you wiggling your bottom around against my...''

"Against your—'' She twisted from his hold and rolled

to the floor, rescuing the lamp from disaster with one outstretched hand. And then looked up at him. "I was only getting comfortable, Beau. I didn't mean to be too familiar."

"Come on, sugar," he whispered, his lips curling in a half smile. "I'll lean against the wall in the corner and you can sit on my lap." Pushing his way upright, he scooted the length of the bench, until his back rested in the corner where the bars met the side of the cell.

"You want me on your lap?" she asked, and then shivered again as a chill brought gooseflesh to her arms and legs. If Beau was willing to spend the night here with her, she would do as he asked. And somehow, sitting on his lap, enclosed in his embrace did not seem too great a sacrifice to make. Beneath the weight of two quilts, they snuggled warmly together and she nestled yet closer.

Her face fit nicely in the crease of his shoulder and neck and she inhaled the male scent of his body. "You smell good," she told him, and felt his laugh vibrate beneath her.

"Not nearly as good as you, sweetheart," he murmured. His hands were firm against her body, one holding her in place, fingers spread wide against her hips, the other on her shoulder blades. His head bent and he nudged her face upward. His lips were damp against her skin, and she turned just a bit, her mouth opening, inviting him to press those warm, wide, expressive lips against hers.

He obliged, and she moaned, the sound held captive in her throat, as she sought comfort in his touch. Long fingers edged their way from her back to slide beneath her arm and then to where her breasts pressed against his chest. He eased her back, just enough to slide his hand between their bodies, his fingers undoing the buttons of her coat and then loosening the front of her dress.

Within moments, he would hold the soft fabric of her

chemise in his hand, and she caught her breath, her mouth moving against his. "Don't tear my new chemise," she warned him, even as one callused fingertip edged between two buttons. The rough skin pressed into the soft flesh, and she whimpered.

"Undo it for me," he told her, his voice roughened, as though he forced the words through gritted teeth.

Sitting upright, she opened wide the bodice of her dress and released the dainty buttons of her chemise, working around the hand he refused to move from the place he had claimed. "You're perfect," he said, his fingertips exploring the tender skin, holding her cupped in his palm, then gently pinching the puckered crest between thumb and forefinger.

She wiggled, unable to withstand the tingling urgency he set into motion with his caress. "I can't hardly stand for you to do that to me, Beau." Her words uttered on a gasping breath, she clamped her legs together, as that forbidden spot between her thighs seemed to swell and burn. "You're making me all twitchy," she wailed.

"Let me touch you, Maggie," he whispered, his hand moving from her breast to slide beneath the fullness of her skirts.

"Not there, you can't." Her thighs tightened even more as his fingers coaxed for admittance, and she squealed as he reached the slit in her drawers. "Beau, don't you be messing with me there. I won't be able to look you in the eye ever again, if you keep on this way."

His hand stilled and then retreated, smoothing her skirts in place, covering her with the quilt. "Can I just touch your breast?" he asked meekly, seeking out the warmth he'd forsaken just moments past.

She leaned back to look at his face, suspicious as she heard the amusement he could not hide. His eyes were dark, his mouth drawn taut as if he fought a smile that begged to be expressed. "Don't you laugh at me, Beau Jackson," she told him.

"I'm not laughing, sweetheart. Just enjoying my wife. I'll behave myself, I promise." He bent and kissed her loudly. "I'm just having a hard time." His brow creased and a rueful expression crossed his features. "And you haven't the faintest idea what I'm talking about, have you?"

She snuggled against him, unwilling to admit that her limited knowledge hovered on the edge of ignorance. "I think I know why Emily and Roberta got married, Beau," she said after a moment. His hand was gentle in its pursuit of her curves and he murmured encouragement beneath his breath, words she ignored, her own mind bent on the reason for her sisters' elopement.

"I'll bet they liked this part of the being married thing. You know, the man and woman stuff we've been doing."

"Yeah, I'll bet they did," he said, his teeth nibbling on the edge of her ear. "The question is, do you?"

Her giggle was muffled against his mouth as she reached to caress his cheek. "I ain't had this much fun since Pa got bogged down in the pig sty and the old sow went after him."

His laughter rang out, and Maggie placed her fingers over his lips. "Don't be so loud, Beau," she scolded. "Anybody'd think we were having a good time in here."

His words were low, dark and filled with promise. "And aren't we? Aren't we, Maggie mine?"

Chapter Twelve

"We want to see our sister, Sheriff." Two voices, almost in unison, spoke the words and Maggie sat upright on Beau's lap, eliciting a groan from the sleeping man. Her hands were frantic as she untangled the quilts that covered them both, stumbling as she slid to the floor, muttering as she straightened her skirts. The dress was hopelessly wrinkled, and the bodice hung unbuttoned.

With fingers made clumsy by haste, she slid black buttons into buttonholes that had suddenly become too small to hold them, looking anxiously from between the bars of the cell toward the sheriff's office. "Emily? Roberta?" Her voice husky with sleep, she shook the bars, her efforts futile against the solid iron framework.

"Maggie?" Beau wakened and sat upright, running long fingers through his hair. "What's going on, honey?" He rose, yawned widely, then tucked in his shirt in an effort to make himself presentable. "Who's out there?" he asked, as the voices from the sheriff's office rose again in volume.

"Where's Maggie?" It was Emily, and Maggie laughed aloud at the sound of her sister's frustrated cry.

"I'm back here, Emily," she called. "I'm in the cell, here in the back."

"I'm here, too, Mags," called Roberta, her deeper tones readily recognizable to Maggie.

"Now listen here, ladies. Your sister is under arrest, and you can't just strut in here and make demands." Tom Clemons was obviously doing his best to maintain order, but Maggie could only grin as she heard the stampede of heels and the muttered threats of the two women as they headed in her direction. Apparently they could indeed make demands, and it would take more than the sheriff of Green Rapids to halt their progress, if Maggie were any judge of the happenings just beyond the nearby door.

It burst open, Emily and Roberta rushing across the threshold, only to skid to a stop as they caught sight of Maggie in the cell. "Merciful heavens, you've locked her in with a man, Sheriff!" Emily said, disbelief coating every syllable.

Roberta strode ahead, as Emily spoke. "Just give me the key, sir. This is not even decent." Tom stumbled in their wake, his haste making him clumsy, and then shoved in front of them to stand directly in front of the cell door.

"You've got this all wrong, ladies. Your sister has not been abused."

"Have you taken a good look at her?" Emily's eyes filled with tears as she reached for Maggie through the bars. "Oh, baby, what has this man done to you? Just look at yourself, all wrinkled and mussed up."

"I don't have a mirror," Maggie said bluntly. "And if this man has wrinkled and mussed me up, it was his right. This is my husband, Emily." She reached behind herself to find Beau and was pleased to find his hand available. "Come here, Beau. Meet my sisters." Tugging him to her side, she glanced up at his amused grin.

"You're married to him?" Roberta asked, tilting her

head to one side as she peered through the dim light at Beau.

"She's not wearing my ring yet, but we'll take care of that today," he said. "You can check with the preacher. The Reverend Bryant married us in his parlor yesterday afternoon, and Willie was the witness."

"Willie?" Roberta answered. "You mean Wilhelmina? Prim and proper Wilhelmina Bryant? And you call her Willie?"

Beau's lips twitched. "Nah, but her husband does."

Roberta shook her head disbelievingly, and then peered past Beau into the shadows of the cell. "How come it's so dark in there, anyway?" she asked. "Doesn't this place have any windows?"

"Looks like Beau covered the bars," Tom observed. "You shoulda closed the shutters before I left, Jackson. I sure didn't think of it."

"We managed to stay warm," Beau said, with a glance slanted in Maggie's direction. "Didn't we, sweetie?"

Maggie groaned, an audible sound that obviously pleased Beau, if his chuckle was anything to go by. He left her side to pull the table from the window, and sunlight poured into the cell. Emily's moan of distress mirrored Maggie's and her hands reached through the bars to draw Maggie forward.

"Are you all right?" she asked quietly, her sharp eyes narrowing as she scanned her sister's face. Her index finger touched Maggie's lips. "Your mouth is swole up," she murmured, her anxious look asking a silent question.

"He's good to me," Maggie whispered. "Beau would never hurt me, Em."

"If you say so," Emily returned. She turned to the sheriff. "What do we have to do to get Maggie out of there?"

"I'm headin' out right now to Beau's place and maybe

I'll have the answer to that within the hour,'' he told her. ''In the meantime, you ladies are gonna hafta be patient. I can't let her out till I make a decision.''

''How about me?'' Beau asked.

''You're free to go,'' Tom said quickly. ''You didn't have to be in there to start with.'' Deliberately choosing the correct key from the ring he held, he bent to the lock, twisting the key and opening the cell door with one easy motion. ''Sorry you can't leave with him, ma'am,'' he told Maggie.

''Beau?'' Her eyes felt damp and she touched his arm as he paused beside her.

He bent to touch her lips with his and whispered a promise. ''I'll only be gone long enough to find you something fresh to wear, and some breakfast for both of us.''

She nodded, satisfied, and watched him walk past Emily and Roberta, nodding politely to both of them. The sheriff closed the cell door with a clang of metal on metal and followed Beau. ''Here's your shotgun,'' he told him. ''I took it out of your buggy last night.''

The men left the office, and Maggie heard the door close behind them. With a rush, Roberta and Emily pressed against the bars. ''Now tell us everything,'' Emily insisted.

''Have you seen Mama?'' Roberta asked, and then the queries flew as the sisters spoke rapidly, their voices overlapping as they prodded Maggie into the details of her stay at Beau's ranch.

''Mama's pretty bad off,'' Maggie said finally. ''She was in the house with no fire going in the stove, and Pa had messed up her mouth. I tried to make her go with me, but she...''

''She's afraid of Pa,'' Roberta finished. Her mouth trembled as she spoke the words. ''I'm still scared to death he'll catch me somewheres without Amos along. I got a good memory," she added, "And I've been worried to pieces about you, Mags. I felt guilty leavin' you there, but I couldn't stand for one more black eye, I swear."

Emily nodded agreement. "Paul says if he ever gets a good shot at Pa, he's as good as a dead man."

"Are you both happy?" Maggie asked, even as she knew the futility of the question. Their faces beamed as the two women nodded in unison. "I got a house to take care of and a baby under my apron," Emily said proudly.

"And my Amos just bought me a new carpet, direct from St. Louis," Roberta added. She cast a longing look at Emily. "I'm hopin' to catch up with Em here right soon. Amos says we can't have Paul and Emily beatin' us to the punch."

And then they quieted, exchanging glances as if the same thought had entered their minds. "Ah…Mags?" Roberta spoke cautiously. "You didn't *do* it, here…last night, I mean?"

Maggie felt a blush rise, and she shook her head. "No, of course not. We just…we just slept. Beau wouldn't…" And then she halted, the events of the night past turning her cheeks even more crimson. "We only got married yesterday."

"I can't imagine he waited," Emily murmured, a tiny smile edging her mouth. "I'll bet he can't wait to get you home."

"You're right there, Em," Beau answered from the office doorway. His hands holding a tray of food, he stepped past the sisters and placed it on the floor. From one corner of the tray he produced a damp towel and passed it through the bars. "Wash up a little, honey," he told her, "While I pour you some coffee. Tom's wife had fresh bread baked already this morning. Said she set it to rise last night."

Maggie inhaled deeply. "It smells wonderful, Beau. So

does the bacon.'' The cloth was rough, but wet and clean and she used it liberally on her face and neck, then scrubbed at her hands with it. Beau waited patiently until she finished, then traded the cloth for a steaming cup of coffee. Backing up to the bench, she settled there and bent to breathe in the fragrant steam. ''I didn't know I was so hungry,'' she told him.

His grin was sheepish. ''I'll have to admit, I sneaked a piece of bread on the way over here. Wasn't easy balancing the tray on one hand while I walked, but I didn't think you'd mind.''

Maggie shook her head. ''I'm just glad you found something to eat.''

''Tom sent me to his place. It's just around the back, and his wife knew I was coming. He must have figured I'd be hungry.''

Emily and Roberta watched as Maggie ate, taking turns as they told her of their husbands and the townspeople they'd met. She listened, her heart swelling with joy, thankful that her worries on their account had been needless.

''Pa said you were like two cats, and you'd land on your feet,'' she said with a grin. ''For once in his life, he was almost right.''

''Anything was better than what we put up with at home,'' Emily vowed, and Roberta seconded her words, nodding her head vigorously.

''Would you ladies go to the Emporium and find your sister something to wear?'' Beau asked. ''You can probably choose better than me. Just make sure you get everything she needs, and don't forget a comb.''

With a chorus of farewells and promises for a quick return, the sisters parted company and Maggie watched as Beau slid down the bars to the floor, resting against the iron barrier. ''It won't be long now,'' he said. He lifted a piece of bread from the plate beside him and took a bite. "Sure you got enough to eat?" he asked. "There's more here."

Maggie watched him, his own shirt wrinkled, yet concerned that she not go out in public without a change of clothes. His eyes were shadowed, his beard a dark growth against his jaw and he'd spent the whole night holding her close and keeping her warm. Her heart felt full to overflowing as she reached through the bars to touch his shoulder.

"Beau? I haven't even thanked you for taking care of me last night."

He shot her a look of surprised pleasure. "You're my wife, Maggie. That's part of my job." A roguish gleam in his eye set her heart to dancing and he turned his head to press his lips on the back of her hand. "The rest of my duties are going to be pure pleasure, sweetheart." His warm breath blended with the brush of his tongue on her fingers as he continued.

"Once we get out of here, we're going to the Emporium again to buy you a ring. I forgot all about it yesterday, and don't think that doesn't make me feel like a poor excuse for a bridegroom."

"I don't need a ring," she protested. "My mama never had one, and she sure knew she was married."

"Don't ever compare yourself to your mother," Beau told her, his hand capturing hers as he turned to face her directly. "She's been through hell, and you'll never know the fear of having an abusive husband. I'll never knowingly hurt you, Maggie."

She clasped his fingers and nodded. "I know that."

It had been a most enlightening session, with Maggie sliding into fresh clothing as Emily and Roberta vied for the opportunity to show off their newly acquired knowledge. Whether or not she was willing to believe the things they'd confided amid whispers and giggles, the coming night promised to be one she would never forget. And should their predictions be on target…Maggie squirmed with delight, tightening her grip on Beau's arm.

He sent her a sidelong glance. "What's got you all in a dither?"

She shrugged and grinned up at him. "I'm just pleased to be out of jail. He sure was mad at Pa, wasn't he?"

"Yeah. The thing is, Maggie, no matter whether you own an animal or not, it's wrong to abuse any creature the way your father did that horse. It's not against the law, but it's wrong, and I think by the time the sheriff got done with him, your father got taken down a peg or two. All his threats didn't amount to a hill of beans when everything came to light." He halted halfway across the street and his expression was stern.

"That doesn't mean you were right, honey. Stealing a horse is about the worst thing you can do in these parts. The sheriff was within his rights to put you in jail. It's just a good thing he persuaded your pa to let me buy the pitiful creature."

"How much did it cost you?" Maggie asked quietly, her good mood forgotten.

"Two dollars."

"You can take it out of my wages," she said, holding on to her hat as Beau quickened his pace, causing her to scamper in order to keep up.

He shot her a quick flash of white teeth and deep dimple. "You don't have wages anymore. You've signed on for a lifetime, girl. From now on you're a full partner in my ranch."

Maggie halted, and Beau swung to face her. "What's wrong?"

"You don't mean that, Beau Jackson. Women don't have their name on a deed. I don't think you can…"

"Watch me," he said firmly. "When you have a ring on your hand, we're going to the bank and change the name on my deed."

And so they did. With a wide gold band gleaming on her finger, Maggie sat on the edge of a burnished walnut chair in the bank president's office, watching as Beau ordered the changes made. Her thumb had about rubbed the finish off the ring, she figured, by the time they left the bank, and she was certain that every eye in town was on them as they rode down the rutted road toward home.

"Now, any other questions?" Beau asked.

"Yes. When can we invite my sisters out to your place for dinner with their husbands and all?"

"It's *our* place, Maggie," he corrected her, his arm nestling her snugly against his side. "And you can invite them whenever you want to."

She rested her hand on his thigh and squeezed it, giddy with the joy of discovery. Eager for the hours ahead when she would help to carry her store of earthly belongings up that wide stairway to the room upstairs. The place where her marriage would truly begin.

"When did you buy me the nightgown?" Maggie asked, holding it up before her. She turned to look in the mirror as Beau met her gaze in the glass.

"When you were changing clothes at the jail," he told her. "Do you like it?"

"How could anybody in their right mind not like it?" she asked, her hands filled with the soft lawn fabric.

''Would you look at all the lace and those bitty little buttons, and the ruffle on the bottom.''

Beau did as she asked, dutifully taking note of the cream-colored lace and the wide ruffle she admired. The buttons were another matter, he thought, wondering how long it would take him to undo them once he got Maggie smack-dab in the middle of his bed. The bedroom door was closed, and they stood in lamplight, the soft glow lending a gleam to Maggie's eyes, and fetching a bloom to pinken her cheeks.

''Why don't you put it on?'' he suggested, turning to sit on a nearby chair. He lifted one foot to the other knee and tugged at his boot. It slid from his foot and he worked at the other, his gaze never swaying from Maggie. She stood stock-still in front of the mirror, and then turned halfway, her knuckles white as she gripped the gown before her.

''You mean right now? Right here in front of you?''

He shrugged as though it mattered little one way or the other. ''I won't peek if it'll bother you to have me look.'' And then he ducked his head to watch his hands unbutton his shirt. He stood, pulling it from the waistband of his trousers, and shed it quickly. ''How would it be if I undid your dress?''

Her mouth trembled, but she nodded and turned her back to him, offering the curve of her spine. He worked slowly at the buttons, his fingers relishing the soft skin beneath the new dress. She wore another new chemise and he ran his finger beneath the strap, sliding it over her shoulder. ''You going to take this off?''

Her nod was an abrupt movement of her head, and she took a deep breath, sliding from the dress, allowing it to pool around her feet. Her fingers worked at the ties of her petticoat and it fell atop the dress. Turning in the circle of clothing, she faced him, her cheeks glowing, her eyes shiny.

"You'd might as well see what you got for your money, Beau. I'm not much to look at under the fancy clothes you got me."

And wasn't that a tall tale, he thought, his breath lodging in his throat. Her waist was slender, her hips rounding, and her breasts…those warm, round, plump treasures he'd only begun to appreciate, tempted him to abandon his plan, and instead to lift her from her feet without another moment's hesitation. Yet, he couldn't do it, could not deprive himself of a moment of this unveiling she'd instigated. Her upper legs covered by drawers, and with pink garters holding white stockings in place at her knee, she was a picture of womanhood such as he'd never seen.

Not that there'd been that many women in his life. He'd been a bit of a rogue before the war, but since Sally's treacherous behavior, he'd steered clear of all but a few women, and those had filled but a temporary spot in his life.

"You're beautiful, Maggie," he breathed, and meant every word. She was not a pampered creature such as the faithless Sally had been, but instead bore calluses on her hands and displayed strong limbs that spoke of long hours of hard work. Some of it for his benefit.

He reached beneath her chemise to undo the ties on her drawers, and her breath hissed past his cheek as he bent to lower the garment to the floor. "Step out of them, Maggie," he told her, and she obeyed.

In white stockings, pink garters and a dainty short chemise, she was a dream he had only dared to hope for. Her long dark hair hung in waves, touching the curve of her hips as she turned her head. "I don't have anything else to take off, except for my stockings and garters, and my shimmy." She leaned closer. "That's what Emily calls this thing. Cora at the store said it was a chemise, but Em said Paul told her it was called a shimmy.''

''I don't care what you call it, honey, so long as you let me take it off.'' His voice sounded rough and raw, as though he'd swallowed a pint of whiskey without pause for breath. His whisper was ragged as he took the hem of her garment in his hands.

''Damn, you're a sight for sore eyes.'' He swallowed, then lifted the chemise slowly, waiting lest she deny him, but she only watched, eyes intent on his face as he stripped it over her head.

And then looked in the mirror behind her. His heart thumped in an unmerciful rhythm as he scanned the length of her. The curves of her lush bottom were firm, the line where her thigh began was a crease that lured his fingers to touch. The rest of her back was covered by the dark veil of hair and he settled for that. Time enough to put his hands on all the places that tempted him. For now, he would be content with holding handsful of that luxurious length of dark silk.

He pulled her closer, and she did as he directed, stepping from her clothing without a second look. His hands were firm against her waist as he lifted her, and she wrapped her arms around his neck, her legs around his hips.

It was almost his undoing. Beneath the trousers, his arousal was firm and throbbing and the soft pressure of her against that rigid member brought a groan from his throat. He bent his head, muffling the sound in her shoulder, turning to kiss the edge of her ear, and then carried her to his bed.

She was deposited in the center and he followed her down, his mouth hot against her skin. Her hands moved to his head, and she whimpered, twisting beneath him as he kissed his way from throat to mouth, and from there to her cheeks and forehead. "Ah, Maggie girl, I've got to slow down. I'll not be able to get my clothes off if I don't take a few deep breaths."

"I'll help you," she offered eagerly, her hands finding the buttons on his undershirt, swiftly moving to loosen them, then working at his belt buckle. A sound of frustration emerged as she tussled with the buttons on his trousers, and he swallowed a laugh, leaning upward to allow her room.

Then the trousers were open and she nudged them down his hips. "Wait, I'll do that," he said, rising from the bed to strip with ease from the constricting garments. His drawers were the last to go, and then he turned back to her. She was flushed, her mouth damp from his kisses, and one knee was lifted as if to protect her female parts. He began there, his fingers working the pink garters down the length of her calf, then returning to roll the white stockings into pale circles. They filled one hand and he leaned to deposit them on the table, beside the garters. He touched the tiny flowers with his index finger, wondering at the delicate stitchery.

"I've never seen such pretty little things," Maggie said, her gaze following each move he made. "I know they cost you dearly."

"And worth every cent if they please you." Her head turned from the distraction and she focused on the evidence of his desire. Reacting as he'd known it would, his arousal increased, and he grinned ruefully, making no attempt to shield her from it.

"You might as well see what you got, too, Maggie," he told her, hoping beyond hope that he hadn't frightened her with the unveiling. She shook her head, almost in wonder, reaching to touch him with her index finger.

"I don't think this is gonna work, Beau," she said softly.

"Emily and Roberta told me it would, but I kinda have my doubts."

"I promise you it will, honey," he told her, tensing as she rubbed that inquisitive finger up and down the length of his male organ, which had grown even more at her prompting, and begun to twitch in response to her touch.

"You want to do it now?" she asked, her voice subdued as she lifted her gaze to his.

"In a little while," he told her, lifting the sheet from the foot of the bed and sliding beneath it, pulling it up to his waist. Perhaps if he covered himself, she would lose that fearful look.

"Are you gonna turn out the lamp?"

"Not unless you make me," he said.

She looked doubtful at that, but her chin firmed and she nodded. "If you want the lamp lit, far be it from me to try to change your mind." She stretched out full length and took a deep breath. "I'm ready, Beau. Whenever you're ready, just go on ahead."

The temptation to smile was strong, but he swallowed the chuckle her words prompted, turning to his side, lifting on his elbow. His hand brushed against her breast and he coaxed the peak to form, aware of the soft hitch in her breathing and the muscles that rippled across her belly at his touch.

He bent to the tiny piece of flesh and took it carefully between his teeth. "You gonna bite me?" she asked, peering down at him.

"Uh-huh," he murmured beneath his breath, bringing his tongue into play and then suckling with gentle tugging movement of lips and tongue.

"I sure do like that, Beau," she whispered, holding his head in place, lest he move from the site he'd chosen, and her bottom lifted from the mattress in a slow, sensuous rhythm, causing her hip to brush against him.

"You'll like this, too, sweetheart," he said, shifting to pay closer attention to her stomach and belly, his hands caressing as he traveled the length of her body. Her legs were strong, well formed and pale, her feet high-arched and narrow. Muscle shaped her hips and bottom, and he explored the crease he'd admired in the mirror, with each movement of his hands and fingers paying heed to the soft sounds of approval she breathed.

"Do I get to touch you, too?" she whispered, shivering as his long fingers slid between her thighs and found a dampness that pleased him.

"Anything you want, Mag," he told her, although if the truth was told, he wasn't sure how much touching he'd be able to tolerate.

She fingered his male nipples, tasted them and laughed with delight at his groaning response. "Hot patootie, Beau. You're about as randy as Roberta said you'd be if I did that."

His laughter pealed out. There was no holding it back, and he rose over her with a smooth movement that placed her directly beneath him. "What else did Emily and Roberta tell you today?"

"They said you'd hurt me a little, but it wouldn't last long, and I'd like it later on."

Her words spoke of confidence in his ability, and he blessed the sisters who had done his work for him. "They've about got that right," he said. "The thing is sweetheart, I don't think I can wait much longer." He nudged her legs apart and found room, there where her soft flesh awaited the hurt he would inflict.

She accommodated him, rising to meet his manhood, her legs twining themselves around his. He met her gaze, saw the dark glimpse of fear she refused to speak aloud and closed his own eyes, dreading to see the tears she would shed. Maggie was small, a virgin, and the path he would take was guaranteed to be tight and unused.

He touched her there, with swirling movements against the tender flesh, parting her gently and moving his fingers to test the taut opening. It was as he had feared, for the muscle that tightened at his touch would effectively bar his way unless he could better prepare her for his taking.

His head bent and his mouth found her breast again, his tongue and cheeks holding her captive. Fingers that trembled caressed her, deftly seeking her pleasure, mindful of her halting breath as he stroked her plush folds. Her fingers clutched at him, her hips rotated against his hand and she whimpered, the sound a plea he recognized.

"I love you, baby," he whispered, his face against her breast, his own breathing harsh. "Let me love you, sweet," he crooned, sensing the tension she sought to ease, and then was rewarded by her soft cry of surprise and pleasure as she shivered against his caresses.

"*Beau!*" She relaxed and he shifted, his arms embracing her as he pushed gently within her depths. She trembled anew and moved to accommodate him, her pleasure seeming to transport her beyond the pain she'd anticipated. "*Beau...*" Again she whispered his name, and he groaned as the thin barrier gave way, his hips surging against her.

There was no use for it. He could no longer resist the lure of her warmth, and the tight grip she unknowingly placed on his swollen manhood. He withdrew almost to the point of losing contact with her flesh, then moved again, losing the last vestige of control he possessed. His teeth ground together as he struggled to hold fast to that magic moment when the hot rush of his seed would explode from within him, to bathe his wife with the proof of his need for her.

His arms trembled and he cast one last glance at the absorbed look she wore, this small, vital woman he'd taken as his own. Her eyes opened and she smiled, even as tears trembled on her eyelids.

"I love you, Beau. I really do."

With cascading pleasure, he was transported beyond himself, and he groaned his satisfaction, covering her with his body, his face buried in her hair. Her arms tightened around him and she hugged him with wiry strength, her murmur whispering the words over and over again.

"I love you, Beau. I love you."

Chapter Thirteen

The sunshine cast a golden glow on the kitchen floor, and outside the snow reflected its brilliance. Maggie stood at the window, bathed in the warmth of the winter sun, even as the ice on the outside of the window pane chilled her fingers. Winter had started early and promised to be hard. And even that thought could not dim her joy. Nothing could touch the happiness filling her soul this morning.

She was truly Mrs. Beau Jackson. The wonderful man had married her and brought her to his bed and given her a glimpse of what heaven must surely be like. She'd spent the whole night wrapped in his long arms and his hands had done beautiful things to her body even this morning. Deep inside, where her woman parts were buried, there was still a feeling of fullness, an awareness of never-forgotten pleasure.

Mrs. Beau Jackson. She shivered and hugged herself, caught up in the delight of knowing she was loved. He'd said so, not just once, but over and over. Her forehead leaned on the window pane as she closed her eyes. Certainly this was one of those times when being thankful was in order. Mama'd always said that God gave us miracles when we least expected them—for sure, the love of a man like Beau Jackson was a genuine miracle.

"You all right?" Sophie spoke from behind her and Maggie whirled.

"I'm more than fine, Sophie," she said. "I feel all brand-new."

A wide smile was Sophie's response to that revelation. She dropped the armload of sheets she carried, stepping over them to meet Maggie in the middle of the kitchen floor. She opened her arms wide and Maggie stepped into her embrace.

Sophie's hug was manna to a hungry soul, multiplying the generosity of her praise. "You're a good girl, Maggie. You deserve Beau, and he's sure a sight happier than I've ever seen him."

"Really? You really think so?" Maggie rejoiced, hope rising that she had brought Beau more than a passel of trouble.

"I know so," Sophie assured her, grasping her hands and holding her at arm's length. "I wondered if you were ever gonna get up this mornin'. Beau's been out and about for two hours and better." Her look was teasing, and Maggie accepted the thrust with good will.

"He didn't wake me up," she admitted. "I must've slept like a dead man."

"Well, get some food in your stomach," Sophie advised. "We've got sheets to wash and it's no fun hangin' them in this weather, but with a sky full of sunshine, we'd better get at it."

Even scrubbing sheets on the ridged board was not enough to dim her spirits and when noontime approached, Maggie was hanging the last of the wash, the sheets from her narrow cot in the storeroom. Pinning them in place, she whispered a farewell to her days of sleeping alone. Beside her hung Beau's long drawers and undershirts, and her own clothing, from petticoat to chemise and even her blue dress.

"I feel like a real wife," she announced to the cat that watched from the roof of the doghouse. "And why aren't you in the barn, where it's warmer?" The cat bent her head to swipe her tongue across her chest, and Maggie laughed aloud. "You're ignoring me, aren't you?" Stepping in the narrow path she'd cleared beneath the clothesline, she scooped the cat up into her arms.

"Why don't you come on in the kitchen?" she asked, nuzzling the furry head with her nose. "You can sleep in the sunshine, right in front of the door. Or maybe in the parlor window." The cat obligingly purred her response and Maggie chuckled, draping her pet over one shoulder as she bent to pick up the clothes basket. She walked back to the porch, the stiff sheets she'd unpinned from the line folded loosely in the basket. At the door, she bent to undo her heavy boots, and the cat scrambled awkwardly to the porch, her three-legged stance toppling her to one side.

As if embarrassed, she rolled to her feet and sat primly, regarding the door. "You gonna accept the invite?" Maggie asked, edging through the doorway, clothes basket in hand. The cat limped regally behind her and eyed the warm kitchen. The side window received her approval and she made her way there, curling up on a small rug.

"She's too good for the barn?" Sophie asked. "I've never cottoned to havin' animals in the house."

"Just for a while," Maggie answered. "It's cold out there."

Sophie softened her stance. "Probably won't hurt anything. Poor crippled thing can't fend for herself anyway." She lifted a sheet from the basket and shook it, then placed it over a rack behind the stove. "This'll warm up quick, once the heat takes the damp out of it," she said. A second sheet was hung beside the first, then the pillowcases. Maggie's dress was shaken, then rolled tightly, to hold the dampness until it was ironed. Sophie repeated the process with petticoat and drawers, finishing with three big aprons.

"I'll iron after dinner, while you start something for supper," she said, then cast Maggie a quick look. "Here I am tellin' you what to do, and you're the woman of the house now. I'd better mind my step, or I'll be lookin' for a new place to live."

"Oh, Sophie, don't even think that." Maggie's spirits drooped for the first time since she'd put her feet on the floor this morning. "I couldn't get along without you. And Beau...you know, I think he loves you like he would his mama." And that revelation, although new, made sense to her. "His mother died during the war, you know, and he was left without any family at all. Don't you think he figures you're the nearest thing to a mama he'll ever have?"

"He's got a mother-in-law now," Sophie reminded her. "She might not be livin' in his house, but when he married you, he picked up a whole family along with you."

"Well, he's not claiming my pa as one of his kin, I'll tell you that," Maggie said bitterly.

"I saw the sheriff and old Edgar go in the barn yesterday," Sophie said. "And then they was back out, yammerin' back and forth, and before I knew it, your pa was in his wagon and haulin' buggy down the lane. He sure didn't look happy, and neither did Sheriff Clemons, now that I think about it."

"Beau paid two dollars for the horse, left the money with the sheriff to give Pa."

"Well, he didn't get any bargain, I'll tell you that." Sophie spoke firmly, and then sighed as her gaze traveled back to the cat, who dozed in comfort near the window. "You got a real yen for helpin' them that can't do much for themselves, don't you?''

"The horse will be good as new, come spring," Maggie assured her. "He's got a few years left yet." She followed Sophie's glance at the cat. "Now, that one. She's about as useless as can be. But she gives me comfort, and that's bound to be worth something I guess."

Voices from the yard signaled the approach of hungry men, and Maggie reached for the heavy china plates in the buffet. "We're behind time, aren't we? They'll think we've been sitting on our hands all morning."

Sophie's look was amused as she carried the stew pot to the table, placing it on a wooden board. "You think Beau cares one way or the other? He's just tickled to death he finally got you out of the cot and up in his bed."

Maggie was blushing to beat the band, and Beau stopped in the doorway, enjoying the rosy hue of her cheeks. "Did I miss something?" At Sophie's muffled chuckle, he pursed his lips and bent to step from his boots. "You ladies had a busy morning. I saw you out hanging sheets, Maggie. I should have cleared the ground for you."

She tilted her chin, feeling cocky-like as his gaze warmed her. "I can shovel as good as the next one, Beau. Me and Sophie make a good team."

That seemed to be making a statement, Beau thought as Sophie nodded agreement. The rest of the men trooped in and in moments they were gathered around the big table and Sophie was dishing up the beef stew and replenishing the bread plate. Pony teased Joe, telling at great length of the youth's problems with feeding the stock, falling from the hay wagon and being surrounded by hungry steers in the far pasture.

And yet, there was no malice intended, Maggie realized, as the men hooted with laughter, even Shay smiling from one side of his mouth. He'd given her one long, approving look upon entering the kitchen, nodding his head in greeting, and then finding his place at the table. The food disappeared rapidly, and then Joe, flushed and triumphant, made a final joke at Pony's expense. In moments, the meal was over, and the kitchen empty as the men trooped out the door.

Outside, the sun played tag with clouds that obscured its warmth, and Maggie stepped down from the porch to remove the last of the washing from the line. A chill gripped her, even through the heavy coat she wore. Snow was coming on again, if she knew anything about it. From the west, heavy, gray weather threatened. Snow before nightfall, she decided. And that would mean that the men would be feeding in the pastures again. There was more snow so far this winter than she'd ever seen in her life. But Beau was ready for it, his loft filled with hay, his silo with grain, and the slat-sided crib next to the springhouse holding bushels of husked corn.

Tilting her head to the sky, she drank in the cold air. Then, mittens in place, she set out toward the clothesline. From her coop, Rascal barked a welcome, then bounded across to where Maggie worked. She dropped a clothespin, and the half-grown dog snatched it up and ran toward the house, turned to drop it and then yapped a challenge.

She could not resist. Dropping the basket to the ground, she plunged after her, and Rascal promptly gripped the clothespin and spun back toward the springhouse, Maggie behind her. And there she halted. "Just keep the thing," she called to the pup. "You got it all mucked up anyway. It won't be fit to use by the time you get through with it."

The door was ajar, and Maggie eyed it curiously. Beau must not have latched it when he set the milk inside this morning. She might as well go on in and tip off the cream as long as she was here. Maybe there was time to churn before supper. She looked back at the clothesline and the waiting basket, and made a decision. The clothes could wait another few minutes.

The door swung open and she peered within. The shutters were in place, and the interior of the building was in shadow. But with the door open, she could see the milk pail on the bench, and there beside it was an empty crock, covered with a clean towel, awaiting the rich cream. She stepped inside, smiling as she thought of the task ahead, when she would wield the dasher and turn the bounty of cream into butter. There was satisfaction in the making of it, joy to be found in the chores she'd thought wearisome in her father's house.

Beau…he made the difference. The now-familiar warmth rose within her as she thought of him. As she bent to pick up the pail, she hesitated, a chill making her shiver. From behind her a sound caught her attention and she half whirled, only to feel the strength of a man's arm around her throat.

"You shoulda stayed out of here, Miss Maggie." From the corner of her eye she caught sight of a whiskered chin and then her eyes closed as his grip tightened.

"I was only waitin' until the coast was clear," he muttered against her head, and she caught the scent of whiskey on his breath.

"Rad?" The name whistled from her throat, and she felt her strength leave her as he laughed, a low, evil sound that brought to mind her father.

"You didn't expect to see me, did you?" he taunted. "Neither did Beau or the rest of them. I snuck in here while ya'll ate your dinner."

She was limp, her eyes closed, and his grip loosened a bit. "I don't want to throttle you, girl. Just be quiet till we're sure the coast is clear. Then I'll get my gear from the bunkhouse and be on my way.''

"They're going to be in the corral," she whispered hoarsely. "They won't see you if you go around the back of the outhouse and behind the chicken yard."

His laugh was bitter. "And leave you here to holler?" He dragged her backward to the wall, where lengths of rope hung from a nail. "I'll have to tie you up, girl. Put a gag in your mouth, I reckon." His arm slid down from her throat and circled her waist, his muscled forearm cruel against the soft curves of her breasts. And then he paused, his breathing harsh.

"Old Beau never did pay me what I was worth. Maybe I'll just take a sample of his woman while I'm here," he said, his words sending fear to her depths. The knowledge of what he intended chilled her, and the thought that Beau had trusted this man saddened her. Beau would feel responsible, no matter what happened. He'd given Radley Bennett his trust, and been betrayed. How much worse it would be if the man succeeded in taking by force that which she'd given Beau so freely.

She twisted in his grip, her voice choked as she attempted to call for help. Rad jerked her around, backhanding her with a sharp blow. The familiar taste of blood was salty in her mouth, and she felt its liquid warmth against her face. A second blow forced his knuckles against the corner of her eye, and she turned her head sharply to escape the punishment he inflicted. Despair settled in her breast as she fought him, silently now, but with every ounce of her strength.

His hands were rough against her, jerking her coat open, sending the buttons flying to the ground. He tugged at her trousers, cursing as he met the resistance of a leather belt. It whipped from her waist and he held it in his hands, his eyes greedy as he lifted her by the front of her shirt, tearing it along the front placket. "I'll use the damn belt on you if you don't behave," he muttered, then methodically tore open the front of her pants.

She choked, his fist thrusting against her throat and he shoved her pants to her ankles, until they pooled around her feet on the floor of the shed. Both hands gripping with cruel force, he pushed her roughly, then released her as she fell. Her head hit the bench, and she groaned, her voice muffled by the palm he slapped against her mouth. On his knees now, he shoved her legs apart, and anguish such as she'd never known brought hot tears to her eyes.

Beau. She could only call his name in silence. Her head throbbed and the light from the doorway faded, her vision blurring as Rad leaned to touch her bared breast. He must not touch her there, she thought sadly. It would stain her forever if he...

In the distance, Rascal yapped sharply, then Sophie's voice called her name. "Maggie? Where are you, girl? Where is she, Shay?"

The darkness enveloped her, and from its depths a voice growled out a vicious oath, even as an unseen hand dragged Rad from atop her. Words she'd never thought to hear from Shay poured out without ceasing, and the thud of a falling body against the wall shook the floor beneath her.

Through the mist surrounding her, she was aware only of a warmth covering her nakedness, and the murmur of Shay's husky voice speaking her name amid words of comfort. And then silence.

The sight of Shay dragging a man from the springhouse was surprise enough, Beau thought, without adding the sound of Sophie's screams echoing from the yard. Rascal's jaw was clenched on the pant leg of Shay's captive, his growls vicious. Beau looked toward the house. Where was

Maggie? Surely in the midst of all this hullabaloo she couldn't still be inside. Not his Maggie. She'd be in the center of things, if he knew her as well as he'd thought.

And then his heart stilled in his chest. Shay was furious, his hat on the ground, his fists pummeling unmercifully at the face and body of the man who reeled from the blows. "What the hell's going on?" Beau shouted, running from the barn door to where Shay's victim lay on the ground, blood pouring from his nose, his groans meshing with the curses that flowed unceasingly from Shay's mouth.

"Rad? What the hell's he doing here?" Beau shouted, his own hands clenching into fists, itching to join the fray. "Shay!"

Shay turned, his mouth twisted, the jagged scar vivid against his crimson face. "Maggie's in there," he said, nodding at the springhouse. And then he bent to pick up the man he'd battered to the ground, dragging him by his coat collar, unheeding of the weak choking sounds his grip brought into being.

Maggie. Beau's fists loosened. Maggie was in the springhouse. He staggered, stunned by the vision Shay's words had conjured. His hand rose to clutch the door post and he leaned inside the building. Shay's distinctive, long leather coat lay on the floor. Below its hem was a pair of crumpled trousers, and from the legs, boots protruded.

Maggie's boots. "Dear God..." If ever he had uttered a prayer in his life, Beau spoke one now. *"Maggie!"* Tears streamed from his eyes and he swiped at them impatiently, falling to his knees beside the still form beneath Shay's coat. Spread sideways across her length, it blocked her form from sight and he lifted it carefully by one sleeve. Blood seeped slowly from a lump on her temple, staining her forehead and matting her hair.

His hands trembled as he touched her cheeks. Her eyes

were closed, one swollen and purpling. Her lips were parted a bit, and blood flowed from the corner of her mouth.

"Maggie?" Drawing the heavy coat down her length, he inhaled sharply. Her breasts lay naked, exposed to view, her dainty chemise torn, her shirt spread wide.

His sobs were no longer silent as he forced his eyes to travel the area of her belly, then down to where her thighs lay apart. Her trousers and drawers, tangled around her boots, forced her limbs into an awkward position and he straightened them carefully. Sophie sobbed quietly outside the door and he called to her over his shoulder.

"Get me a quilt. I want to carry her into the house." He bent, his ear against Maggie's breast, relief flooding him as the steady beat of her heart gave him assurance.

Beside Beau, the pup nosed at Maggie's limp hand, whining softly. Rascal's pink tongue touched lax fingers and as Beau watched, they twitched, then lifted to stroke the eager pup. Her eyes flickered open, and Beau was sickened by the horror reflected there, her lashes fluttering as she looked past him at the doorway.

"Where is he?" she whispered, her voice rasping. "I heard Shay hitting him, didn't I?"

"He's gone. Shay's got him, sweetheart." Drawing the handkerchief from his pocket, he wiped the corner of her mouth. "I'm going to take you to the house," he told her. His fingertips lifted her hair from the knot at her temple, where the blood still seeped. Her eye was rapidly closing and his distress dissolved into cold anger as the image of Rad's hands causing this damage filled his mind.

Rad had been more than a fool to set foot back here. He was a dead man. If Shay hadn't already done the job, Beau vowed to see to it himself, before the sun set on this miserable day.

"Here's the quilt," Sophie said from the doorway. "Do you want me to help?"

Beau shook his head. "No, just get a bowl of warm water and some towels. I'll bring her in and get her cleaned up." His hands slid her boots off, then stripped the trousers and drawers from her legs. Lifting Shay's sheep-lined coat, he lay it to one side and quickly covered Maggie with the quilt, lifting her and wrapping her in its warmth in one easy motion.

She moaned, her head rolling against his arm, and he whispered words of comfort as he carried her across the yard. "Almost there, sweetheart. We'll get you cleaned up and tucked into bed. You'll be fine. You'll see."

Maggie turned her face against his shoulder, groaning as her damaged skin rubbed against the wool fabric. "I can do it," she said. "Just fill the tub for me."

"No, not now," he told her. "Maybe later on." He stepped onto the porch and Sophie held the door wide. Through the kitchen and up the stairs, he carried his precious bundle, set on ridding her of her torn shirt and the delicate chemise. With care, he placed her on the bed and she shivered beneath the warmth of the quilt. Her teeth chattered and she closed her eyes tightly.

"I'm so cold, Beau. I've never been so cold," she whimpered, turning to her side and drawing up her knees.

"Here's the basin," Sophie said from the doorway. "Should I get her out of those things?"

"I'll do it," Beau told her. "Close the door." He heard the latch click as he took off his coat, tossing it to the floor. Reaching for the pillows, he stacked them against the metal headboard and then bent to lift Maggie into his arms again. Even with the heavy quilt, she shivered almost uncontrollably, and he settled himself against the pillows, tucking her feet beneath the covers and cradling her on his lap. He rocked with her, pulling the quilt around the back of her head, until only her face was exposed. She was pale, her features pinched, and swelling marred the fine lines of her cheek and forehead.

Weeks ago, she'd come to him in almost this same condition, he thought, remembering his first sight of the defiant young woman who'd sought shelter in his hayloft. He'd not been able that time to deliver justice to her attacker. Today would be different, he vowed.

Reaching to the table beside the bed, he squeezed the washrag with one hand, then lifted the warm cloth to her face, his touch gentle as he cleaned the blood from her mouth. He rinsed it and squeezed it again, this time placing it on her forehead, allowing the blood to soak up into the cloth. Wiping carefully, he exposed the cut, a small one, right at the hairline. Head wounds always bled fiercely, he reminded himself, noting that the cut was already beginning to clot.

"Thank you," Maggie whispered. Her trembling had become less noticeable, and she curled against him, her arms warming against his chest. "Why would he come back?" she asked. "He might have known someone would see him."

"Joe went through his things in the bunkhouse yesterday," Beau told her. "He had a couple of guns and over two hundred dollars. He hid the money in the mattress. My guess is he must've thought it was worth the risk."

"Where's your horse? The one he took."

Beau shrugged. "I don't know. Probably in the woods beyond the orchard. Shay will find it."

"I'm sorry, Beau. I know I upset you, letting him get the best of me thataway. He caught me by surprise and I couldn't get my hands on anything to smack him with."

He made a sound of disbelief. How like Maggie to apol-

ogize for that which she had no control over. "You're a
small woman," he told her. "You couldn't be expected to
protect yourself against a big man like Rad." He turned
her, sliding her to the bed and his hands were gentle as he
unwrapped her from the quilt.

"I can do this," she told him again. Her eyes pled with
him, but he ignored her protest.

"If you're worrying because you haven't got anything
on, sweetheart, you must be forgetting that I saw you this
way last night." His words were teasing, and he forced a
smile.

"That was before Rad touched me," she said, turning
her head away. "Please, Beau." Gripping the quilt tightly,
she smothered a sob, and he relented.

"All right. I'll go down and get the tub ready for you.
It'll take a while to heat the water. Will you be all right?"

She nodded. "Just leave the basin here please."

"The water's not clean," he told her. "I'll bring up
fresh."

"Fill the tub." Her head turned stubbornly away, she
waited, and he allowed her defiance.

Rising from the bed, he picked up his coat and left the
room, closing the door behind himself. From the foot of
the stairs, Sophie watched his slow progress down the steps.
"Is she all right? Did you get her cleaned up?"

"A little," he said tersely. "She wants to take a bath."

"The wash boiler's on the stove. I filled it, and there's
a full reservoir. It won't take long. I stoked up the fire real
good." She stepped back as he walked past her into the
kitchen. "Beau?"

Stalking to the window, he looked out onto the yard.
"Yeah?"

"What will happen to Radley?"

Nothing stirred beyond the window. Even the pup had

taken refuge on the porch, and lay with her head resting on her paws. "You don't need to know, Sophie," Beau said after a moment.

"Will you get the sheriff?"

He shook his head and heard her swift intake of breath. "Beau, don't get in trouble over the man."

One thought spun through his mind and he spoke it aloud. "He hurt Maggie."

"She wouldn't want you to…" As if she could not speak the unthinkable, Sophie paused, and then she was there at his elbow. "You don't want his blood on your hands."

"He has Maggie's blood on his." His jaw tightened, and he cursed. "Damn it, Sophie. Do you think I'll ever forget seeing her there like that?" He spun to the door, shoving his sleeves into his coat. "Where the hell's my hat?" he growled.

"In the shed, I think," Sophie told him.

The door slammed behind him as he leaped from the porch. "Joe!" he shouted, and then called again. "Joe? Pony?" His stride was long as he went to the shed. Shay's long coat lay on the floor, Beau's hat beside it. Crushing the brim, he jerked the hat onto his head and slung Shay's coat over his shoulder.

From the barn door Pony and Joe watched his approach and he looked beyond them into the shadowed interior. "Where'd Shay take him?"

"Last I saw, Shay was draggin' Rad by the back of his coat, out past the orchard, into the woods."

"Get my horse saddled," he told Pony, then turned to Joe. "I want you to bundle up all Rad's belongings. Wrap everything in his slicker and bring it out of the bunkhouse."

"What about the money, and his guns?" Joe asked.

"Leave them out. He won't need them."

"There's not much else, just a couple of pants and shirts

and his old boots.'' Joe shrugged and turned away. ''Sure fooled us all, didn't he?''

And therein, Beau decided, lay the reason for his anger. That he had been made a fool of by a man he'd trusted. He'd look harder at the next cowboy that rode up, that was a sure bet. He'd almost lost Maggie, and all because he'd been blind to Rad's dark side.

Pony led the big stallion from the barn, and without a word Beau was in the saddle. Shay's coat over his lap, he turned the stud with a movement of his reins and touched his heels to the animal's sides. With a toss of his head, the horse broke into a quick trot, and Beau turned him into the orchard, making his way between the rows of fruit trees to the heavily wooded area beyond.

There was no sign of Shay as he entered the woods, and he leaned over his horse's shoulder to peer at the ground. The trail was easy to follow, footsteps obscured in places by the burden Shay had dragged behind him. Beneath the trees, the snow was not as deep and Beau made slower progress. Shay had had a good fifteen-minute start on him. He couldn't have gone far on foot, not dragging Rad's considerable weight through the brush.

''Beau.'' So quietly he might not have heard it had not his ears been attuned to every sound, Shay's voice came from a cluster of pine trees on Beau's right. He turned in the saddle and faced the man he sought.

''You need your coat,'' he said, handing it down. Shay walked closer and took the heavy garment, sliding his arms into the sleeves and adjusting the collar.

''Where is he?'' Beau asked.

''You don't need to know,'' Shay told him. ''Fact is, you're better off if you don't know anything about it.''

''What're you talkin' about?'' Beau snapped, anger

flooding his mind as he glared at Shay. "He's not leaving my ranch standing up, Shay. He's a dead man."

Shay shoved his hands into his coat pockets and nodded. "You got that right, boss." A glimmer of satisfaction stirred in his eyes as he spoke. "He won't lay his hands on another woman, I promise you that."

"He's dead?" Shay's words shot holes in Beau's hopes for at least one good solid punch before he shot the man, and he felt frustration take hold.

"You don't know where he is or where he's goin', boss. That's the way it has to be. Otherwise you'll be answerin' a whole heap of questions when you go visit the sheriff. This way, you're in the clear. You don't know what happened to the man."

"And you do." Beau's jaw clamped tightly as he read between the lines. Shay would not budge. He knew the man well enough to realize that. "Now what, Shay?"

"I'm leavin'. I'll get my things and be gone by nightfall."

"I can't let you do that. Maggie would have my hide if she finds out you left because of her."

"I won't have her shamed every time she looks at me, Beau." It was personal now. Shay's use of his given name brought Beau up sharply. "Remember? I found her there. I covered her with my coat, but she'll always remember that I saw her and knew that Rad had torn her clothes off."

"You're not thinking that he..." Beau could not speak the words, and Shay spared him the need.

"No. He didn't have time. Not that he wouldn't have, given a couple more minutes. He didn't even have his pants undone." Shay looked at the ground and cleared his throat. "He touched her, Beau. That was enough to earn him a one-way ticket to hell."

And that was that, Beau realized. The anger drained from

him, only a sense of sorrow remaining. Rad Bennett had stolen more than his money. He'd taken from him the man who'd proved himself to be a friend. That Shay would leave was a given.

Maggie would recover. She was tough, too much woman to be laid low by this. With some care, and a lot of love, she'd be healed.

And to that end he would devote himself, heart and soul.

Chapter Fourteen

She wore the nightgown. And that fact in itself was a message. The glowing bride of last night had become a woman he recognized all too well. He'd seen her first, barefoot and defiant, descending from his hayloft, weeks ago. Now, after lifting the bed coverings, he found her small, huddled form. Well-garbed in yards of white lawn, her feet hidden from view within the deep ruffle, she was as close to the far edge of his bed as she could get.

Sheet in hand, he looked across the expanse of mattress and sighed. "Ah, Maggie."

"Cover me, please," she asked politely, and he allowed the white sheet to billow like a sail caught in the wind, drifting to hide her from his sight. She tugged it up to her ear, only her long braided plait, spread across her pillow, exposed to his gaze. "Thank you." Muffled in the bedding, her polite response was the spark that lit his fuse.

Bending to the bed, he grasped the sheet, lifting it again. Flinging it over the footboard, he waited. The response was not long in coming.

"I'm cold."

"Well, sweetheart," he told her, in a voice that struggled to be gentle, "I'm more than willing to get you warm."

His fingers busy with the ritual of undressing, he watched her, and felt a twinge of remorse as she groped for the sheet he'd tossed aside.

Stark naked, more than aware of her discomfort, he settled himself behind her, drawing up the bedding to cover them both. He slid his arm around her waist and tugged her across the bed, ignoring the stiffening of her body, the soft sounds of protest she uttered, and the stirring of arousal she must surely feel nudging her backside.

"I want to look at you, Maggie."

"I'm not a pretty sight," she told him. "You've already seen me lookin' like this."

"Looking," he reminded her. "And I think you're pretty no matter how many bruises you wear."

"Don't, Beau. I don't want you touchin' me."

Touching. The word remained unspoken on his tongue as he considered her request. More than anything on God's green earth, he wanted his hands on her. Not with passion, for her condition tonight precluded that, no matter what his needy body proclaimed. He wanted, no, needed, to inspect her face. His hands yearned for the soft curves of her body, and his mouth was hungry for the taste of her skin, but for tonight he would put aside his needs, and play the part of comforter. As his mother had done, in those long ago years of his childhood, he wanted to kiss every inch of swollen flesh, touch his lips to the bruises and blow warmth against the hurts she'd received today.

"Maggie…" He heard the echo of sadness as his voice spoke her name. "I only want to talk to you, and hold you, sweetheart."

She rolled to her back, and his arm lay loosely against her midriff. "I'm sorry," she whispered, her uninjured eye staring at the ceiling. "I thought if I scrubbed real good, I could wash away the feel of his hands on me." The eye closed and a tear slipped from beneath its lid. "It didn't work."

Beau lifted up on his elbow and leaned over her, his hand leaving her waist to cradle her cheek. "You look clean to me, honey," he said softly. And then he bent to her, fulfilling the desire of his heart, his mouth blessing her wounds of battle. "You smell good, too."

"Beau?" She looked at him and the pleading in that single word was almost his undoing. "I feel like I'm not the same person I was last night. Like Rad's hands left big old black marks on me, and I'll never get them off, no matter what I do."

"You're still my wife, Maggie. I still love you. That hasn't changed, not one little bit." He brushed a gentle forefinger against her forehead. "It's already scabbed over. In just a few days, that crusty old scab will fall off and you'll have new, pink skin underneath." His mouth touched like butterfly wings against her eye, and he winced inwardly at the purple lump that hid its beauty.

"This is going to fade, Maggie. The bump on your head will go down, and the cuts inside your mouth will heal. It won't hurt for me to kiss you after a few days." He smiled, willing her to understand.

"By the time all that happens, the memory of what happened today will begin to fade. You won't forget it," he went on, one finger touching her lips as she would have protested his words. "But it won't hurt like it does tonight."

"How can you want to touch me?" she asked, tears clogging her voice. "*He* had his hands on me, Beau."

"I'll never stop wanting to touch you," he vowed, and knew in his heart that it was true. The love he felt for Maggie was deeply ingrained, far outweighing the affection he'd felt for any woman in his past. His lips pressed warmth against her forehead and he recalled the first night they'd been alone together, when he'd played his guitar.

He'd known even then that he loved her and had soothed her apprehension, lest she be fearful of him. Those words returned to him now. "You're my friend, remember? And you're the girl who pitched in and helped when I needed someone to heal my cow. You were there when the colt stepped in the barbed wire."

"I was only trying to earn my keep," she reminded him. "And I'm not real sure I ever did that, what with all the things you kept buying for me."

He kissed her gently. "Maggie, Maggie. You fill my life with joy. There's no price can be put on that." Leaning back, he took assessment of the nightgown she wore, his arousal demanding attention. "Are you determined to wear this thing all night? Or is there a chance I can persuade you to let me take it off."

"Shay saw me," she said abruptly. "He didn't really look, just put his coat over me."

"I know." *And that fact had sent Shay on his way.*

"He's a kind man, isn't he?" Maggie asked, her fingers clasping the front of her gown.

If she'd seen Shay earlier, he thought… But she hadn't, and that was a blessing. One day she'd realize Shay's sacrifice on her behalf. For tonight, he would be the only one to mourn the man's leaving. Tomorrow would be soon enough for Maggie to recognize Shay's absence.

"Do you want me to put more salve on your forehead?" he asked.

She shook her head, a minute movement. "No, it hurts to touch it. Matter of fact, my whole head aches."

And he'd been trying to persuade her to— His pang of remorse forbade all but succor at his hands tonight. He slid his arm beneath her neck, easing down to rest against his own pillow. She turned her head away, allowing him only the sight of an unblemished cheek and the solitary teardrop that slid into her hair.

"Aren't you going to turn out the lamp?" Her words were whispered, her swollen lips barely moving.

"Are you afraid I'll see you cry?"

"You feel bad enough without me blubbering all over you. I'm nothing but trouble, Beau. And now you're stuck with me."

"I'm not complaining." He eased from her side and sat up on the edge of the bed. The lamp was a small matter, easily solved. What to do with Maggie was another story, he feared. In all the time she'd been with him, he'd never seen this degree of desolation. Even her father's abuse had left her defiant and feisty.

"Maggie? I need you," he whispered. He dropped his head into his hands, his own soul sickened by the wedge driven between them. If they could not survive the events of this day, he would have lost a part of Maggie he cherished. That exuberant nature she possessed that allowed her to be ever hopeful.

The mattress shifted and her hand touched his back. "I can't deny you anything, Beau. You know that. I can't kiss very good tonight. My mouth hurts too bad. But I can do the rest if you want to." Her fingers applied pressure, and he closed his eyes.

"I only need to hold you, sweetheart," he said, ashamed of his lie, hoping against hope that his manhood would cooperate in this venture. Turning to her, he plumped his pillow and faced her. She waited, willing to do as he directed and he tugged at her pigtail. "Just let me take your hair down, all right?"

The string she'd tied in place slid off easily and his fingers wove through the strands, loosening the silken bounty.

"Now, just put your head on my arm, if it doesn't make your headache worse."

She obeyed silently, forming herself against his long frame. One slender arm slid up to his neck and she sighed, nestling closer, until her breath warmed his throat. "I think it feels better, layin' here," she murmured. One long breath followed another, and her body softened, a soft sob escaping only once as she drifted into sleep.

Beau circled her with his free arm, his hand at the small of her back, his fingers rubbing in circles, then moving upward to stroke the length of her spine. She murmured something, and he heard his name whispered softly. Inhaling the scent of her hair, he closed his eyes. She was safe, she was secure in his embrace and she would heal.

And for all of that, he owed a debt to Shay, a debt he would never be able to repay.

Daybreak brought more snow. Sophie cooked for all of them, and breakfast was a quiet meal, Pony and Joe talking quietly to Beau about the snow and the cattle they intended to check on later. Feeding the horses would come first, they decided and they left the table together, Beau donning his big coat while the men headed for the barn.

"I'll go with you," Maggie said, and he only nodded when she stated her intentions. She watched as he set off, shoveling a wide path to the barn, then donned her boots and heavy coat, wrapping the long scarf around her head.

"I wanted to tend to the horse," she told him, catching up as he neared the barn door.

"I figured as much." Inside the barn the animal heat allowed Maggie to undo her coat and let her scarf fall around her neck. She found the small step stool and took it into the gelding's stall, then fed him generously before she began the uncovering of his wound. Standing on the stool, she spoke softly to the horse, caressing its ears and neck. With gentle hands she changed the dressing on his withers, applying more salve to the healing laceration.

"He's gonna be fine," she announced, draping a blanket over the animal's back and stepping down to the floor to strap it into place. "He ate pretty good, Beau. I gave him an extra measure of grain."

"You feel like milking?" he asked. "Pony and Joe are heading out with hay for the stock."

She glanced at him quickly. "Will you go with them?"

He shook his head. "I'll be here. I'm going to clean up the tack room and spend some time in the corral. A few times around with those yearlings and they'll have a track made in the snow."

"I'll help after I milk," she offered, and then looked beyond him where the back door of the barn stood open, Pony visible as he harnessed the workhorses to the wagon. "Shay wasn't here for breakfast, Beau. Where is he?" she asked, and even as she spoke the words, she wished them back. Beau's eyes darkened.

"He decided to move on, Maggie. Left last night." A smile curved his mouth and he shrugged. "He's a wanderer, always has been, I guess. With winter here and all, he knew we could handle things with just Pony and Joe."

She picked up the three-legged stool and placed it beside the cow, settling in place with the pail between her feet. Her hands rubbed soothingly against the cow's hind quarter, and then against her side, stroking with familiarity. Her hands grasped the two far teats and she began the ritual of filling the pail with foaming milk.

Her head leaned against the warmth of the animal's side. "He left because of me, didn't he?" Sadness crept in, and her fingers tightened their grip a bit, even as she released her hold on the small bits of pleasure she'd accumulated since arising.

Rad. "Where's Rad?" she asked, a chill taking her as she spoke his name. And then a thought too enormous to speak aloud seized her. Had Shay sent Rad on his way? Or worse? The cow shifted and Maggie relaxed her grip, speaking soothing nonsense words to ease the animal's uneasiness.

"Rad's gone," Beau said quickly. "He got quite a send-off. Shay made sure he got the message that it wouldn't be safe for him to ever come back here."

"We don't have to tell anyone what happened, do we?" she asked, unwilling that her shame be a topic of conversation.

"No, of course not. You know the men won't say anything." Beau stepped to the door of the tack room. "Let me know when you've finished and I'll carry the milk to the springhouse."

She shook her head. "No, I'll do it." Better that she enter that place today, that room that held terror within its walls. She would never again cross the threshold of the springhouse without the knowledge of evil that would forever stain the memory of that small building.

Her hands worked more slowly as the cow's bag emptied. The milk splashed in the pail in smaller spurts and Maggie sighed. "There's no putting it off," she whispered, rising from the stool and backing from the stall. Beau watched from the doorway of the tack room, his gaze searching her.

"Want me to go along?"

"No." She turned from him, fearful that he would notice the trembling of her mouth. The door slid open and she stepped into the cold, tiny snowflakes glittering in the crisp air. Reaching behind her, she closed the door.

"Leave it open, Maggie," Beau said sharply. She turned to him and he nodded encouragement. "I'll be here."

"Yes." He'd be there. She'd known it, yet how like him to want to watch as she made the trek to the springhouse, opened the door and carried the pail of milk inside. Her footsteps did not falter as she trudged across the yard, her hand barely trembled as she lifted the latch, and with firm movements she entered the dim interior. Her heart beat more rapidly, and she ignored it. Her eyes sought the corners, and she forced them back to the bench before her.

And then she was done, finished with the task. A clean towel covered the pail, and she turned to leave. A leaf blew across the doorstep and she started, wide-eyed as it skittered across the floor. The rustle of its movement in the silence around her sent her pulse soaring, but then she smiled.

"I'm not afraid of you, Radley," she whispered. Wherever the man was, he was no threat to her, of that she was certain. And why that should be so was a mystery she had no chance of solving. She only knew that right now, in this moment, Radley Bennett was no longer a menace. He was a bad memory, one she would not allow to poison her mind.

Beau watched as she left the building, visible through the open barn door, and he met her as she hurried to him, drawing her inside the doorway and holding her against himself. "Are you all right?" he asked, his mouth touching her forehead. His lips pressed warmth against her skin and she smiled, remembering his words from last night.

The memory of what happened today will begin to fade... And it already had, she realized. She'd taken the first step and it had been difficult. The next would be easy. Maggie tilted her head, then with one palm on Beau's face, she drew him closer, until their lips met. It was a gentle kiss, with no other reason for being than to offer him her thanks for his kindness. For being her friend.

And then he turned his head a bit, taking a new angle, a new approach, still gentle but easing his way past her tender lips to the hurt she'd suffered from teeth that cut into soft flesh. He touched her with care, murmuring sounds beneath his breath that brought a fluttering pulse beat to life. He left her mouth, left her still wanting, still hungry for his kiss, only to move to her throat, there where her heartbeat vibrated against the tender skin beneath her jaw.

"You taste so sweet, Maggie, so good."

She embraced him, her body aching for a closer union, charmed by his wooing, beguiled by the soft phrases he whispered. "I love you, Beau." It came unbidden, this declaration. And she repeated it, her heart giving voice to the deepest emotion it had ever known.

He straightened and shook his head. "I'm not going to bed you in a stall, Maggie, and if I don't behave myself, that's what's going to happen." His grin was lopsided and he clasped her shoulders in his big hands. "You better just remember all this after dark, when I hide that nightgown of yours. You hear me?"

She nodded, her vision blurred, cocking her head to one side, the better to see him from the undamaged eye. Tears threatened to overflow its lower lid and she blinked them back. "I'll remember. I promise."

A horse neighed loudly from the corral and another answered the challenge from beyond the yard. "Sounds like company," Beau said, releasing her and stepping back to open the big door. From the lane, a farm wagon approached, the driver lifting a hand in a casual salute. "Looks like Cord McPherson," Beau announced. He shot Maggie an assessing look, and she winced.

"He'll see me, Beau. There's no helping it."

"He'll know something's happened, honey. I'll have to

tell him. But, remember this. Cord's no gossip. What I tell him won't go any further.''

The wagon pulled close to the door and from its bed, two smaller figures stood erect, waving and shouting greetings. ''Hey there, Mr. Jackson. We come for our yearlings.'' The tallest of the two boys leaped to the ground even before the wagon halted near the barn. ''Cord said it was a good day for a holiday, and Rachel couldn't come 'cause it's too cold for the babies, so she's makin' pies for dinner.''

And wasn't that a conglomeration of reasons, Maggie thought, her smile unbidden as she caught the eagerness of the youth. Two of the yearlings would leave here today, and her mind turned in that direction. She'd chosen the best of the lot for these boys, and whether they picked her selection or not, they were guaranteed top quality animals. Her pride in Beau's stock was second only to his own, she decided.

Cord looked at her over Beau's shoulder and his smile faded. ''Maggie?''

''Hey,'' she replied, stepping backward into the shadows, her joy dimmed by his concern. ''I'll turn the yearlings out into the corral,'' she told Beau in an undertone. And before he could form an answer, she picked up a bucket, filled it with grain and headed for the back door of the barn.

Across the near pasture, the yearlings gathered beneath the sparse shelter of a grove of trees, bare of leaves, but the natural gathering place for the small herd. Maggie approached the gate, shaking the bucket of grain, calling for their attention, her voice radiating a coaxing timbre they heeded. With uplifted heads and snorts of welcome, they trotted across the pasture, drawn by the woman they recognized and the rattle of feed in the bucket she held. The gate opened readily to her touch and she lured the yearlings into the corral, closing them in swiftly. They swarmed around her and she spoke to them, allowing one, then another to dip their heads in the pail, pushing them aside with a burst of laughter as they nudged her for attention.

"You've got them all eating out of your hand, Miss Maggie," Cord said from the other side of the corral fence. He'd climbed up to sit on the top rail and the two boys peered between the rails at the yearlings that surrounded Maggie. Their eyes were eager, their mouths pressed into identical, thin lines as if they held fast to exuberant laughter that begged to be released.

"They're all beautiful," the younger lad said. "Which ones can we have, Cord?"

"I think maybe Beau has some ideas about that," Cord replied, looking at Maggie, his eyes kind, his expression knowing. "Or maybe Miss Maggie might be the better one to ask."

"How'd you get all banged up, ma'am?" the eldest boy asked, concern marring the lines of his brow. "You take a tumble off one of Beau's horses?"

"Something like that," Maggie answered, thankful for the assumption he'd made. That the thought of a beating such as she'd survived wouldn't enter the boy's mind said a lot for his rearing at Cord McPherson's hand, she thought. A small glimmer of envy tainted her mind as she watched the two boys, and then she chided herself for such an unworthy thought. She'd survived her childhood, and put it behind her. She was beyond the reach of her father's hands.

"Have you chosen your favorites for my brothers, Maggie?" Cord's words broke into her thoughts and she smiled, her mouth painful as it stretched.

"You could say that," she told him. "There's three actually that catch on real quick. They're all good-natured, mostly, but sometimes you just can't help liking one animal more than another.''

''Kinda like people?'' Cord asked.

She nodded, reaching for the halter of a blood-bay gelding. His tail and mane were lush, long and black, and ebony stockings brought attention to his slender legs. He tossed his head, and Maggie spoke firmly, a command he heeded. His eyes were intent and he followed her willingly as she approached the two youths who watched eagerly.

''This is one of the best Beau owns,'' she told them. ''He's eager and smart, and if you're not careful, he'll lead you a merry chase.'' She met the gaze of the eldest boy and nodded invitingly. ''Come on over the rail and talk to him.'' He obliged quickly, and she watched as his large-knuckled hands took the halter, one lifting to rub firmly against the horse's nose.

''Hey, there, boy. Do you like me?''

Succumbing to the lure of the animal he held, the boy bent forward, placing his face against the proud head, already well smitten by the horse Maggie had chosen for him.

''Lead him out the gate,'' Maggie told him, nodding at Beau, who jumped obligingly from the top rail to assist. Holding the gate ajar, Beau nodded with satisfaction as boy and horse ambled past him.

''One down,'' Cord said. ''That takes care of Henry. What do you have for Jay, Maggie?'' His eyes narrowed as he took her measure, and then he nodded approvingly. ''You've made a fine choice so far, ma'am. What about the chestnut with the wide blaze?''

''You have a good eye, Mr. McPherson.'' Maggie pushed several horses from her path, and laughed as they milled around her. The chestnut stood firm, watching her approach and then nickered softly, ducking his head, nudging her shoulder. She slipped a piece of carrot from her jacket pocket and the yearling found it, taking it daintily from her palm.

"Come on, baby," she crooned, leading him to where Jay watched through the rails. "Do you like him?" she asked the boy, knowing the answer as his wistful expression blossomed into a wide grin.

"Wow!" he breathed. "Do you think he'll like me? Can I pet him like Henry did?"

Maggie nodded, and the boy scrambled over the fence, almost tumbling on the ground at her feet in his eagerness. The horse shied a bit, then leaned to nibble at the cowlick atop Jay's head. A soft whuffle of greeting brought Jay to his feet and he clutched at the yearling's neck with both arms. "Oh, Cord! Can I really have this one?"

Cord chuckled, his amusement contagious, for Beau joined in, laughing aloud. "I don't think there's much doubt about it, Jay. He likes you, all right. Bring him on out the gate and through the barn. Maggie will attach a lead line for you. Henry, too."

Maggie followed the boy, pleased that the feisty colt was proving amiable today. They would have their hands full with the yearlings, but she could rest easy, knowing they were going to a good home. Attaching short lead lines to each halter, she walked with the two boys from the front of the barn.

"Did Beau talk to you about a pup?" Maggie asked quietly, catching Cord's eye.

He nodded. "He said you might have one left." Behind her, she heard indrawn breaths, and then two voices spoke, almost in unison.

"A dog?"

Cord nodded, his grin wide. "Might as well take all we can get, boys. If Maggie's pup is as well trained as these yearlings…"

Her laughter caught them all off guard, and Maggie stifled it behind one hand. "I fear you're in for a surprise, Mr. McPherson. We're talking about a puppy here, half grown, maybe, but still a scallywag."

"Just the kind we'd like to have, Miss Maggie," Henry said eagerly.

"Yes, ma'am, the very kind," Jay added, peering toward the house where two half-grown dogs sat at attention.

There was no choice involved this time, and even though Rascal howled mournfully, the last of Maisie's litter was lugged without ceremony to the wagon.

In moments, the horses were tied to the rear of the wagon, and Cord had concluded his business with Beau. Money exchanged hands and Beau stuffed the bills into his pocket, uncounted. Maggie stood beside him and they watched in silence as the wagon turned in the yard, to head back toward the road.

"Part of this is yours, you know," Beau said, patting his pocket. "Horse trainers are high-paid people hereabouts. Not to mention the money for the dog."

"I got my pay," Maggie said. "Just watching those boys was wages enough for me." She sniffed, wiping her nose with Beau's kerchief. "At least I'll get to see the pup when we visit at the McPherson place."

Beau's arm circled her waist. "I hear Pony and Joe coming back. I'll give them a hand. Why don't you go on in the house where it's warm. Must be almost time for Sophie to be getting dinner ready, don't you think?"

"Yes, all right."

"Maggie?"

She turned to face him, backing slowly toward the house. "What? What's wrong?"

He smiled. "Nothing. I just wanted to tell you that I'm

proud of you. You did really well with the yearlings. Cord thinks you're top rate.''

The praise brought satisfaction to her heart.

''Maggie? I think you're the best,'' Beau said. ''The very best.''

She came to a halt. ''And now you expect me to just turn around and go in the house and tend to dinner? Are you sure we can't put some fresh straw in that stall you were talking about?''

He grinned, a boyish expression crossing his face. ''You make me feel young again. Like all the bad things that ever happened to me never really mattered.'' He stepped toward her, wide strides that covered the ground between them. ''I told you this before, but I want to say it again, Maggie Jackson. You bring me joy.''

His hands circled her waist and he lifted her, boots and heavy coat seeming as nothing, and she felt weightless. Her hands reached for his shoulders and she clutched there for purchase. Then, clasped in his strong grip, she looked down at him, straight into the glowing eyes and smiling lips that promised enough love to last a lifetime.

Chapter Fifteen

"Are you going to lay there all night, not talking to me?" She'd waited long minutes, staring into the darkness, until her eyes became accustomed to the variations of light and shadow cast by the glow of moonlight. Reflecting from the snow below, it diffused an unearthly glow. In its light, she looked from the corner of her eye at Beau, there in the bed beside her.

"Beau?" He was silent, and, stricken by a sense of shame, Maggie wondered if he thought her brazen. Better to find out than ponder the thing to death, she decided, and turned onto her side to face him. He met her gaze, his eyes hooded and deep set.

"I was thinking about doing more than just talking," he said. "And then I was wondering about where all your bruises are, Maggie. And thinking maybe I shouldn't be pushing you too fast. You've only been a bride for a couple of days, and I don't want to make you think that—"

Her hand moved rapidly, smothering his words. His lips moved against her fingers and she pressed more firmly. "Hush, Beau. You listen to me. I'm fine as frog hairs, maybe a little battered up, but shoot—that's nothing new." She felt his lips purse, then pucker and her fingers were kissed, then tasted. Made bolder by his response, she grinned.

"Last night," she began, aware of the mischief glittering from his eyes, "you told me something, and I been wondering ever since how it could be."

His head moved against the pillow, dislodging her palm, and he captured it against his cheek in a swift movement. "Which thing are we talking about?"

Now she was hesitant, but the words spilled forth, and she found that simply speaking them gave her courage. "You said you needed me." He had said it, and in just that way. His head bent, his posture weary, he'd spoken the words, and she'd yearned to comfort him. Why such a thing should be so, that this strong, capable man *needed* Maggie O'Neill was beyond her, but if Beau said it, it must be true.

"So, did you mean you just need me to stay here, helping out? Or here, laying in your bed? You know, so you can do that same thing we did the first night?"

His laugh was a whisper of sound, and his grasp was firm as he turned her hand to his mouth, his lips against her palm. "I suspect I could live without you, Maggie, but I sure don't want to try. Not now…" His mouth sent tendrils of fire the length of her arm as he whispered words that set her heart beating like she'd been running full tilt through the woods. "Now that I know what it's like to see you every day and watch the way you do things." She felt his tongue as he measured the width of her callused palm. "I like kissing you, and feeling all your curves up against me…"

"Beau!" He inhaled sharply as she fetched her hand from his grasp, then moved to take up the scant space between them, lifting over him to peer anxiously into his face. "You're making me all prickly down inside," she hissed, "making me want to do all the things you said."

"You picked up on that real quick," he said, sliding his hands down the length of her back. "Go right ahead and do what you please." His voice was deep, growling inside his chest, and his hands moved unceasingly, yet slowly, exploring now beneath the white gown she wore.

"You don't need to be still thinking you'll hurt me," she whispered, wiggling a bit as she slid one leg between his knees.

"Are you sure?" he asked, his fingers stroking the curve of her hips. She was motionless, admiring the skill of his callused hands on her warm flesh. Her head dipped, her forehead resting against his chest, and she inhaled his scent. "Maggie? Are you sure?"

"Um…I'll hurt something fierce if you change your mind about me. If ever you don't want to touch me this way again," she murmured, her voice a whimper now as his fingers ventured further.

"Slim chance of that, sweetheart," he said firmly. And then his fingers moved again. "Do you like this?" he asked, lifting her a bit, arranging her against his body, his hands measuring curves and hollows.

She winced as his palm fit firmly against her bottom and he stilled the movement. "I think I got a bruise there. I hit the floor pretty solid," she told him. He lightened his touch, and she shook her head, a quick movement. "It doesn't pain me any, Beau. Maybe my head a little, and my mouth is still a little raw feeling. Not enough to make me squirm, though. You can do me any which way you want to."

His words were even and without inflection, as if he would not influence her to his will. "And how about you, Mag? Do you want to touch me?"

"Well, I was thinking," she whispered, her lips brushing the curls at the base of his throat. "You know, when you kissed my bubbies, and it made me squirm all over the bed, and then you kinda pinched them a little bit with your teeth, and they got all puckered up and hard…'' She lifted her head, peering through her one uninjured eye to see his face. ''Maybe I shouldn't be talking like this, Beau.''

''You can say anything you like, honey.'' His hand snaked up her spine, his palm coming to rest on the back of her head. ''Feel what you've done to me, Maggie.'' His fingers cupped her nape and he pressed gently, guiding her face until her cheek brushed against the rise of his chest. There, where the muscles were firmest, a small, impudent button nudged her skin.

''My,'' she whispered softly, turning her head to taste his faintly salty flavor. Her lips formed against his male nipple, tugging it within her mouth.

From deep in his throat, a groan vibrated, and she grinned, the small bit of flesh escaping her mouth. Again, she found it, captured it and savored the male scent of him, a strangely musky aroma that wafted from his body. Deep inside her, where the memory of his presence remained, she felt a flutter of response, and her thighs clenched, gripping his leg in a firm hold.

''Maggie…'' A guttural whisper, like sandpaper against a wooden board, sent another quiver of excitement cascading to meet the first, and she felt the ridge of his manhood against her belly. It fascinated her, that hard, masculine portion of him that seemed to respond so readily to the pressure of her female parts. She'd felt it that first time, and even then, touching it with her fingertip, had wondered at his body's ability to prepare for the marriage thing they'd done together.

Lifting from him, she shifted to one side, her eager fingers seeking the solid flesh of his arousal. ''Can I do this?'' she asked politely, hesitant, yet yearning to discover for herself the measure of that masculine member.

"Sweetheart, you surely can," he whispered, and she felt a shiver vibrate beneath her touch. His hands fell to his sides and a sense of power such as she'd never known made her laugh aloud. She bent, smothering the sound against his chest, and his fingers clenched tightly in her hair, then loosened, weaving through the strands.

Against her palm, he twitched, and the flesh she held thickened and pulsed, a drop of fluid seeping against her fingers. "You gonna leak on me, Beau?" she asked, lifting to peer up at him anxiously.

"No." The single word was forced from him on a puff of air, and he inhaled quickly, shaking his head. "It's just part of what happens," he told her, shifting again, his body rising from the mattress. "Hold me tighter, Mag."

Her fingers tightened and she moved them, awkwardly at first, then more readily, in the rhythm he set. He was solid, yet the skin was soft, like the underside of the pups Maisie'd borne. But beneath the pulsing flesh was a heavy, firm shaft, and some hidden part of her own body ached to possess it within her. Her breath quickened at that thought. And then he moaned softly, his head tilting back against the pillow. Teeth bared, he shivered again, and his words were strained and harsh. "I think you'd better quit, honey."

"Am I hurting you, Beau?" Her hand released him and she lifted against his chest, peering fearfully at his half-closed eyes, his flaring nostrils and the intent expression he wore.

"It's a good hurt, a needy thing you've made me feel, Maggie." He rolled with her across the mattress, his arms coming to enclose her as he nudged his way between her thighs. He knelt there, lifting her legs to accommodate himself and she knew a moment's unease, the moonlight exposing her lower body to his gaze. He lifted her gown higher, and his hands were warm against her breasts, his fingers shaping her.

"I'm gonna pull this thing over your head," he told her, easing it up, then lifting and entangling her in the yards of white material. Arms caught up in the long sleeves, she wiggled to escape, and his whisper soothed her. "Just lay still there. You're fine, Mag." Her head was freed from the neckline and she twisted a bit, aware of his hands holding her arms, keeping her captive.

"Let me loose," she told him, and watched as he shook his head, bending to form her fingers to the iron bars of the headboard.

"Just hang on there," he said, and his mouth twisted in a smile that sent hot shards of fire to the center of her belly. "I want to show you something."

Her fingers gripped tightly, and she smothered a rush of apprehension. "I'm all naked, Beau. All but my arms." And even as the words were whispered, his head lowered and his lips formed against the crest of her breast.

"So you are," he murmured, his teeth and tongue once more rendering her helpless, suckling that tiny bit of flesh he held captive.

"I guess I know why you were wigglin' to beat the band." Her words sounded hoarse and her fingers curled against themselves around the metal bars, anchoring her to the bed.

"I like it when you wiggle," he murmured against her breast. "Do it again, honey."

She obliged him. Indeed, she could not have resisted the movement that sent her hips into motion, lifting against him, shifting, then settling once more against the mattress, only to rise again, to rub against the delicious friction of his body. A heated core deep inside her body demanded her attention, and her hips thrust again, her movements rapid and erratic.

"Let me help you," he said softly. His hands firm against her soft flesh, he touched her carefully, and she could not capture the small whimpers that surged from her throat. All else fled from her mind as he prepared her for his taking. And when she thought she could endure no more, that the pleasure he brought her would surely cause her heart to beat beyond bearing, he hesitated. She sobbed aloud, her cry a plea she could not stifle.

"Beau..." Her hands clenched tightly to the bars he bade her hold fast in her grip. Her hair was a heavy mass she'd tangled beneath her head, damp strands clinging to her forehead and cheeks.

"Shh..." As if he comforted her for what pain he might cause, he hushed her sharp cry, then easing carefully he pressed his way into her tender flesh. She rose to meet him, welcoming the thrust he could not halt. "Maggie, Maggie girl." Head bent, he rose from her and she whimpered, some instinct tightening her muscles.

And then he surged against her again, and she lifted her legs, enclosing him, lest he leave her bereft, with her need not met. For even now there was a promise of pleasure, foretold in each penetrating thrust, each anguished breath he drew, every shifting of his hips against her body. There—a shiver of delight pierced her to the core of her being, and she cried aloud. His mouth smothered the half-uttered sound and his tongue pressed for entry, imitating the movement of that male member deep within her.

How could it be? How could her body withstand the swirling, aching pleasure he gave? She formed her lips around his tongue, drawing it deeper still. Her hips heaved upward from the bed and his hands were harsh against her bottom, holding her fast for his own use. She ached for a breath, and as if he sensed her need, he released her mouth and her head whirled as she gasped wildly for air.

"Beau..." High and thin, her cry was desperate now, and as his fingers found her once more, she was engulfed by a madness that knew no name. *Complete.* She was complete, and the bliss of that single thought vibrated in the whispered syllable of his name.

He lay against her, heavy and replete, his breathing harsh. "Maggie...Maggie mine." He inhaled deeply, as if his lungs were starving for the scent of her, and his nose burrowed against her throat. "Sweetheart," he murmured, his lips blessing her skin, his mouth open and damp, his harsh breathing eased, his sigh a whisper.

Her womb knew his presence, felt the depth of his penetration, absorbed his seed, and welcomed it. Her grip on the bed loosened and he lifted his head, then leaned upward on his elbows, one hand reaching to release her from the bonds of her nightgown. Her arms slid readily from the sleeves and he murmured an apology.

"I shouldn't have done that to you." Taking her hand, he brought it to his lips. "I wouldn't have kept you captive for the wrong reasons, Maggie."

"I know that," she told him with a laugh. "You don't have it in you to cause me hurt." She flexed her fingers and spread them wide against his cheek. "I didn't know a body could feel such things as you did to me. It was a wonderment, all the aching and burning...and then when you were inside me—I felt so full, Beau, and so *complete.* It was like when you fold your fingers together to pray and they're all tangled up and nothing can make them come apart unless you want it to happen."

She laughed, feeling sheepish as she considered the words she'd allowed to pour forth. "You'll think I'm daft, saying all that foolishness in your ear."

"No." His head shook solemnly. "Not daft, never that. And it's not foolishness. Never think so, Mag. It's just another way of saying that you love me, and that you could tell how much I love you—when we were a part of each other."

"You make it sound real elegant," she told him. "I don't know the right words to say sometimes, but…"

"I know exactly what you mean," he said reprovingly, and then softened his words with kisses against her cheek. "*You* are elegant, Maggie. You carry yourself well. And sometimes you move like those pretty little weanlings out in the pasture, when they leap into the air and run the length of the fence line and you think that their feet aren't even touching the ground."

"You think so, Beau? Truly?" She was awed by his description, that he should think her akin to those beauties he cherished.

"Truly, Mrs. Jackson. Truly." He eased from her and drew her into his arms, tossing the nightgown to the floor beside the bed.

"Shouldn't I put it back on?" she asked, even as she snuggled against him.

"You want to?" His chuckle was lazy against her forehead.

She shook her head. "I don't believe I'll wear it at all anymore. Maybe just while I brush my hair and tend to things."

"Things? I'll agree to that," he said, his words slurred, and she smiled, a secret, warm delight filling her to the brim. "Maggie?" She tilted her head, listening to the sound of his voice speaking her name. "I liked it when you tended to me. I liked it real well."

Tom Clemons's big horse stood in front of the barn, the sheriff holding his reins. Maggie left the porch and walked across the yard, a sense of foreboding slowing her steps. Catching sight of Beau, inside the barn, her heart plummeted. He looked beyond serious, she thought, standing there in the shadows. Whatever the reason for the sheriff's visit, Beau did not welcome it.

He looked up, his gaze meeting hers, and she checked her pace. Perhaps this was none of her business. She drew to a stop next to the springhouse, glancing at the closed door. Distaste soured her throat, and she stepped closer, lifting the latch. It would get easier each time she entered the small shed. She'd already decided that. The milk from last evening's milking would be ready to use, and that task gave good reason for staying clear of the barn.

"Maggie?" Beau called her name and she halted, midway across the threshold. "Come on out here, honey. The sheriff wants to talk to you."

Surely Pa hadn't caused another fuss over the horse. That was water under the bridge. Sheriff Clemons wasn't the sort of man to allow Edgar's nastiness to reopen that mess. Well, whatever the problem, there was no stepping aside. Somehow, she was in the midst of it. Pulling the door closed, she walked toward Beau. He held out his hand and she grasped it, then found herself hauled against his side.

"There's news from your folks' farm," he said quietly.

Maggie's throat tightened and her single thought was spoken aloud. "Mama? Is my mother all right?"

Tom nodded. "She'll be fine, Maggie."

The words sounded ominous, couched in tones that spoke of past danger, and Maggie's head shot up, her eyes fixed on the sheriff's face. "What's happened to her?" And then she knew. Knew without a shadow of a doubt that Edgar had been at it again. "What did Pa do to her?" And wasn't that a foolish question. She'd seen her mother too many times with bruises and cuts and scrapes to be unaware of the damage a man's fists could cause.

Tom's flat statement gave proof to that assumption. "Looks like he pounded on her, Maggie. I sent your sisters out there to get her. She wouldn't leave with me."

Maggie's heart raced at that thought. "If Pa sees them he's liable to do his worst, Sheriff. You don't know what he's like." And then another thought intruded. "They didn't head out there without their husbands, did they?"

The sheriff shook his head. "All four of them went out this morning. They're probably on their way back to town now." He shifted uncomfortably, for the first time allowing his gaze to focus on her eye, then slide to her still-swollen mouth. "What happened to you?" he asked.

She cast a look at Beau, and found him to be no help whatsoever. If he was willing that she speak of Radley Bennett and Shay, she would do so. If Beau would rather she didn't tell of Rad's leaving, she'd keep quiet.

"Maggie?" Her silence prompted a nudge from Tom. "Who hit you, girl?"

"It wasn't my pa," she said defensively. "I haven't seen him since you threw me in jail."

"Well," Tom said slowly, "your pa's the reason I'm here."

"What did he do now?" Maggie blurted. "Besides pounding on my mother again."

Beau's arm tightened around her waist and she glanced up. "Someone shot your father, Maggie. He's dead." His eyes narrowed, as if he sought her reaction. If Beau thought for one minute she was going to sob and carry on over the death of a reprobate like Edgar O'Neill, he had another think coming. Her jaw tightened as she thought of the man who'd made her life a misery for nineteen years.

"I hope he died hard." Through gritted teeth, she uttered

words that would have shamed her, had they concerned anyone but Pa. With no sense of grief to bring tears, she lifted her head. "Who did it?"

Tom shrugged, glancing at Beau before he answered. "Don't know yet. A fella from west of here came into town last night and told me he'd stopped by your pa's place to pick up a jug of whiskey. Found Edgar on the ground near the porch. A shotgun was next to him."

"Did the man see my mother?" The thought of Verna alone in the house with a body in the yard just outside the kitchen made Maggie's stomach roil.

"Nope, just came into town and let me know that Edgar was dead. I went on out and found him and trundled him back on a wagon. Your ma was in the house, but she wouldn't let me in. I saw she was banged up pretty bad, but she was on her feet. So I told your sisters first thing this morning, and they went out to get her."

He shifted uncomfortably, allowing his gaze to return once more to Maggie's face. "Who hit you, Maggie?"

"If you're thinking I went over there and shot him, you're wrong, Sheriff. If I'd done that, I'd have brought my mother back here with me."

"I didn't think you'd shot him," Tom said. "How about you, Beau? Were you out to Edgar's place yesterday?"

"I had no reason to visit Edgar," Beau told him. "What've you got in mind, Tom? You think—" He shook his head. "You're wrong, you know. Maggie hasn't been anywhere but right here for the past two days. Neither have I."

"You had good reason, Beau. If someone hurt my woman, he'd have me after him in a skinny minute."

And didn't that sound reasonable? Maggie thought. Not true, but certainly worth a second thought. Especially if the sheriff was looking for a likely suspect. In this case, though, he was off the mark.

"The man who hit me worked for Beau," she said quietly. "Radley Bennett came around, looking to pick up his belongings, and he caught me in the springhouse."

"Rad Bennett? Thought he skipped town with your horse, Beau. I hadn't heard that he came back." A skeptical look slanted in Beau's direction, Tom thrust his hands into his pockets. "And you let him waltz off after he gave Maggie here a black eye?"

"He's gone," Beau said shortly. "Left in a big hurry a couple of days ago. Same day he hurt Maggie."

"You sent him on his way? Alive?" Tom repeated, his sober visage holding more than a mite of speculation.

"He was alive when he left here." Beau's jaw was tight, and even the narrowing of his dark eyes could not diffuse the heated anger in their depths. "I saw him heading for the woods beyond the orchard."

But not under his own power. The words burned in Maggie's mouth and she swallowed them.

Tom looked incredulous. "Let me get this straight. After hitting your wife, you let him walk away." He shook his head. "Somehow, I doubt that, Beau."

"Don't call Beau a liar, Tom Clemons." Anger blurred her vision as Maggie's hand flew up to push against the sheriff's chest. "Shay pounded the bejabbers out of the son of a pup. Rad left. If Beau says a thing is true, then you can bet your bottom dollar that it is."

"Maggie..." Beau's eyes crinkled with laughter as he drew her back from the assault. One-sided, to be sure, but Maggie in a snit was a sight to behold. For the first time since her arrival, she'd sailed into someone. And for his benefit. She stood stiffly in his grasp, obviously unwilling to back from her stance.

Tom eyed her askance, a crooked smile giving homage to her temper. "Sorry, Maggie. I didn't mean to discredit your husband. But, you can see that I'm between a rock and a hard place here. We got a dead man waitin' to be buried, and not much to go on. From the looks of you, Beau might have good reason to lose his temper with your pa." He shrugged and glanced at Beau. "Can't say that I'd blame you any."

"Well, you'll have to look elsewhere, Tom. I didn't shoot Edgar." A thought entered his mind and he squeezed Maggie closer to his side. "Matter of fact, you might want to talk to Cord McPherson. He was here yesterday, and bought a couple of yearlings from me. I think he'll tell you that I was at home and Maggie was already wearing the bruises she's got today."

"You don't say." Tom rocked back on his heels. "Well, we'll leave it at that for now, Beau. Probably the judge will hold a hearing next week, just to clear things up."

"We're not going anywhere," Beau told him. "We'll do whatever you like."

Tom swung into his saddle and turned the horse with a movement of his reins. "I reckon I'd better start lookin' further, hadn't I? That gun's got to belong to someone. I just can't figure out why a man would walk off and leave his shotgun layin' in the dirt."

Maggie slid her arm around his waist, fitting herself neatly against his side, and Beau held her snugly. "You all right, Mag?" She would not grieve, of that he was certain. Worrying about her mother would be enough to keep her occupied. And he'd guarantee that a trip to town was in the offing.

"I hated him."

Forlorn didn't begin to describe her words, Beau decided. He turned her, lifting her chin with his index finger.

"Don't let it be a canker inside you, honey. He can't hurt you anymore."

Tears filled her eyes as he watched and her chin trembled against his touch. "Why couldn't he have been like you, Beau? Even a little bit?" Jerking her head away, she swiped at the tears angrily. "It's not fair that one man can make four lives so miserable. He didn't do diddly squat for my mama, just acted mean as sin every livelong day."

"He's gone now, Maggie. You need to think about your mother."

She spun back, tears forgotten. "Can we go see her? I'll bet she's with Emily. Em was always her favorite."

"She'd choose Emily over you?" Beau shook his head. "Can't imagine such a thing." His levity produced the desired effect, and Maggie smiled, fishing in her pocket for a handkerchief.

"You been stealing my kerchiefs?" he asked, taking it from her hand and wiping gently at the mute evidence of her distress.

She nodded. "I don't have any."

"We'll have to solve that problem today. We'll stop at the store and buy some."

Her chin set and her glare was mutinous. "There you go again, Beau Jackson. Every time I open my mouth, you're off buying me something else."

Making Maggie understand her position in his life would take more than a day or so, he decided. "You can earn it out."

"Doing what?" She glanced up at him. "How much do I have to do for you to buy me a couple of hankies?"

"Come on," he told her, hustling her toward the house. "Put on a dress and we'll go to town to see your mother. I'll think of a chore for you to do later on."

"Boss?" From within the barn, Pony caught his attention, and Beau turned. "Do you need the mare harnessed to the buggy?"

Beau nodded. Pony was never far afield. "That'll work," he said. "We'll be ready to leave in a few minutes."

"Miss Maggie?" Pony stepped across the threshold, removing his hat. "I know your pa wasn't much good, but he was still your pa. It's too bad, the way he died."

Maggie inclined her head. "Thank you, Pony. I reckon there wouldn't have ever been a good way for him to kick the bucket. He was a hateful man from the word go. I'm just glad my mama doesn't have to put up with him anymore."

"What will she do, Mag?" Beau asked. "It's going to be hard on her. She must have known he was out there with a hole in him. No matter what, she's got to be upset over things."

They turned to the house and Maggie leaned against him. "I wonder who did it?"

"Did your pa have a shotgun?"

She nodded. "He kept one in the barn and another in the house. Said that a man in his business had to be ready for trouble." Her shoulders slumped beneath his arm. "I can't believe it, Beau. That he's dead, I mean. I wished him gone so many times, and now, I don't have to worry about him anymore. I can go visit Mama without looking over my shoulder."

And that was another issue they needed to face, Beau thought. Apparently Maggie hadn't thought that far ahead. "I doubt your mother will want to stay on the farm by herself," he said. "She probably isn't strong enough to do the barn work, let alone anything else."

Maggie cast a scornful look at him. "What barn work? Pa put all his apples in one bushel, Beau. That still was his livelihood. The animals were only there for what he could get out of them. He used the horses to haul his whiskey barrels on a sledge, and made Mama take care of the chickens and milk the cow. The damn stalls wouldn't ever have been cleaned if I didn't do it, nor the chicken house mucked out. I grew up with a pitchfork in my hand, back when he had four stalls full of livestock.''

"And now what?" Beau asked. "Is there a cow out there, waiting to be milked?"

Maggie's jaw dropped. "I didn't even think of that. She must be in misery by now."

Chapter Sixteen

"What am I supposed to do with two cows?" Beau asked in bemusement, watching as Joe led the rescued creature into the big barn.

"Maybe you can find someone needy enough to take her in," Maggie suggested. "I have a notion Mama won't be going back to the farm. It looked like Emily and Roberta gathered up every blessed thing she owned when they took her to town."

"Probably the smartest thing to do. As for the cow, we'll check around," Beau said agreeably. "Let's get a bite to eat first, then we'll go to Green Rapids and see to burying your pa." So sleekly he slid in the words, and Maggie waited for an aching to commence. *Burying Pa* held no pain for her, only the knowledge that from now on she would know freedom from the bygone fears she'd harbored for so long.

And Mama would never again suffer at his hands. That alone was cause to rejoice. Maggie's step was firm as she walked beside Beau to the house. He would tend to things. And she would let him. Leaning on a man's strength was getting to be easier by the day.

Sophie spent long moments helping Maggie prepare for

what she deemed would be an ordeal. "Let me fix you up a little, girl," she said firmly, and without waiting for permission, she began. Standing behind Maggie, she brushed her hair until it shimmered. Then, beginning at the crown, she worked the long locks into an intricate braid. Then, winding it into a circle at the back of Maggie's head, she pinned it in place.

"Now you look like a dignified lady," Sophie announced, standing back to view her work. Maggie's hands rose to investigate, and her fingers splayed wide over the arrangement.

"It feels pretty."

"You look beautiful," Beau told her, aware that his words spoke the truth. She was a beauty. Even with the evidence of cruelty apparent, she looked every inch a woman to be proud of. Perhaps the tilt of her head, or the erect posture she'd gradually assumed over the past weeks made a difference. Or maybe the clear honesty of blue eyes that met his without hesitation. She bore little resemblance to the ragamuffin he'd taken into his household.

Her strength amazed him. Not just the physical stamina she possessed, but the maturity with which she met obstacles and surmounted them. She was ready now to comfort her mother and bury her father. Even the distress she would face in the day ahead was not enough to bow her head. No doubt her fertile mind was already awash with arrangements to be made.

Sophie retied the sash at Maggie's back, then stood back. "Turn around," she said gruffly, her narrowed gaze taking in her handiwork. "Hate to see that pretty dress covered up with your coat," she said after a moment. And then shot a look at Beau.

He'd forgotten. In the confusion of the past days, the memory of the package in the storeroom had fled from his mind. "Wait a minute," he said, turning to retrieve the bundle from where he'd stowed it. "I want your mama to see you this time as Mrs. Beau Jackson. She needs to know I'm taking care of you."

And then he winced as he thought of the black eye Maggie sported. There was no help for it. At least he could present her with a flourish upon arrival at Emily's house. No doubt Verna wouldn't take much notice of a bruise, so inured to the condition herself.

The package fell open once he tugged the string from place and brown paper scattered as Beau lifted a cloak from the wrappings. It swirled through the air and settled in folds of maroon wool, the fastenings of black braid accented by velvet of the same hue, lining the hem and front facings. Maggie looked at him, ignoring the gift, her eyes focused on the giver.

"You spoil me, Beau. I don't feel worthy of all this." Tears gathered, then overflowed and she allowed them to fall, unheeded. "I have so much, and Mama always had to get by on less than nothing." Her mouth twisted, her lips folding tightly as she lifted her hand to touch the soft fabric. "Maybe..." She was hesitant, and yet he knew her mind, knew the intricate path her reasoning took.

"We'll get her one just like it, if you want to. I had Mrs. Lewis make it for you. She can sew another in a few days, I'm sure."

"You had it made up special for me?"

"I wanted a long cape to keep you warm. Cora, at the Emporium, told me Mrs. Lewis sewed nicely. I'm glad you like it, Mag. Let me help you put it on."

Her gaze was hungry, her nod hesitant. "Maybe I'll just wear it to town, and take my coat along. We can give it to Mama and you can order up another for me, if you want to."

"Will that make you happy?" he asked, knowing the answer even as he spoke.

Her nod was quick. "Happier, Beau. I'm already about as full of pleasure as a body can get, and seeing Mama in this will make it overflow, I'm sure."

He wrapped her in the garment, showed her the intricate braided fastenings, and watched as her fingers brushed the surface of ebony buttons and fancy black loops. Reaching for the hood, he drew it over her head, settling it with care, so as not to muss her hair. Then, extending his arm, he gestured toward the door.

"We need to be on our way, Maggie. Pony's got the buggy waiting." He snatched her coat from the hook and carried it over his other arm, then led her from the house.

He'd managed to insert some small amount of happiness into this grim undertaking, and he reveled in Maggie's quiet joy as they traveled the road to town. She was silent, and he glanced at her, recognizing the depths of her fears for her mother's well-being. Yet, even that could not spoil her pleasure in the gift he'd offered. Her fingers brushed the fine fabric, her eyes took full measure of the enveloping folds surrounding her, and she nestled beside him, chin held high, defiant in the face of despair.

A quick burial suited the family. Since her daughters decreed Verna unfit to walk behind the undertaker's wagon to the churchyard, the three sons-in-law trudged along in their stead. There was a certain irony in the whole thing, Beau thought, that such a heathen be buried in the hallowed ground, and yet it was Verna's choice. Perhaps there was some spark left of the love she'd borne him in the beginning. Whatever, he would not deny her any small amount of comfort this ceremony might bring.

Back in Emily's kitchen, the womenfolk settled around

her table. The upright, well-starched Wilhelmina Bryant became as one of them in that hour, her stern visage a thing of the past as she took on the guise of friend. Reflecting on the future they would face as four women freed from the tyranny of Edgar O'Neill, the sisters drank tea from china cups and ate cookies baked in the parsonage kitchen.

Verna ate slowly and Maggie knew her pain, her own mouth still painful. "Will you come home with me?" Maggie asked, seeking her mother's gaze. "Beau has room enough, and you'd like Sophie."

"She can stay here if she wants to," Emily put in.

"Amos won't care if she stays in our spare room," Roberta said stoutly. "I'll bet she'd like it here in town."

Verna shook her head. "I need to go back to the farm. The cow and chickens will need tending. I only came to get your pa put in the ground, decent-like."

"Beau went out and got the cow already, Mama," Maggie said. "He fed the chickens plenty for a couple of days. You don't need to worry about going back to the farm."

Wilhelmina stood and reached for the tray of cookies she'd brought, replenishing the plate on the table. "Sounds to me like you've got a slew of choices, Verna. You're lucky your girls all want you close at hand. I'm not even going to offer my extra bedroom. I'll just fix you a cup of tea now and then and have you come to visit."

So quickly they had drawn together, Maggie thought. Five women, sharing tea and planning for the future of one who had lived without hope. Verna looked around the table and she sighed. "Mercy sakes, I don't know what to tell y'all. With so many places to go…" Her voice trailed off and she brushed her hand across her mouth.

"Paul said he thought he could sell the farm for you, Mama," Emily said quietly. "I, for one, don't think you should go back out there. Roberta and me brought all your stuff along.''

Verna nodded slowly. ''Maybe I'll go home with Maggie. She'll need help with her chickens and I can still milk a cow. I'd feel like I was payin' my way.''

So easily it was solved. Maggie drew in a deep breath. There was only one more question to be asked, and she dreaded it being voiced aloud. But, it could not be helped. So long as the sheriff thought Beau suspect, the person who pulled the trigger and blasted a hole in Edgar O'Neill must be identified.

''Mama?'' she asked, drawing four pair of eyes in her direction. ''Did you see Pa get shot? Do you know who it was?''

Verna's pale skin grew even more ashen, the purpling of her cheek a vivid hue. She glanced away from Maggie, her gaze seeking the floor, and then she rose from her chair and walked slowly to the window, lifting a hand to touch the glass pane.

''I never thought to see so many windows in a house,'' she murmured. ''All these bitty little panes, all shiny in the sunlight. It brings the world right inside, don't it?''

The women at the table watched her, a hush enclosing them. Maggie's heart fluttered in her chest as a thought awakened within her, and she stifled it quickly, rising to go to her mother. ''You don't have to talk about it now, Mama,'' she whispered. ''But, when the judge holds a hearing, he'll want to know what you saw.''

''Don't you think they're about done with the burying?'' Verna asked, looking past Maggie to where the women waited.

''Maybe so,'' Wilhelmina allowed. ''I doubt there was a lot to be said. I know my husband wasn't looking forward to this.''

"Why don't we get your things packed up?" Emily said brightly, rising from the table. She clasped Verna's hands and led her from the room, casting a worried glance behind her.

"Does she know what happened?" Maggie asked softly. "You went out there, Roberta. What did she say?"

Roberta shrugged, shaking her head. "You wouldn't believe it, Mags. She acted like nothing happened at all. We walked past where Pa got shot, and the snow was all messed up and she didn't even give it a second glance." Her eyes swept to the doorway and beyond as she leaned forward, speaking quietly. "Do you think she's tryin' to forget? Maybe she knows and maybe she doesn't. I don't think she's about to tell us, either way."

"How did you manage it?" Beau asked, settling between the sheets, his sigh of contentment muffled against Maggie's forehead.

She snuggled closer, fitting herself to his masculine frame, delighting in the strength of his body. "She just packed her duds. The fact is, she'd barely taken things out of the pillowcase she brought them in, so it didn't take long."

Beau's hands ceased their motion against her back. "You mean to tell me that everything your mother has in this world is in that sack I carried in?"

Maggie nodded, her head moving against his shoulder. "Everything she'll need from the old place. Just her clothes and house shoes." She leaned back, seeking his face in the darkness. "She never had much. Just a change of clothes. Sometimes not even that."

"She'll have more here, Mag," he vowed. "We'll let her pick out clothes at the Emporium, maybe next week.

In the meantime, if she needs anything, Sophie should be able to put something together for her."

Maggie smothered her laugh and hugged Beau, winding her arms around his neck. "Poor Sophie. You keep giving her strays to tend to and she's liable to quit."

"Not a chance, honey. Didn't you see how she took to your mother? They'll be old friends in no time flat."

Maggie's eyes felt moist, imagining her mother, even now half buried in the thick feather tick, in the room across the hall. "She's never had such beauty around her, Beau. Mama always had to make do, and Pa never gave her much, always just enough to get from one day to the next."

"Why did she put up with him?" Beau's voice was gruff against her ear, rumbling in his chest. "You'd think she'd have been fed up a long time ago."

"Where would she go? And what would she do when she got there?" Maggie asked sourly. "There's no place for a woman in this world, lessen she's got a man to keep her in food and clothing. We're all beholden to whatever man is willing to take us on."

She held her breath as Beau seemed to digest her words. Then with a quick movement, he rolled her to her back, looming above her. "Is that how you feel? That you're beholden to me, because I've *taken you on?*" She heard the abruptness he made no attempt to soften, caught the trace of pain in his words and rued the harsh reality of her words.

Lifting her hand to his cheek, she breathed a denial. "Not you, Beau. Never you."

As if deaf to her concession, his pain spewed forth. "You own half of my ranch, Maggie. Does that sound like I'm trying to make you bow down to me? As if I'm keeping you under my thumb?"

She shook her head, rebuking his words. "I was raised

by a man who was cruel and mean and hateful. But that's not reason enough to lump you in the same pot—and God help me, I didn't mean to." She gripped his nape with a strength honed by long hours of toil, dragging him from his position above her, catching him off guard. His mouth was before her, tempting, yet narrowed with a residue of anger she could not fault.

In the darkness, she caught only glimpses of deep-set eyes and ridged cheekbones. And then as she lifted her head, she inhaled the masculine essence he wore. She would recognize it anywhere. Given a roomful of men, she would scent him out, as would any female creature when offered her choice of mates.

Her mouth claimed his and for the first time she sensed a withholding in his kiss. His lips failed to part, his jaw remained tense beneath her fingertips, and against her cupped palm his nape was firm, with taut tendons that refused to obey her command.

"Beau—please, Beau." She'd thought never to beg for anything in her whole life, not even mercy at her father's hands. And now, here in her marriage bed, she beseeched the man she'd married, asking for a softening, a warming of his harshness. This was a side of Beau Jackson she'd never been exposed to, for when he turned his rage upon Rad Bennett she had not suffered for it.

Tears slipped from her eyes and she closed her lids, hoping to contain them. Deep within, she knew it would be unfair to ask for sympathy, and she prided herself, above all things, on the innate fairness by which she judged her actions. Her fingers released him, sliding from the dark hair, brushing against his neck, across his jaw and finally resting against his broad chest.

"I love you." It was all she had to offer, more than an apology for her thoughtless words, yet perhaps not enough to dispel the pain she'd inflicted. "I love you, Beau." Barely whispered, they were the cry of her heart. He hadn't moved, and from that fact she found comfort. Surely, if his anger did not abate, he would roll aside, turn from her, rise from the bed and stalk away, perhaps to gaze from the window into the starry sky.

Yet he held himself above her, for long moments only the harsh sounds of his breathing marring the silence. And then he bent his arms, resting against the mattress, hands on either side of her head, elbows enclosing her. She felt the soft whisper of his sigh, and then her name, spoken with an intonation she recognized.

"Maggie...Maggie girl." He bent his head, barely an inch, his mouth gifting her with the sweetest of caresses, lips touching and tasting with tenderness, and all the while the soft, subtle speaking of her name. "I spoke harshly." Barely audible, his mouth touched her ear and the words were like manna to her soul. "I love you, sweetheart."

He rolled with her, tucking her against himself, his face against her hair, his hands filled with its dark length, holding fistfuls, then spreading it behind her. "I love everything about you, Mag. Your blue eyes, the way your hair hangs down your back, the way you smile at me, and the magic way you touch me."

"I'm sorry, Beau. I say mean things before I think—"

"No, it's not that, honey. It's a matter of trusting me to take care of you, knowing that I'll always share everything I have with you. You haven't learned that yet. But, so help me, if it takes the rest of my life, I'll make you understand that I'm in this for the long haul. And I don't do things halfway."

"I *know* all that," she whispered. "I do trust you, Beau. You'd ought to know that by now. It was just for a minute there, thinking about my mother and..."

"Hush." His fingers found her mouth and he pressed them there, stilling her protest. "We won't talk about it, not ever again. I jumped on you." His chuckle was low, his words humble. "I caused you pain, Maggie. As much as you hurt me, I returned the hurt, and that's not fair. You needn't ever beg me, not for anything. Not ever again."

"My mother won't know what to make of you," she whispered, her lips moving against his fingers. "She'll think she's died and gone to heaven, and you're one of the archangels."

"You know about archangels?" he asked.

She nodded. "Mama told us about angels when we were young enough to believe in such things."

"You don't believe now?"

He expected an answer, and Maggie searched her heart for the right words. "I didn't, not for a long time. I about made up my mind that Mama was wasting her breath, praying every day for something that was never going to happen." She closed her eyes and knew a sense of profound sorrow as she remembered the words her mother had whispered only days past.

"Maggie?" Beau spoke her name with urgency. "Maggie. Look at me."

"She prayed for him to die, Beau. I heard her, more times than I can count, praying that God would..." Her eyes opened wide and she stared into Beau's shocked expression.

"Beau? Do you think...did Mama kill him?"

Verna was changing, right before Maggie's eyes. Not once, but on two occasions, she'd chuckled at Rascal's foolishness. And for the first time in years, Maggie saw her mother as more than the target for Edgar O'Neill's miserable temper. As her bruises faded, her bowed head lifted higher. Her voice became stronger, and wonder of wonders, she'd laughed. Now, in the early morning hours, that same sound drifted up the stairway, reaching the bedroom.

"Beau? Did you hear that?"

"Hmm…" He turned from the window, buttoning his shirt. Maggie clutched the bedpost, her head tilted to one side. "Did I hear what?"

She lifted her hand, finger touching her lips. "Shh… listen, Beau."

And then it rose again from the kitchen below, the unmistakable sound of two women, one of them speaking, the other laughing in response. "Your mother?" he asked.

Maggie nodded, her eyes glazed with tears. "I haven't heard that sound…maybe it's been forever. Mama doesn't laugh. Once in a while, she smiles, but most of the time, she just looks hopeless."

"Not lately, she doesn't," Beau reminded her. "Between her and Sophie, they've about baked and cooked the pantry full, and had a good time doing it." He tucked his shirt in and fastened his belt. "We're going to be celebrating Christmas in a big way, if they have anything to say about it."

"I think Mama's looking better, don't you?"

He nodded. "Give her a couple of weeks, and she'll be rounding out, same way you did." Stepping closer, he stood behind her, his hands itching to possess the curves he viewed.

"Me?" Her tone was offended as she looked down at her slender form in a critical survey. "You think I'm getting fat?"

"Not yet, sweetheart. But one of these days you'll be rounding out, right about here," he murmured over her shoulder, his arms circling her waist, allowing his hands to rest against her belly.

Maggie bent her head, and her fingers covered his. "Would you like that?"

"You betcha, I would," he stated emphatically. "Now that we've got your mama here to help out, we can concentrate on making it happen." Beau nuzzled her neck and she obliged him, tilting her head. She smelled sweet, her skin was smooth and soft, and he pulled her firmly against himself.

Again, laughter pealed from below, and Maggie turned quickly in his embrace, winding her arms around his neck. "You made this happen, and I love you for it," she whispered. "I don't know what all they're having such a good time over down there, but my mama's acting like a young girl, Beau. She's not walking all stooped over anymore, and she's been taking a bath almost every day, just because she can."

"I'm thinking we need to put that tub in the storage room and leave it there," Beau said. "In fact, I'd ought to order a regular bathing tub and install it. Conrad says he's gotten them for most everyone in town. I'll get some pipe and lay it under the ground come spring, let it drain out back."

Maggie's eyes widened. "You can do that? We could take a bath without having to carry the water out to the porch?"

"Folks do it all the time in town," he said. "I don't know why we can't." He bent to kiss her and then whispered a suggestion that elicited a gasp from her lips.

"Beau! There's no way two people can fit in a tub, not at the same time." She pushed against his chest. "You're just pulling my leg."

"We could give it a shot," he told her. "It'd sure be fun to try."

The brown scarf was almost completed. She'd only had a scant few minutes here and there to work at it for the most part, and compared to Sophie's work, it was woefully inadequate. Maggie held it before her, her narrowed gaze critical as she noted several lumpy areas, and the uneven edges. It hung from her hands to the floor, certainly long enough to wrap around Beau's neck with enough left over to tuck across his chest beneath his coat.

"You might want to cast off the stitches now," Sophie said from across the room. "I believe it's about as long as it needs to be." Amusement colored her words and Maggie ignored the gibe.

"I don't know how," she said after a moment. "I'm not very good at this."

"He'll like it, no matter now long it is," Verna assured her, turning from the stove. "He likes everything you do, girl."

Maggie felt her cheeks burn. Beau was not above wrapping his arms around her, no matter who watched, and her mother had viewed more than one embrace right here in the kitchen. "He's good to me, Mama. I wanted to make him something, just from me."

"All you gotta do is exist, Maggie. Just being his wife appears to be enough for Beau. I heard him singing to you last night after we went to bed. He plays that guitar real pretty."

"He's teaching me," Maggie told her. "One day I'll show you the books he got me." Her hesitation was long, aware that her mother felt keenly her own lack of education. "I'm learning to read, Mama, and Beau taught me to cipher."

"I should have done that for you, girl, at least taught you what little I know." Verna spoke softly, her words heavy with regret. "There wasn't ever book number one to read from, and your pa made it hard to do any teaching.

He didn't ever hold with girls getting any schooling. I was lucky I got to send Emily and Roberta for a couple of years. By the time it was your turn, he thought y'all needed to stay home and work the fields.''

"It's all right," Maggie told her, clutching the scarf and needles to her chest as she rose from her chair. She turned, deposited the project on the table, then went to her mother's side. Her arms enclosed the frail woman and she bent her head to rest against Verna's shoulder. "I love you, Mama. You did the best you could."

"I didn't protect you, Maggie. You took too many licks from your pa. He made you the scapegoat, mostly 'cause you was the spunkiest of the lot." Her tone was gruff. "I reckon you needed to be, runnin' away like you did." Her hand was soothing against Maggie's face. "And now, just look at you."

"You better hide that scarf." Sophie stepped to the window. "Rascal's makin' a fuss. Sounds like the men are on their way in for dinner."

Maggie snatched her project up from the table and stuffed it in a tapestry bag. Too small for her own handwork anymore, Sophie had passed it along for Maggie's benefit. "When can you show me how to end this thing?" she asked, brushing past Sophie to stash the evidence on a pantry shelf.

"Maybe tonight."

But it was not to be. Midafternoon brought the sheriff to the door, and before the day was over preparations were being made for a trip to town. Tomorrow morning was designated as the time for a hearing, and Sophie spent the evening taking in a dress for Verna to wear. The three women worked in the kitchen long after dark, and finally Maggie slipped into the parlor, where Beau sat in the overstuffed chair, next to the lamp table. A book lay across his lap, and his head was tilted back.

She hesitated in the doorway, watching the rise and fall of his chest, aware of the soft sounds he emitted as he succumbed to slumber. And then her stockinged feet moved quickly across the carpet and she knelt beside him, her head resting against his thigh. The warmth of his palm cupped her head and he shifted, bending forward.

"Maggie? Are you all right?" he whispered, his long fingers slipping through her hair. He loosened the braid she wore, lifting it from her back and releasing the short piece of yarn she'd tied it with. Brown yarn.

"About as all right as a body can get," she murmured. "All but for worrying about tomorrow, I suppose."

Beau drew her hair onto his lap, admiring the shimmering depths of color in the lamplight. "Tomorrow will take care of itself," he told her. "Things will work out."

"The judge is going to want to know what happened, Beau. And no one has any answers, at least not that I know of." She clutched at his wrist and brought his hand to rest against her cheek. "Did the sheriff say anything to you?"

Her face was flushed and he traced the line of her jaw, massaging the tension there. "He's got some ideas, I suppose. It might have been one of your pa's customers."

"Maybe." She sounded dubious and Beau privately agreed. And then her head lifted and she met his gaze. "Will they question Mama?"

"Probably. She was there, honey." He'd held it in for three days now, and it was time to tell her what he'd found out. "When I went to the farm the other day to gather up the chickens I brought your pa's shotgun from the barn, Maggie. You told me he kept one in the house, too."

A flare of comprehension lit her gaze. "The one in the

house? It was gone, wasn't it? Probably the one that killed him, Beau.''

''We'll let the judge figure it out, honey. Myself, I don't care how it happened. I never thought to be joyful over a man's death, but I was proven wrong.''

''It's sad that no one mourned him,'' Maggie whispered. ''And I can't bring myself to be the first, Beau.''

''Come up here on my lap.'' He lifted her from the floor and she curled in his arms, her head against his shoulder. ''No matter what happens tomorrow, your mother will be all right. Sheriff Clemons might know more than he's saying, but my guess is that he's as much in the dark as any of us.''

The judge looked like any ordinary man, sitting behind the tall desk in the courtroom. His collar was too tight, and his glasses slid down his nose as he looked at Verna and her daughters. ''I understand y'all are the survivors of Edgar O'Neill,'' he intoned, peering back at the papers in front of him. ''Now we need to decide just what happened to the man.'' Still perusing the document, he waved his hand. ''Take a seat, ladies.''

The three sisters settled into wooden chairs, Verna in their midst, their husbands in a row behind them. The judge leaned to one side, murmuring in Tom Clemons's ear then sat erect once more, clearing his throat. His gavel pounded the desk, and Maggie stiffened in her seat.

From the back of the small courtroom, a man entered, carrying a shotgun. Reaching upward, he placed it on the desk before the judge. ''This here's the gun they brought in with O'Neill's body.'' Turning on his heel, he shot a quick grin at the four women. ''Nuthin' to worry about,'' he whispered, bending to offer encouragement.

The judge took note of the weapon. ''Anybody here in

the courtroom recognize this weapon?'' he asked sternly, his gaze raking the group assembled.

''I can't tell one gun from another,'' Emily said firmly, and Roberta nodded her agreement.

''It looks like the one my pa kept in the barn,'' Maggie said quietly. Beside her, Verna moved restlessly, and Maggie's hand reached to enclose the woman's fingers, halting their fitful movement. Verna looked up at her, her chin trembling, her lips pressed into a tight line. ''Hold tight, Mama,'' Maggie whispered. ''We'll be out of here in no time.''

''Well, I'd say the perpetrator is unknown,'' the judge said, his eyes kindly as he inspected the women before him. If he took special note of Verna's fading bruises, he did not linger, but allowed his gaze to sweep past the four women to the men behind them. ''I think you gentlemen need to take your ladies home now. We'll probably never know what happened to…'' He bent to read the name from the paper in his hand. ''Edgar O'Neill died from an unknown hand,'' he repeated, banging his gavel twice against the desk. ''And that's the decision of this court.''

''I didn't even have to testify,'' Verna whispered. ''He didn't even ask me anything.'' She stood, her daughters rising as one, surrounding her with loving arms. Behind them, Beau met the judge's eye and nodded his thanks. The statue of justice in the corner of the courtroom made more sense to him today than ever before. She was blind, perhaps because she saw with her heart, as did the man sitting at the bench.

Emily's kitchen was once more the scene of a family gathering, and in the midst of voices raised and relieved laughter, Verna was silent and subdued. Around her the talk was of Christmas and gifts and the church service to be held only two days hence to celebrate the holiday.

Maggie was vigilant, watching as her mother sat quietly, listening to the family around her. Trembling fingers held the teacup to her lips and then replaced it carefully in its saucer. Pushing back from the table, Verna rose, and the voices around her were silent, hushed by the pale, anguished look she cast from one to another of her family members.

"I got something to say to y'all, and I need to tell you this, so don't be hushin' me up." She walked to the far wall where a wide window looked out upon Emily's garden, and then turned to face her daughters. Her words fell like stones against hard ground, firm and implacable.

"I shot Edgar myself. Didn't anybody else pull the trigger but me. I hit him with two blasts, just in case one didn't do the trick."

Facing her audience with defiance evident in her uplifted chin, she drew in a deep breath. Bruised and battered she might have been in the past, but today Verna spoke without fear. "It was time and beyond that somebody called a halt to his meanness, and I couldn't see that anybody else was about to do it." With deliberate movements she unbuttoned the cuff of her sleeve and shoved it up to her elbow. Bruises, yellowed but still evident, came into view and Maggie smothered a cry of pain.

"There's more like this just about everywhere you look," Verna announced, and then with care, she replaced the sleeve and fastened the cuff. "I figured I could either let him into the house with his jug of whiskey and watch him get drunker than a skunk again, or I could use his shotgun and save myself another day of misery. When he started up the steps I just opened the door and let him have it, both barrels right in the chest."

She tightened her jaw. "I should have done it a long time ago, instead of lettin' my girls be worked like slaves." Tears flowed now as Verna's gaze touched each of her daughters. "I'm sorry I ever let him touch y'all the first time."

"It's all past now, Mama," Roberta said quickly.

"We love you." Emily's words were fierce, and her eyes snapped as she spoke. "And no one else needs to know about this. There ain't a judge in the world would blame you for what you did."

"There ain't a judge in the world will ever get the chance," Amos said firmly. "What we know goes no further. Agreed?" The other two men nodded without hesitation.

"The judge made his decision," Beau reminded them. "It's finished. No matter what, it's over."

Epilogue

"'There were in the same country shepherds abiding in the field, keeping watch over their flock by night.'" Verna lifted her head, pausing to wipe at her eyes with a brand-new white hankie. "I haven't read those words in years," she said. "Not since—well, not in a long time."

"Keep reading, Mama," Maggie urged. Sitting on the floor beside the sofa, she smiled up at her mother. "What's the next line say?"

Verna read on and Beau heard the familiar story anew, each word already tucked away in his memory, brought forth now on this Christmas Eve he would never forget. The days of childhood, when his father read the verses with majestic, booming tones, then later, when he'd sat in the back pew of various churches during his wandering years, listening as black-frocked ministers told the ancient story anew to their people.

"'...a multitude of the heavenly host, praising God, and saying...'" Verna's voice was stronger now, and Maggie leaned even closer, one hand clasping her mother's knee.

So might his children one day sit, Beau thought. Watching the candles flicker on the Christmas tree, hearing the familiar words of the story, maybe even listening to their grandmother's voice. Family was a wondrous thing. His children would know the love of parents and a grandmother, probably grow up with Sophie in their midst.

Verna looked up and met his gaze. Her index finger marked the stopping place and she veered from the words to speak directly to Beau. "My Maggie girl said you wouldn't take offence by her givin' me your mama's Bible. Did she speak true?"

Beau nodded. "I gave it to Maggie. It was hers to do with. If it pleases her to see it in your hands, then I'm happy, too. When you've finished with it one day, it can come back to Maggie." Her hand brushed the crown of Maggie's head, her smile in agreement with his words. "Maybe," he suggested, "you can use it to help her with her reading, evenings when we sit in the parlor."

Verna nodded. "Reading words puts them in your mind. You never forget. Even when you don't get a chance to dwell on the music, you can hear it in your head."

"Music?" Puzzled by her choice of words, Beau lifted his brow.

"Can't you hear the music?" Verna asked him. "The good book's got melodies all through it. You just hafta listen for them." She bent her head once more.

"'…and on earth peace, good will toward men.'" The parlor was silent, snug against the wind blowing beyond the windows, warm with more than the heat from the woodstove. In the circle of light shed by the parlor lamp, Maggie shifted, rising to her knees.

"Beau, do you want to open your present?" she asked, and he caught a look of apprehension in the depths of blue eyes. Not waiting for his bidding, she rose, turning toward the tree to search amidst the wrapped gifts. A bulky package, bundled carefully and tied with a length of yarn was deposited in his lap and he touched it with care. No matter the contents, it would be priceless, for Maggie's were the hands that had given it.

His fingers fumbled a bit as he untied the brown yarn, and his memory traced a night not long gone when her braid had been tied with a piece of the same color. When her hair had shimmered in lamplight and his hands had found silken treasure there, her scent rising to tempt him.

The wrapping was simple, but Beau's instincts told him to move slowly, and he did, each corner lifted and examined, peering within the folds to find a soft, misshapen length of knitted wool. His mind noted the uneven stitches, his fingers touched the imperfect edges, and his heart rejoiced. That Maggie should have spent her time in the making of a gift for him was reason to reach for her, gather her in his arms and draw her onto his lap.

"Put it around my neck," he told her, amused at the blush riding her cheeks. Then watched closely as she obeyed, his gaze taken by the graceful movement of her hands, his skin warmed by the brush of her fingertips. "Thank you," he said solemnly as she adjusted the length of knitted yarn across his chest, as he would wear it beneath his coat. "No one's ever given me so wonderful a gift."

Maggie's mouth curved in a smile that denied his words, her eyes crinkling at the corners as she shook her head. "I'd wager you've had…" She hesitated, as if determining some enormous number to quote.

Beau filled the expectant silence. "Nothing I've ever received, no Christmas gift, that is, has given me more pleasure than this." He lifted his hand from where it rested in her lap, and his fingers gathered brown yarn into his palm. And thought of that other gift he'd not mentioned, here where propriety deemed it inappropriate.

He'd tell her later, tonight in the darkness, when his arms held her close and their hearts beat in tandem. He'd speak of her love and the manifestation of it, when she'd come to him, unwrapped the gift of her body in his sight, and given it with joy.

Maggie. His Maggie, who made his life complete, taking the pain of the past and replacing it with promise for the future.

Christmas morning fell on a Sunday, and to Maggie's delight, Beau prompted their departure for the small church in town. Breakfast was eaten quickly, the wagon readied by Pony for the trip. Hay filled the bed, and quilts covered it, in preparation for the two women who were assisted there. Sophie and Verna laughed with delight as they were ensconced behind the wagon seat. Maggie sat with Beau, who wore a white shirt for the occasion, while Joe and Pony rode behind on prancing horses.

The church was filled to capacity, and the beaming Reverend Bryant greeted them before the service. In a pew to their left Cord and Rachel McPherson sat beside Lorena. And beside her, in the far aisle, a wheeled chair held a dark-haired man who bore a resemblance to Cord. The brother, Maggie realized. Jake was his name. Maggie bent forward a bit, the better to see, and spotted a wrapped bundle in Lorena's arms.

She'd had the baby, and not long ago from the size of the armful she held. Rachel looked across the aisle in that moment and smiled, then nudged Lorena, speaking in her ear. A long, slender hand lifted the blue covering and a tiny, round face came into view. Dark hair crowned the infant beauty and a small fist waved in the air.

Lorena's mouth formed two words. *A boy.* And Maggie nodded her understanding. A thrill traveled the length of her spine as she gazed in awe at the yawning babe and beside her Beau's hand reached for her. Their fingers entwined and his gaze followed that which hers had taken.

"We'll see them later," he whispered, and Maggie nodded, her attention caught by the resounding chords of the organ. She sat back, looking forward eagerly to where small figures darted to and fro. At the front of the small chapel a giant pine tree took much of the space, and beneath it was a rough manger, where robed children gathered to portray the Christmas story, nudging and elbowing each other as they found their places.

"I've never been here for such a beautiful thing before," Maggie whispered. "Mama brought us once when I was little, but Pa always said it was a waste of time. There was no sense in going to town unless you had a da—a good reason," she said hastily.

The music was simple now, and Maggie recalled the words from deep in her memory, a song of shepherds and stars and the infant King. Before them the tableau was acted out, children moving as directed, tripping on long robes, singing in treble voices, and waving to watching parents in the congregation. In the back row, garbed in striped robes, Rachel's brothers stood, holding curved staffs and looking properly solemn for the occasion.

And then it was over and the assembled cast stood in a ragged row, the blue-robed Mary holding a doll upside-down. Maggie covered her mouth to hold back the chuckle and Beau bent his head to nudge hers in acknowledgment of her mirth. As the organ burst into triumphant sound, the congregation rose as one. Maggie looked around, picking up a hymnal as did the others, and then waited as Beau found the correct page.

"'...and heaven and nature sing...'" The words were a thing of beauty, she thought, listening as the assembled congregation sang lustily. Beside her, Beau grinned in her direction and beyond him, Sophie mangled the melody, obviously uncaring if her notes matched those on the page.

"'...and wonders of His love...'" Verna sang softly, sweetly, and Maggie rejoiced at the happiness displayed on her mother's face. That the love spoken of in the Christmas song was not of this earth, but of heavenly origin was a fact. Even in her untutored state, Maggie was aware of that much. But today, they could apply to the man beside her, she decided, and in her heart she sang them in silence, translating them into a paean of joy.

"'...and wonders of His love...'" They tasted sweet as she whispered them in barely audible tones. "'...and wonders of His love...'"

The wondrous love of Beau Jackson, given to her...Maggie O'Neill. To have and to hold.

* * * * *

Be sure to look for Carolyn's next book,

THE SEDUCTION OF SHAY DEVEREAUX,

on sale in April 2001.
It's fantastic!

Please turn the page for an excerpt...

Chapter One

A man sat astride a black horse, bending his head to move beneath the open doorway. His shirtsleeves were rolled up to his elbows and a large pistol was holstered against his thigh. To the left side of his saddle, just touching his hip, a scabbard held a long gun, probably a rifle, she thought. And yet he was relaxed, both hands visible, fingers curved against the pommel of his saddle.

"Jennifer Pennington?" he asked. His gaze was penetrating, his eyes shaded by the brim of his hat, and his voice deep, almost rasping. No trace of a drawl softened his words, and no smile curved those wide lips.

"Yes, I'm Jennifer." And if he wanted to take her horses or rummage through the house for whatever booty he might find, she would forever curse her lack of caution today.

"Was your husband Carl?" At her nod, he glanced behind him, through the barn, toward the house. As if he was determined to be in the right place, he mentioned the facts that made up the boundaries of her life. "And is the boy yours?"

She nodded. "What do you want with me?" Her voice came out sharper than she'd intended. The mention of Carl's name did that to her, put her on the defensive and brought resentment to the surface. As much as she'd loved him, and still loved him, she reminded herself. The fact that he'd gone to war and left her to cope with impossible odds was enough to make her angry, whenever she thought about it. And lately, she'd thought about it a lot.

He slid from the horse's back in an easy motion that did little to reassure her, dropping the reins to the ground. His horse stood, immobile but for an ear that flicked, and then was still. Before her, the man was sleek and agile, garbed in dark clothing. He looked…threatening. It was the only word she could think of to describe him.

There was an almost tangible sense of menace about him, a sliver of danger in the depths of dark eyes shadowed by a wide-brimmed hat. It shadowed his face, but could not conceal the scar that slashed one cheek from jawbone to temple. White against deeply tanned skin, it proclaimed a message of danger, of battles fought, and apparently won, since the man wearing it was alive. And, she'd warrant, there were those who'd died at his hand.

His gaze raked over her, measuring and weighing, and she stiffened, squaring her shoulders. "What do you want?" she repeated. "There's not much left if you're looking for a handout."

She thought one corner of his mouth lifted in a faint sign of amusement, and then he shook his head. "Carl sent me."

A rush of heat rose to envelop her, and she drew in a trembling breath. "What are you talking about? Carl is dead. He died in the north, in a prison camp."

Her visitor nodded. "I know. I was with him."

"You knew him? You were there when he died?" The words sounded fragile, as if they might disappear on a breath of wind, and she gasped for air, filling her lungs.

He stepped closer and gripped her elbow with strong fingers, steering her into the barn. She tottered, her legs barely holding her erect. An upright log against the wall provided a seat and Jenny sank onto its surface, grateful that her trembling limbs needn't carry her farther.

He crouched in front of her, one long finger nudging at his hat brim. Silent, unmoving, he watched her as she drew in deep breaths, thankful for this short respite before Carl's name would once more be spoken between them. A chill took her unaware, and her arms wrapped protectively around her waist as she bowed her head.

Closing her eyes, she blotted out his image, the black shirt, the gleaming dark hair, and the ragged scar. "Who are you?" The whisper was faint, but he responded with a single word.

"Shay."

"Is that your last name?" she asked, looking up from beneath her lashes, aware suddenly that tears blurred her vision. She folded her hands atop her knees and straightened her shoulders, attempting to gain some small measure of control.

He shook his head. "No, but it doesn't matter for now."

Harlequin® Historical

PRESENTS

SIRENS OF THE SEA

The brand-new historical series
from bestselling author

Ruth Langan

Join the spirited Lambert sisters in their
search for adventure—and love!

THE SEA WITCH
When dashing Captain Riordan Spencer arrives in
Land's End, Ambrosia Lambert may have
met her perfect match!

On sale January 2001
THE SEA NYMPH
Middle sister Bethany must choose between a
scandalous highwayman and the very proper
Earl of Alsmeeth.

In June 2001
THE SEA SPRITE
Youngest sister Darcy loses the love of her life
in a shipwreck, only to fall for a man who
strongly resembles her lost lover.

Harlequin® Historical

Harlequin proudly brings you

STELLA CAMERON
Bobby Hutchinson
Sandra Marton

in

MARRIED IN SPRING

*a brand-new anthology in which three couples
find that when spring arrives, romance soon
follows...along with an unexpected
walk down the aisle!*

February 2001

Available wherever Harlequin books are sold.

HARLEQUIN®
Makes any time special ™

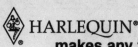

Take a trip to the Old West with four handsome heroes from Harlequin Historicals.

ON SALE JANUARY 2001

MAGGIE'S BEAU
by **Carolyn Davidson**

Beau Jackson, former soldier/rancher

and

BRIDE ON THE RUN
by **Elizabeth Lane**

Malachi Stone, ferry owner

ON SALE FEBRUARY 2001

SWEET ANNIE
by **Cheryl St.John**

Luke Carpenter, horseman

and

THE RANGER'S BRIDE
by **Laurie Grant**

Rede Smith, Texas Ranger

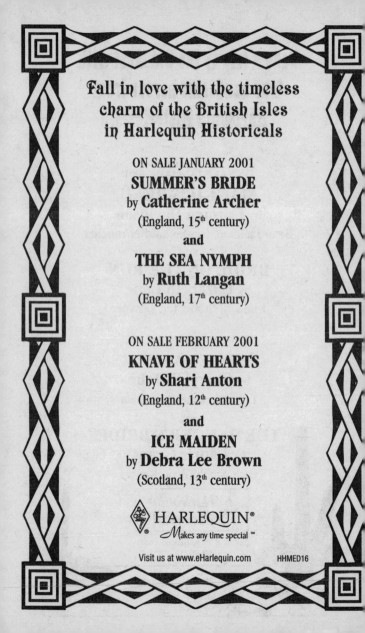